I0535857

THE UNIQUE MAGAZINE

Summer 1988   All art by Stephen Fabian

Published quarterly by the Terminus Publishing Company, Inc., P.O. Box 13418, Philadelphia PA 19101-3418. Application to mail at second
class postage rates pending at Philadelphia PA and additional mailing offices. Single copies, $3.50 (plus $1.00 postage if ordered by mail). Subscription
rates: Eighteen months (six issues) for $18.00 in the United States and its posessions, for $24.00 in Canada, and for $27.00 elsewhere. The publishers
are not responsible for the loss of manuscripts, although reasonable care will be taken of such material while in their possession. Copyright©
1988 by the Terminus Publishing Company, Inc.; all rights reserved; reproduction prohibited without prior permission. *Weird Tales*™ is a trade
mark owned by Weird Tales, Limited. Typeset, printed, and bound in the United States of America.

THE EYRIE

The response to our 65th-Anniversary issue was gratifyingly favorable. Your Humble Editors feel a certain trepidation, perhaps even awe, at filling the shoes (size 14-E) of such giants among our predecessors as Farnsworth Wright and Dorothy McIlwraith. We have spent much of the past few months attending conventions and promoting the magazine, and the signs are encouragingly good. The magazine's newest revival seemed particularly welcome at the World Fantasy Convention in Nashville, this past Halloween weekend.

What direction should the magazine take? We have discussed this among ourselves and with our readers, both in person and in correspondence. The illustrious **Forrest J Ackerman** writes:

Welcome back, Weird Tales™.

Your inspiring editorial augurs well for the future of the periodical.

If (in)humanly possible, see if you can conjure up a miracle and find an unpublished work by David H. Keller, Catherine Moore, and/or Charles Beaumont. Also, any unseen art by Bok or Finlay, although of the modern illustrators George is perfect, Barr none.

As the near editor or quasi-editor or phantom editor (I leave it to posterity to determine my status) of the last incarnation of WT, I congratulate you on the revival and wish you a 31-year run to equal its original span.

Thanks for the kind words, Forry, and let us mention here that we appreciate the graceful way you have taken the whole bizarre experience. Indeed, we hope history *does* straighten the whole story out, because we're still not sure we understand what happened with the previous incarnation of this magazine. But your letter also raises a serious point about this one: Yes, we would like to publish new stories by Keller, Moore, or whoever, but *only* if those stories would actually do those famous writers credit. If a *good* C.L. Moore story turned up, you can be certain we would grab it. But if it were a bit of juvenilia or a fragment or other barrel-scraping, we would sadly have to pass.

And, in the course of correspondence with another previous *Weird Tales™* editor, **Lin Carter**, we touched on this further. Writes Lin:

I have a dreadful feeling that you are making a big mistake with Weird Tales™. *From your remark about trying to "publish the magazine* Weird Tales™ *would have been if it had survived to the present day" as uninterrupted as* Analog *has, you confirm the worst fears of my friends and me about this most recent incarnation.*

In other words, what you plan to publish is not Weird Tales™ *at all, that juicy old pulp magazine with all its corn and hokum, but a "serious" " '80s" horror mag. The mind reels. Why bother calling it* Weird Tales™, *then, unless you plan on reviving* Weird Tales™ *as we who love the mag remember it?*

Since the Cthulhu Mythos was born in Weird Tales™, *anyone who subscribes to* Weird Tales™ *today expects to read an occasional new Mythos story — no? After all, the original magazine was still publishing*

4

THE EYRIE

Mythos stories up to its last year. August Derleth's "The Black Island" was in one of the very last issues. True, Derleth is gone now, but still — And why not something like Jules de Grandin? For thirty years, de Grandin was the most popular series Weird Tales™ *ever ran and the stories regularly placed first or second in the issue-by-issue readers' poll.*

Lin has clearly raised serious points here, but our overall reply is that, try as we may, we can't make it 1930 again. *Weird Tales™* in its original incarnation published what was *new* in the fantasy field at the time, and not pastiches of material from fifty years earlier — which would have been harkening back to 1880 or thereabouts. So, to best duplicate the experience those readers had back then, we hope to retain the spirit of the original incarnation by likewise offering what is new *now*. We don't intend to be just another horror magazine, as should be evident from the last issue and this present one. But when Lin goes on to say that *the people who subscribe to* Weird Tales™ *rather naturally expect to get all the pulpishness, purple prose, and hokum that implies*, we cannot agree. No, we think they would rather have good writing.

Remember that the resurrected (not exhumed!) *Weird Tales™* is aimed at a relatively large readership, not a handful of nostalgic fans. Stories like the Jules de Grandin series (tales of a psychic detective, by Seabury Quinn, which were indeed the most popular thing the old magazine ever published) are more inadvertently funny than thrilling today. For a small audience of fans, one or two such pastiches might be campy fun; but for the mass readership, they would seem incomprehensibly and inexcusably bad. Now were someone to offer us a *modern* psychic-detective series which could give 1988 readers the same sort of thrills that de Grandin's adventures gave the readers of 1930, fine. That would be another matter. The same goes for Cthulhu Mythos stories. We are not opposed to them. But we are tired of protagonists who exist to be eaten; one more addition to the library of nameless tomes; and, indeed, all the *hokum*. If a Mythos story as good as, say, T.E.D. Klein's "Black Man With a Horn" turned up, of course we'd buy it. But one more old-fashioned romp would be about as

Darrell Schweitzer
John Betancourt
George H. Scithers
Editors & Publishers
Leslie Smith
Dainis Bisenieks
Karl Würf
Vincent Evangelisti
Assistant Editors
Richard Kabakjian
Circulation Manager
David J. Williams III
Computer Consultant
Yale F. Edeiken
Of Counsel
Advanced Litho, Inc.
Photographer
The Twin Company, Inc.
Campus Copy Center
Typesetters
Malloy Lithographing, Inc.
Printer

SUBMISSIONS?

Like most editors, we get unsolicited manuscripts, *lots* of them. We survive, as do other editors, only by imposing Rules.

Yes, we read unsolicited manuscripts — *if* they are in proper manuscript format. Each must arrive with a self-addressed, stamped return envelop big enough to take that manuscript back to you, or with a stamped, addressed, business-letter-sized envelope *and* instructions to dispose of the manuscript if not bought. And no, we will not read manuscripts in unacceptable format.

This proper format is described in numerous reference works. One of them is *On Writing Science Fiction: The Editors Strike Back!*, by George H. Scithers, Darrell Schweitzer, and John M. Ford — which also goes into the whole art and practice of writing and selling fantastic literature. *On Writing* is available for $19.50, postpaid, from Owlswick Press, PO Box 8243, Philadelphia, PA 19101 (if you live in Pennsylvania, add $1.17 for sales tax).

appropriate, we feel, as a revival of the Hawk Carse space-opera series (fabulously popular in *Astounding* circa 1932) in the contemporary *Analog.*

To which Lin replied, *All kidding aside, if they* did *run an occasional Hawk Carse yarn, I might be persuaded to read an issue of* Analog . . .

We don't think most *Analog* readers would agree, Lin. Times change.

But one thing that doesn't change is that the editor is occasionally wrong. Case in point is the explanation we gave you last issue of this famous, apocryphal "quote" from H.P. Lovecraft:

"All my stories, unconnected as they may be, are based on the fundamental lore or legend that this world was inhabited at one time by another race who, in practising black magic, lost their foothold and were expelled, yet live outside ever ready to take possession of the Earth again."

This is the celebrated "black magic" quote, often repeated on the dustjackets of Lovecraft books, which has so confused and altered Lovecraft's Cthulhu Mythos. August Derleth and his followers turned the whole thing into cosmic cops-and-robbers, in which the evil Old Ones were "expelled" from the Earth by Forces of Good, which come to mankind's rescue in tight moments. Lovecraft's own view of things left little room for such optimism. As a result, his Mythos stories tended to be considerably scarier than anyone else's. (Would-be writers of Mythos stories for *Weird Tales*™ should, we think, follow Lovecraft's rather than Derleth's model if they want to put the *fear* back in what has lately been an entirely too cozy Mythos.)

When we wrote last issue's editorial, the best current scholarship held that this perversion of Lovecraft's *Weltanschauung* (if we may wax philosophical) did indeed result from a misquotation of the Lovecraft letter to Farnsworth Wright, which we reprinted correctly on page 6 of our 65th-Anniversary issue.

But now *Crypt of Cthulhu* tells us otherwise. This admirable magazine, published by Robert M. Price ($36 for one year, from Cryptic Publications, 107 East James St., Mount Olive NC 28365), is in the forefront of modern Lovecraft scholarship. What

we most like about Bob Price's "pulp thriller and theological journal" is its lack of pretension and its sense of humor. This is the magazine that even published what purported to be "Lovecraft's Letters to Santa Claus." But it is also a magazine of genuine substance, often featuring rare, lost fiction or verse by the great names of the past (a whole issue was devoted to *previously unpublished* Clark Ashton Smith material — barrel-scrapings much of it, but Price is a barrel-scraper with real flair) and scholarly articles which genuinely add to our knowledge of this important writer.

In *Crypt of Cthulhu* #48 (St. John's Eve, 1987), which appeared about the time *Weird Tales*™ 290 went to press, there appeared an article by David E. Schultz, which seems to have definitively proven that the "black magic" quote was actually manufactured by one Harold Farnese, an occultist with whom Lovecraft corresponded. After Lovecraft's death, Farnese wrote to August Derleth, quoting from his own (Farnese's) somewhat faulty memory various things Lovecraft had written. So the scientific materialist Lovecraft's views were filtered through the mind of the occultist, and Derleth took Farnese's inaccurate paraphrases to be actual quotations. Derleth, as Lovecraft's publisher and chief advocate, spread the error far and wide. Now it has come to rest at last.

We recommend *Crypt of Cthulhu* to fans of all things Lovecrafty and eldritch.

Getting back to readers' responses, **Steve Roy** of Ottawa, Canada wrote: *Having read* Amazing *and* Asimov's *during George Scithers's editorial reigns at each, I've noticed that he enjoys such humorous poetry as F. Gwynplaine MacIntyre's* Improbable Bestiary *verses. So I can only apologize for the following:*

While browsing through shelves
 full of comic book elves
I encountered a magazine mystery.
I espied, with a gulp,
 what resembled a pulp,
So far from its true time in history.
But this one looked new;
 I looked closer; 'twas true,
This was George Scithers's Weird Tales.™
With Betancourt and Schweitzer,
 they edits and they writes 'er,

And with Gene Wolfe et al. to aid sales.
Yes, Weird Tales™ *is back*
   though there's nary a hack
To be found in its crisp clear new pages.
And as for the art,
   Barr's made a good start
At depicting barbarian rages.

And so, in conclusion...

'Twas truly a swell anniversary,
No need to expect controversary
(Sic? Why, the genre's never been healthier
And with luck, George,
   you'll all grow much wealthier).

If I may be serious for a moment, I'd like to request that George Barr continue to do the illustrations for WT in the future. A longer review column would also be appreciated. The mix of fiction was good; I trust you can keep it up.

Ken Wisman — whose "My Mother's Purse" appears in this issue — writes:
First, let me get my one criticism out of the way. This is in the choice of cover art. I assume that the cover was taken from an old issue of WT. It's okay for its nostalgic value but is not really in keeping with your manifesto: "We intend to resurrect the magazine, not to exhume it . . . we recognize that nostalgia can be a trap . . . the new Weird Tales™ *will try to be what the magazine would have become had it survived, continuously and uninterruptedly up to the present, as a living, changing, viable publication."*
Actually, the cover — by George Barr — was brand new last issue, but very much in the manner of the old style covers. We thought that a nod to the past was appropriate for the first issue — and we put it together on the run; to get the issue out in time for the World Fantasy Convention we had to commission the cover before most of the stories were in hand. This is why the painting didn't illustrate a specific story.
Of the quality of the cover stock, paper, and printing — all first rate. No other magazine in the field, that I've seen at least, equals it.
And of the fiction — you are to be commended for your choices. Specifically for:
1. Gene Wolfe's "The Dead Man"
2. Darrell Schweitzer's "The Mysteries

of the Faceless King"
3. Tanith Lee's "Death Dances"
These are not the typical stories found in the professional magazines. With these you are out of the realm of mere fiction and in Jung's, Joseph Campbell's, and Eliade's realm. The realm from which the Greeks wrote. A timeless place that speaks in universals. I'm talking about the place where myths are made, the collective unconscious.
I think Tanith Lee, of all writers I've read, writes most consistently from this realm. Her fiction is not "now" nor is it "past" nor is it "future." A lot of her fiction is out of the timestream — much like Hoffmann and Dunsany, and with the latter's eye for poetic beauty.
She is a wise choice for Featured Writer in the second issue. By the way, I'll be nominating her story as well as Gene's and Darrell's for the Horror Writers of America's annual award so they can get the recognition they deserve.

Paul A. Roales of Tulsa, OK, writes:
Congratulations on the revival of Weird Tales™.
The first issue contains several very good stories. My favorites were:
"The Other Dead Man," by Gene Wolfe
"Sister Abigail's Collection," by Lloyd Arthur Eshbach, and
"Ménage à Trois," by F. Paul Wilson.
The art work was also quite good. The cover illustration conveys a sense of continuity with the old Weird Tales™ *and its Brundage covers. However, the cover should illustrate a story. The monsters on the cover are not found inside this issue. The best inside illustrations were the title illustrations for "The Other Dead Man" and "Death Dances." I also liked the filler illustrations on pages 104, 120, and 146.*
I know that psychological thrillers are in vogue right now, but every story in your initial issue was about "human" horrors. Where are the monsters, the creatures from other times and other dimensions, the elder gods? Please don't ignore that type of story. You evoke the names of H.P. Lovecraft, Robert Howard, August Derleth, etc. in your ads . . . remember they all wrote many "creature" stories.
Actually, they wrote all kinds of stories — for all his cosmicism, many of Lovecraft's

best efforts turned on the evil of humans or semi-humans. "The Thing on the Doorstep" and "Dreams in the Witch-House" come immediately to mind. And I'd hardly call the horrors in Keith Taylor's "The Unlawful Hunter" and Gene Wolfe's "The Other Dead Man" purely psychological. As for elder gods, certainly "The Mysteries of the Faceless King" had those in abundance. But, if you want monsters, we have everything from vampires to zombies "coming up" so to speak.

But enough of such grave matters. We were particularly pleased to receive the following postcard from one of this magazine's most distinguished contributors, **Robert Bloch**:

It looks great — and, even better than that, familiar. You've captured the essence in its appearance, and I'm delighted to see it. Many thanks, and much, much success.

And, similar sentiments from another old-time *Weird Tales*™ regular, **Joseph Payne Brennan**:

I'm delighted with the WT. You have very faithfully kept the format, features, and "feel" of the original. The old, brittle pulp paper is gone, and that, of course, is a great improvement. I am not up to a critique of each contribution. With a possible exception or two, the contents maintain a high level of excellence. Congratulations.

And one last word on the subject of pulp paper from **F. Gwynplaine MacIntyre**:

Your new Weird Tales™ *arrived direct from 1938 via time-warp. Congratulations. Now if only your paper supplier could replicate that great old pulp-wood* smell . . .

Can odor be a matter of editorial policy? Here, maybe. This is, after all, the Unique Magazine. The bitter-sweet odor of oxidizing pulp paper is indeed beloved of collectors, but in *our* magazine that would actually be a violation of the "revival, not exhumation" policy. After all, we are trying to give today's readers the same experience the *Weird Tales*™ buyers of the '30s had then. They were reading a *new* magazine, not something fifty years old and moldering. *New* pulp paper doesn't have that distinctive tang. So, alas, no . . . Nostalgic fans will have to go on *sniffing* the old issues. But we hope they'll be *reading* ours.

Long-time fan and noted essayist **Ben P. Indick** writes:

I received Weird Tales™ *with much delight. Excepting its superlative production values, it is a loving continuation of "the unique magazine" indeed. (Those values include splendid cover and interior stock, such as would have set old Wright foaming at the mouth in jealousy. Of course, the price exceeds the 10¢ or 15¢ he was able, with difficulty, to get.)*

The most outstanding quality is the wonderful art of George Barr, as himself and as a pastichist. As openers, the cover, a loving, amusing reprise of old Weird Tales *covers (no* ™ *in referring to the oldtime WT) — complete to the frightened girl. His Virgil Finlay (pp 54-55) and his Boks, in headpieces and a tailpiece, bring reminiscent tears to the eye. Heck, he even has a "Dolbokov" on p. 120. (Or, let's just give credit to Boris Dolgov, whose name has not remained alive.) I hope Barr will remain with you. He might come up with one of Mrs. Brundage's famous* whips next time.

I admire Gene Wolfe, but I think it is an error to have so lopsided a concentration of his work. Six stories, a profile, and an interview — Not even Seabury Quinn, most beloved of all WT's stable to its readers half a century ago, rated such a treatment. HPL was sometimes lucky even to get into an issue. Imagine, if a potential reader were, for some benighted reason, not a Wolfe admirer, voilà. You have lost a customer. I suggest in the future you have no more than one story by any author in any single issue.

Alas, Ben, we can't agree. Most of the six Wolfe stories last issue were very short. The total wordage was no more than that of a good-sized novelet. So, if someone didn't like Wolfe, there was still quite a lot left in the magazine.

This issue, as you see, we have two Tanith Lee novellas, which take up a lot more space than all the Wolfe material last time.

Do readers approve? We'd like to hear from you on this. Our plans in the future do indeed call for several stories (or else one very long one) by the Featured Author each issue, the better to demonstrate that author's full range.

As for Mrs. Brundage's famous whips, well, our own feeling is that there are now numerous . . . ah . . . specialist publications available for that sort of thing.

SSgt. Chester L. Cox writes:
For the third time in less than thirteen years, I applaud the resurrection of Weird Tales™. Let us all pray to the Elder Ones that this time, the magazine will stick around. We have to admire the courage of the Trinity of Betancourt/Schweitzer/Scithers; WT is not a magazine with the best track record for investors or owners, and this group of talents could easily find greener pastures elsewhere.

The first new issue (what '84 and '85 issues?) shows a professionalism that made it leap right off the racks of the local SF/comics store. Here's hoping that it gets on the racks of more stores.

I can find no faults with this first issue; you obviously set out to put your best foot forward. However, I hope this doesn't cause you to become set in your ways. Though George Barr's artwork is excellent, would we want a WT to showcase exclusively George Barr's artwork? Likewise the "special" issues

showcasing one writer; this gets old quickly. And that exciting, nostalgic cover uses the theme which can become overused easily: the loinclothed swordsman, the monster, and the nearly-naked helpless woman. The archetype becomes cliché, and Weird Tales™ need not become known as a Conan-type magazine.

Weird Tales™ lives up to its considerable reputation with this issue. The stories are all unique; not all are horror or even fantasy. This is the sort of magazine I expect when I hear the phrase "unique magazine." If I may, I'll list the top five favorites, in my humble opinion.

1. "Ménage à Trois" by F. Paul Wilson. A truly weird tale, subjective and moody. Clever introduction of the fantastic into the mundane setting.

2. "The Wonderful Wallstretcher" by Felix Gotschalk. Recalls the young Bradbury, and his empathetic viewpoint of the small-town youngster. I could almost smell the weeds in the backlots. No fantasy here at all, other than a young boy's fanciful dreaming.

3. "Mary Beatrice Smoot Friarly, SPV" by Gene Wolfe. Seems a shame that the featured author comes no higher than #3, but it speaks highly of the other stories. Normally, "deals with the devil" stories are old hat, but Wolfe interests us so much in Mary and her hobby that we follow a problem we know she's predetermined to succeed in solving.

4. "Boiled Alive" by Ramsey Campbell. Campbell takes us right inside a paranoid's mind, crawls around with us, then leaves us feeling alone and abandoned in there. After reading this, one feels sticky and races to the shower to clean off.

5. "The Mysteries of the Faceless King" by Darrell Schweitzer. No real surprises here, just a solid, entertaining story.

Really, it was difficult to choose favorites from the excellent material within the 290th issue of Weird Tales™. May I have such difficulties with all future issues.

You've said it yourself. A "considerable reputation." For all the Editorial Trio (a better phrase, perhaps, than "The Gang of Three," to which John Betancourt objected on the grounds that at six foot six he is much too tall to be a Chinese Communist) may have shown courage or foolhardiness, or

THE EYRIE

We've met a few delay problems with both of our Weird Tales™ Library books, but our first -- The Devil's Auction, by Robert Weinberg -- will be out as you read this. (Our second, The White Isle, by Darrell Schweitzer, will be out later this year.) Part of the delay comes from our decision to use full color covers instead of the three-color covers we'd been planning . . . and once you see the spectacular wrap-around cover Stephen Fabian did for The Devil's Auction, you'll know how right that choice was!

The Devil's Auction is an occult adventure in the tradition of Seabury Quinn and Sax Rohmer . . . but with a distinctly modern feel. Weinberg is also the author of over 50 books on the fantasy and horror fields, including (appropriately enough) The Weird Tales Story. Color dustjacket, frontispiece, and chapter headings by Stephen Fabian. Hardcover. Trade edition limited to 900 copies -- sure to be a collector's item! Only $18.95. (There is also a 50-copy signed, limited, boxed edition for $40.00 -- but only a few copies are left, so if you want one, buy now.)

The White Isle is a dreamlike fantasy novel by Darrell Schweitzer, reminiscent of LeGuin's A Wizard of Earthsea and Clark Aston Smith's Hyperborea series. (Schweitzer is not only one of the editors of Weird Tales, but a critically well-received author in his own right, whose books include The Shattered Goddess and We Are All Legends.) The White Isle was originally serialized in Fantastic Stories, and has never appeared in book form before. This edition has been expanded and revised from the serial version. Color distjacket, frontispiece, and chapter headings by Stephen Fabian. Hardcover. Only $18.95 -- available late in 1988. Cover price will be $18.95, but if you order in advance it's only $14.50 -- save $4.45!

- -

Yes, I'm interested! Here is U.S.$_____ for the following:

[ ] Trade Edition of The Devil's Auction (only $18.95).
[ ] Trade Edition of The White Isle ($14.50 until September, 1988).

[ ] Signed, numbered, boxed edition of The Devil's Auction ($40.00).
[ ] Signed, numbered, boxed edition of The White Isle ($40.00).

Send to: Name: _____

Weird Tales™ Library   Address:_____
PO Box 13418
Philadelphia, PA 19101   Address:_____

whatever, we also went into this venture in a very professional way, with profit afore-thought. Yes, *Weird Tales™* has had a somewhat spotty record in the immediate past, but this was not, we reasoned, because there was anything wrong with the magazine itself. Rather, each of the previous attempts was flawed in some fatal, obvious, and easily avoidable way. We were quite certain there would be a large market for *Weird Tales™* done *right*. The important thing is to make sure that the magazine really *is* what we claim it to be, and not just a famous name. But that name *does* indeed matter. A certain book dealer in the field ordered a thousand copies of issue 290. If that same content had been packaged as *Scary Stories* Vol. 1 No. 1, he probably would have ordered twenty. So it works both ways. If we meet our responsibilities — and reader expectations — then we can reasonably hope to take advantage of the *Weird Tales™* name. The future of this magazine is, we think, far more secure than it is for most new ventures at this stage of the game.

As for one-artist, one-author issues, we plan to do three or four to start out, then go on to "regular" issues, featuring no single writer so prominently and illustrated by a variety of artists, with a featured-author issue perhaps once a year thereafter. We agree that such a device can go stale, but, for openers, there are several authors we'd like to devote special issues to, and it *is* a nice excuse to run a lot of first-rate fiction and art, isn't it?

Certainly we *don't* intend to make *Weird Tales™* a "Conan-type magazine." As our contents amply show, we have a much wider range than that. And we don't intend to run sword and sorcery covers exclusively, either. Darrell says he wants some very modern-looking ghouls or zombies before long.

And now a few words from the leading British scholar, editor, and lately Algernon Blackwood biographer, **Mike Ashley**:

It's beautiful. Fiction aside, what makes this issue is George Barr's artwork. He has so captured the spirit of WT *with his range of Finlayesque, Bokish, and St. John style artwork, that one has only to look at that cover and flick through the pages to feel transported back to those great old days. It was a magical moment opening this issue*

for the first time.

The fiction lives up to expectations. Tanith Lee's piece is predictably excellent and highly atmospheric. The Gene Wolfe tribute was just about at the right pitch. The great thing about the old WT *was the odd story that would crop up, the kind that could appear nowhere else, and I wonder if Felix Got-schalk's "The Wonderful Wallstretcher" isn't a little like one of those.*

You are all to be congratulated for bringing back the real WT. *It's a treasure and a delight.*

Yes, we hope to publish some stories which could indeed not appear anywhere else. *Weird Tales™* is still the Unique Magazine, and part of that uniqueness is that you *can't* automatically figure out how a story is going to end — or even if it will turn out to be fantasy. It merely has to be, in the correct sense, *weird*.

Long-time reader and poet **Walter Shed-lofsky** offers the following tribute to the most famous of this magazine's many editors, Farnsworth Wright:

After fifty years my recollection is still keen of Farnsworth Wright, editor of Weird Tales *during the 1930s. Like a bedeviled character that might have appeared in* WT, *Wright was a cadaverous figure, extremely thin, well over 6 feet tall. His light blue eyes peered quizzically from a haggard face. Wright suffered from Parkinson's Disease. There were no drugs at that time to control seizures, so Wright continually trembled. He had a hard time walking, and his body and hands shook and quivered. In order to read, Wright would place a manuscript on a lectern, read a page by leaning forward, then with a trembling hand turn the page on the lectern so as to read the next page. Despite his infirmity, Wright was very amiable. He liked to talk with his authors. Vaguely I recall his mentioning that Howard liked to submit his manuscripts on yellow paper. He was very disappointed that August Derleth did not receive proper acclaim. Smith, Howard, Lovecraft, and Quinn received accolades, but Derleth was also a fine craftsman. Wright's rapport, sensitivity, and encouragement of talent converted "pulp" stories into literature. An extremely high percentage stories that appeared in* WT *later were anthologized by Arkham House.*

THE EYRIE

Walter followed this with a charming acrostic poem in memory of Farnsworth Wright which, alas, will not reproduce as it should with modern typesetting equipment.

A Weird Tales Club

Back in the 1940s, this magazine featured a Weird Tales Club, a kind of roster masquerading as a department, whereby readers could get in touch with one another. This was a common feature in the pulps of the day. *Thrilling Wonder Stories* still maintained the Science Fiction League that way, and *Super Science Stories* had something similar. But the Club is one feature we of the Editorial Horde don't have the time to become involved with. Fortunately, **Tony Oliveri** has started a discussion group on his own. While his group is not affiliated with the magazine in any way, we encourage interested parties to get in touch with him at 4512 MacArthur Blvd. N.W. Apt 3, Washington DC 20007.

The Most Popular Story

Another *Weird Tales*™ feature we *would* like to revive is the voting for the most popular story of the issue. This customarily appeared at the end of the Eyrie, which is where we intend to put it. So, what was your favorite story this issue? We have no conclusive winner for issue 290, although Gene Wolfe's "The Other Dead Man," Tanith Lee's "Death Dances," and Darrell Schweitzer's "The Mysteries of the Faceless King" seemed to draw a lot of praise. Felix Gotschalk's "The Wonderful Wallstretcher" was certainly the most controversial story in the issue.

Do write us soon. ∎

MOVING?

Don't risk leaving The Unique Magazine behind! Just send us your mailing label (on the enveloped this issue came in) plus your new address, and we'll update your subscription information right away. If you no longer have your mailing label, just send us your old address (complete with zip code) and your new address; we'll take it from there.

NOT A SUBSCRIBER YET?

If you move and you're not a subscriber, there's no guarantee you'll be able to find *Weird Tales*™ in your new neighborhood. So, don't risk missing out — turn to the inside back cover of this issue and fill out the subscription form. (Or send a Xerox copy of it if you don't want to damage your copy.)

by John Gregory Betancourt

This issue of *Weird Tales*™ is something of a landmark for the book review column: it now has a "proper" name, The Den, which seems uniquely apt. A den is a place for weird beasts (witness the logo) as well as a cozy place to curl up with the odd tome of eldritch lore. Or, lacking that, with a good fantasy novel. And, too, I've decided to change the format of the book review section a wee bit. One of the most common comments about last issue was that there simply weren't enough reviews. This issue I have almost twice as much space (unless a flood of last-minute advertisements comes in), so . . . to business.

A Mask for the General, by Lisa Goldstein
Bantam Spectra, 201pp., $14.95

A few years ago, a small group of very vocal critics began claiming that "pure" science fiction was being somehow subverted (read: lessened) by fantasy. To prove this, they pointed at the growing number of books mixing standard elements of fantasy with standard elements of science fiction. Never mind that fantasy has been around far longer than genre science fiction, or that science fiction is in fact a subset (albeit a very large and influential subset these days) of fantasy. And never mind that science fiction has always had strong elements of fantasy at the core of many stories — time-travel and faster-than-light-travel stories are almost certainly fantasy. And, of course, never mind 'classic' novels like *Dune*, which mixed genres twenty years

14

ago.

One superb new example of science fiction and fantasy blending to create a powerful story that couldn't exist without either element is Lisa Goldstein's brilliant novel, *A Mask for the General*. Here Goldstein sets up a 21st-century world in which the United States has suffered an economic collapse and become a third-world nation, subservient to Japan and other economic powers. A dictator, the General of the title, is in complete charge; and under his harsh laws the country is slowly starting to recover, but at the expense of its citizens.

A new way of life is at hand, however. A kind of tribalism is spreading through the country, one marked by spiritual journeys to lands inhabited by spirit-totems. These spirit-totems take the form of animals, each with its own personality and traits. For instance, Mary, the protagonist, belongs to the sea-otter tribe; other characters belong to the bear, lion, and spider tribes. The General is a crow.

Goldstein has done her research into the beliefs of American Indians and African tribesmen. But she's also up to date: the spirit-totems are an extension of the "power animal" fantasies in which an animal guides a human on a spiritual journey, fantasies that some yuppies are experimenting with today. In both our world and in Goldstein's, these fantasies are a way to retreat from technology to a more primitive mindset.

In *A Mask for the General*, it is taken for granted that spirit-totems are real; after all, the protagonists can see them, speak to them, and interact with them. The whole point of the book lies in getting the oppressive General to wear a mask so his spirit-totem can find him and give him a soul ... which will then free the United States from the worst excesses of his tyranny. Yet even though mysticism drives the novel's plot, science fiction does too, for the story simply wouldn't work if set in today's New York or San Francisco, partly because many of the characters' decisions are based on their future environment. Several of them escape from one of the General's "rehabilitation camps," for instance; and others use not-yet-invented drugs to mimic spirit-trances which otherwise would require many days of fasting and meditation.

Beyond its synthesis of fantasy and SF, *A Mask for the General* offers clear, crisp writing, well-drawn characters, and a believable background. It's easy to see why Lisa Goldstein's first novel, *The Red Magician*, won an American Book Award: she's one of the best writers to emerge in the last few years. Don't miss this one.

The Year's Best Fantasy Stories: 13,
edited by Arthur W. Saha
DAW Books, 238pp., $2.95

In this latest volume of his Year's Best, editor Saha has selected an extraordinary range of stories, from modern-scene to historical to alternate-world backgrounds. There are tales by Tanith Lee ("Beauty is the Beast"), Richard L. Purtill ("Something in the Blood"), Judith Tarr ("Pièce de Résistance"), R. Chetwynd-Hayes ("Long, Long Ago"), Kevin J. Anderson ("The Old Man and the Cherry Tree"), Nancy Kress ("Phone Repairs"), Michael Rutherford ("The Tale and its Master"), Kim Antieu ("Sanctuary"), Jane Yolen ("The Uncorking of Uncle Finn"), Jim Aiken ("A Place to Stay for a Little"), and Nancy Springer ("The Boy Who Plaited Manes").

Rutherford's story is, without a doubt, the centerpiece of the collection; it's a mythic adventure set in Smunsk, detailing the life of a storyteller. The tale has the richness of texture; and the story itself, the pathos, excitement, and thoroughly believable characters that will make this a classic of the field. Rutherford is certainly a writer whose name I intend to watch; he may well

turn out to be one of the major fantasists this decade, if this story is any indication.

And if Rutherford's story isn't enough to get you to buy the book, the stories by Kress and Springer are absolutely top-flight as well. In fact, there's not a clunker in the lot. Recommended.

Land of Dreams, by James P. Blaylock
Arbor House, 264pp., $16.95

James Blaylock has quite a following for his weird fantasies. They've won him both the World Fantasy Award (for his novella "Paper Dragons") and the Philip K. Dick Award. His fiction can be very murky at times, but beneath that murk stir images of startling beauty. *Land of Dreams* is exactly like that.

Set in the same world as "Paper Dragons," *Land of Dreams* is an often exciting, often dull, often murky story about travel between worlds with different realities; an evil carnival that shows up once every 12 years during the 'Solstice'; a migration of hermit crabs, each succeeding crab slightly larger; articles of giant clothing which keep washing ashore; and all manner of strange creatures. All that plus a coming-of-age story.

The book's real problems lie in its structure: although interesting things are happening, Blaylock goes up blind alleys, pursuing various plot threads, then wanders back to the storyline, then wanders off again on yet more tangents. The effect is something like examining a mosaic with a magnifying glass: you can see a few of the tiles at once, but never the whole picture. To his credit, Blaylock manages to tie up all the loose plot threads at the end. But it's still an unsatisfying book — ambitious, certainly, but critically flawed. I understand the hardcover is now out of print, so look for a paperback if you're interested; it should be out soon, I imagine.

The Secret Ascension; or, Philip K. Dick is Dead, Alas, by Michael Bishop
TOR Books, 339pp., $16.95

It's become almost a cliché these days for "literary" science-fiction writers to publish stories with Philip K. Dick's name in the title, purporting to be tributes. Bishop's book is the latest in the series, and it's certainly the best of the lot I've read. The fact that Bishop has real feelings for Dick as a person and as a writer certainly shows.

In Bishop's alternate America, Richard Nixon has assumed complete control of the country and is now in his fourth term as President (a lot of people refer to him as King Richard). Nixon's United States is reminiscent of Nazi Germany, with travel restrictions, censorship, and secret police. In this world Philip K. Dick is a writer famous for his mainstream novels (books which, in our world, weren't published until after his death). Dick's science fiction remains unpublished because it's too full of anti-government propaganda.

When Dick dies, God (or aliens, depending on how you look at it) brings him back as a sort of astral projection of himself. The purpose of his new existence is to change the present reality for the better. Unfortunately he can't remember who he is anymore. But he sets about contacting people anyway, slowly working toward the altered reality in which Nixon is no longer President.

Bishop mimics a number of Dick's story devices — an unraveling reality and multiple third-person viewpoints being the most obvious — with seeming ease. Further, he builds on a number of Dick's real-world hangups, chiefly fear of secret police (Dick's apartment was broken into and his files searched several times in the early 1970s) and religious obsessions (at one time Dick claimed to be receiving messages from God). Would Dick have liked *The Secret Ascension*? Probably not; it hits awfully close to many of his private phobias. Will readers? I imagine so. The book would work just as well as a novel if Philip K. Dick weren't mentioned, which must remain the ultimate criterion.

Polyphemus, by Michael Shea
Arkham House, 245pp., $16.95

Michael Shea — as all horror fans know — is a talent whose work is to be savored time and again. He won the World Fantasy Award in 1983 for his dark fantasy *Nifft the Lean*; he is also the author of *A Quest for Simbilis*, *The Color Out of Time*, and *In Yana, the Touch of Undying* (all DAW books) which have given him a cult following. These novels, along with his idiosyncratic, often pyrotechnic short stories that have appeared in *The Magazine of Fantasy and Science Fiction* and *Whispers*, form a body of work which hasn't received the critical and popular attention it deserves.

Collected here are the best of Shea's shorter works, plus an excerpt from *Nifft*, which provide an excellent overview of his career so far. Stories included are: "Polyphemus," "The Angel of Death," "Uncle Tuggs," "The Pearls of the Vampire Queen," "The Horror on the #33," "The Extra," and "The Autopsy." There is also an introduction by Algis Budrys. The stories range from graphic horror to psychological terror to dark fantasy à la Jack Vance's *The Dying Earth*. If you're unfamiliar with Shea, this is the place to start.

Haunted Castles: The Complete Gothic Tales of Ray Russell
Maclay & Associates, 187pp., $12.95

Another short story collection of note is *Haunted Castles*, by Ray Russell. Russell is probably best known in the horror field for being the author of *The Case Against Satan*, even though he's written quite a few other novels and short stories of note. All his gothic tales are here, and they're quite a set, full of gloomy castles, weird menaces, grotesqueries and deformities, and evil incarnate. The 19th century is wonderfully evoked. All the stories are good, but I found the opening novella, "Sardonicus," particularly compelling: it's the story of a man whose face has been paralyzed so it's always grinning, and of the agonies and tortures to which that eternal grin drives him.

Russell is deft at characterization. I can't imagine any serious horror fan skipping this book, unless he already has the stories in other collections.

Since Maclay & Associates is a regional publisher, you should probably order directly from them for fastest service: Maclay & Associates, P.O. Box 16253, Baltimore MD 21210. Add a couple of dollars for postage and handling.

Yellow Fog, by Les Daniels
Donald M. Grant: Publisher, 191pp., $30.00

One always expects elegant books from Donald Grant, and *Yellow Fog* is no exception: a striking dust jacket, interior illustration, acid-free paper — the whole works. The price may seem a bit high, but on closer

examination one sees the reason: this edition is limited to 800 copies, all of them signed by author and artist (Frank Villano). My only quibble about the book as artifact is that it's simply too short — the type is *very* large, and there is a lot of white space between the lines. It took me less than two hours to read, and I like to savor my books.

As for the writing itself . . . this is decidedly minor Les Daniels. The vampire Sebastian is again a character, but very much off-stage throughout. When I think back to the last book of Daniels's I read (*Citizen Vampire*, about Sebastian's life in the French Revolution), this one seems pale by comparison.

Nevertheless, the writing is still rich and absorbing, the characters believable, and the evocation of London by gaslight striking. Daniels is without a doubt an excellent writer; I just wish he'd put more meat into this story.

The Moon's Revenge, by Joan Aiken
Knopf, 30pp., $12.95

This is a large-size children's storybook, illustrated very ably by Alan Lee. I normally wouldn't review a children's book here, but this one is pretty special . . . it's a fairy-tale more suitable for adults than children, and it has the sort of charm you don't find in many stories these days.

It starts: "Once there was a boy called Seppy, and he was the seventh son of a seventh son. This was long ago, in the days when women wore shawls and men wore hoods and long pointed shoes, and the cure for an earache was to put a hot roasted onion in your ear." It continues in the same delightful vein. If you see it in a store, take a glance — if you have a young relative I bet you'll leave with it tucked under your arm.

The Dark Descent, edited by David G. Hartwell
TOR Books, 1011pp., $29.95
The Oxford Book of English Ghost Stories, ed. by Michael Cox and R.A. Gilbert
Oxford University Press, 504pp., $18.95

The last six months have been good for horror short fiction, witnessing the appearance of *two* major horror anthologies. *The Dark Descent* is a mammoth compilation of horror, emphasizing more modern writers like Clive Barker, Ray Bradbury, Michael Shea, and Stephen King (plus some names less associated with horror, such as Joyce Carol Oates, John Collier, and Philip K. Dick). Of course there are the obligatory classics like Poe's "The Fall of the House of Usher," Lovecraft's "The Call of Cthulhu," and Ambrose Bierce's "The Damned Thing," as well as stories by M.R. James, Lucy Clifford, Russell Kirk, Shirley Jackson, Harlan Ellison, Nathaniel Hawthorne, J. Sheridan Le Fanu, E. Nesbit, Karl Edward Wagner, Robert Aickman, Fritz Leiber, Robert Bloch, Charles L. Grant, Manly Wade Wellman, Thomas M. Disch, Theodore Sturgeon, Michael Bishop, Charlotte Perkins Gilman, William Faulkner, Robert Hichens, Richard Matheson, Joanna Russ, Dennis Etchison, D.H. Lawrence, Tanith Lee, Flannery O'Connor, Ramsey Campbell, Henry James, Gene Wolfe, Charles Dickens, Walter de la Mare, Ivan Turgenev, Robert W. Chambers, Oliver Onions, Fitz-James O'Brien, Edith Wharton, and Algernon Blackwood.

The Dark Descent is a must-read for all readers newly come to horror. It provides an overview of past and contemporary horror that's unmatched in any other collection.

The Oxford Book of English Ghost Stories is a seminal collection of a more specialized form of horror: the ghost story, most specifically, the *English* ghost story. Not all the authors are English, interestingly enough, though their stories have the 'proper' flavour and atmosphere. All the stories are arranged in order of publication, from Sir Walter Scott's "The Tapestried Chamber" (1829) to T.H. White's "Soft Voices at Passenham" (1981, a posthumous publication). Sandwiched between these are stories by Amelia B. Edwards, J. Sheridan Le Fanu, M.E. Braddon, F. Marion Crawford, Vernon Lee, Bram Stoker, E. Nesbit, Sir Arthur Quiller-Couch, Henry James, H.G. Wells, W.W. Jacobs, Mary E. Wilkins, M.R. James, Algernon Blackwood, Oliver Onions, Barry Pain, E.F. Benson, Richard Middleton, E.G. Swain, Arthur Gray, W. Somerset Maugham, May Sinclair, L.P. Hartley, John Buchan, W.F. Harvey, H. Russell Wakefield, Edith Wharton, A.M. Burrage, Hugh Walpole, A.E. Coppard, Thomas Burke, Charles Williams, L.T.C. Rolt, A.N.L. Munby, Elizabeth Bowen, V.S. Pritchett, Christopher Wood-

forde, Walter de la Mare, Simon Raven, and Robert Aickman.

Anyone with a good horror collection will have most of these (the same goes for *The Dark Descent*), but it's still a good collection. As with *The Dark Descent*, this would be a terrific starting place for someone new to the horror field. Both taken together would be perfect.

Whispers 23-4, edited by Stuart David Schiff
Whispers Press, 176pp., $8.95

I suppose, considering the infrequent publishing schedule, that *Whispers* is more of a trade paperback anthology than anything else these days. The price has also gone up, since Schiff attended a small press publishers' meeting and found out that (according to them, anyway) he was underpricing his magazine; but it's still a good buy.

Included here are stories by Steve Rasnic Tem, Ray Russell, Julie Stevens, Joe R. Lansdale, Carl Jacobi, Kit van Zandt, Barbara W. Durkin, Hugh B. Cave, Jayge Carr, Manly Wade Wellman, Brian Lumley, Phyllis Eisenstein, Bill Pronzini, William Relling, Jr., William D. Cotrell, and David Drake. There's also an excerpt from the next Fafhrd & the Gray Mouser novel by Fritz Leiber.

Somehow, I found this issue less satisfying than any so far: the Fritz Leiber excerpt is excellent — but ends annoyingly on a cliff-hanger. Many of the stories are shorts with "surprise" endings, and they become tiresome rather quickly. I particularly enjoyed "Century Farm," by Julie Stevens, about farmers and their ties to the land, and "Where Did She Wander?" by Manly Wade Wellman — Wellman's last story, a tale of John the Balladeer fully as good as most of the others in that series.

I note that this is the first issue in quite a while which does *not* devote special attention to one author. The production values remain high, with good paper, color cover by Stephen Fabian, and lots of interior illustrations. Order from: Whispers Press, 70 Highland Ave., Binghamton, NY 27514. A subscription for two double-issues costs $13.95; if you missed the previous issue, I'm sure you could get both that and the current one as your subscription.

Psycho II, by Robert Bloch
Whispers Press, 223pp., $15.00
Lost in Time and Space with Lefty Feep, by Robert Bloch
Creatures at Large, 258pp., $12.95 (trade pb); $40.00 (hc)
The Complete Robert Bloch, by Randall D. Larson
Fandom Unlimited Enterprises, 123pp., $10.00 (trade pb)

It seems Robert Bloch is a hot item these days — in the last few months I've received no less than 5 books by or about him. Admittedly, several of them are old, but all are still in print. The three above seem the most interesting.

Psycho II — originally published in 1982 — is still in print in a handsome hardcover edition. With the way book prices are climbing, $15.00 for a small-press hardcover on acid-free paper seems like a decided bargain. And, too, Bloch does interesting things with Norman Bates, since this one is entirely his story and not based on the movie of the same title. For psychological horror, you can't do much better. (And there is a bit of blood, too, splattered here and there . . .)

Lost in Time and Space with Lefty Feep is a collection of humorous fantasy stories originally written for *Fantastic Adventures*, plus one new story, all about a hip '40s guy who's somewhat on the shady side of things, if his tales are to be believed. Bloch himself is the narrator, hearing an improbable yarn each time he meets up with Lefty. Tacky clothes and people make an irresistible combination. The humor's a bit dated in places, but I liked it anyway. I'm looking forward to the next two collections of Feep stories, which have been announced as forthcoming. Write to: Creatures at Large (P.O. Box 687, Pacifica CA 94044) for complete ordering information, and for info on their other publications.

Finally, *The Complete Robert Bloch*, a detailed bibliography. It's well designed and illustrated with covers from what seem like hundreds of books and magazines; for anyone interested in collecting Robert Bloch's work, this is certainly an essential tool. Order from: Fandom Unlimited Enterprises, P.O. Box 70868, Sunnyvale CA 94086.

The Art of Segrelles, by Vicente Segrelles

NBM, 30pp., $13.95

Vicente Segrelles is a Spanish artist whose work has been appearing on book covers in this country with increasing regularity. I found this collection of his color work good, but a bit uneven; some of the covers have a roughness to them I didn't like, while others were polished to perfection. When Segrelles wants to, he can come up with work comparable to the best of the field.

If you like art books, this is probably one you won't want to miss. If you can't find it locally, write to: NBM, 35-53 70th St., Jackson Heights NY 11372.

Clive Barker's *The Damnation Game*
Books on Tape
Warner Audio, 2 hours 30 minutes, $12.95

It's been a couple of months since I listened to this 2-cassette dramatization of Clive Barker's *The Damnation Game*, but I can still remember some scenes vividly. The tape would seem to be very true to the book (which I haven't read yet) because I'm familiar with Clive Barker's writing style, and this dramatization comes close. It horrified me at times, nauseated me at others, and kept my rapt attention throughout.

It's basically an occult revenge story, with lots of interesting horrors and ghastly characters along the way. Marty Straus is released from prison and takes a job as bodyguard to a rich industrialist named Joseph Whitehead. Unfortunately, Whitehead owes his soul to the demonic Mamoulian, and Mamoulian has decided to collect. There are plenty of plot twists, and all the actors do superb jobs with their rôles.

If you listen to books in your car (as I do), and have a tough stomach for grue and gore, this is a good one to have.

Shorts: News and such

Darrell Schweitzer has been quite active in the non-fiction, scholarly end of our field of late. His latest essay anthology, *Discovering Classic Horror Fiction I* is due momentarily from Starmont House. The book contains articles by S.T. Joshi, Mike Ashley, Sam Moskowitz, and other leading scholar-critics; their subjects include the authors Arthur Machen, M.R. James, J. Sheridan Le Fanu, all three Benson brothers, and others. Further down the line are several more such books, plus *Pathways to Elfland: The Writings of Lord Dunsany*, from Owlswick Press. Schweitzer is also working on a bibliography of Lord Dunsany, in collaboration with S.T. Joshi and Douglas Anderson.

George Scithers (with co-editor Schweitzer) is busy putting together a companion volume to his Avon Books anthology, *Tales from the Spaceport Bar*, called (appropriately enough) *More Tales from the Spaceport Bar*. Look for Morgan Llywellyn's story "Princess" to be included.

And, lastly, and without further comment, I point out *The Blind Archer*, a fantasy novel published by Avon Books in February, 1988, and *Johnny Zed*, a science fiction novel to be released by Warner Books in July, 1988, both by John Gregory Betancourt. Funny coincidence, that.

See you next issue. ∎

Lin Carter

June 9, 1930

February 7, 1988

The Unrequited Glove

by Tanith Lee

Jason Drinkwood had many advantages. He was both young enough and old enough, and good-looking enough, and well enough off, that nothing very much need lie very much out of reach for very long. During the Amerenglish season along the coast, he was generally known by sight, and by name, for at that time, "Jason" was an uncommon appellation, particularly augmented by such dark wavy hair, bright blue eyes, expensive garments and ice-cream-coloured car. His code of conduct, nonetheless, was quite decorous. He did not belong to the artist or poet caste whose seasons sometimes ran in tandem with the Amerenglish one. He was seen to drink, but never drunk, to gamble a little, but never recklessly. He would dance, and he would dine, but with the air of one only performing a natural duty naturally well. Though the ice-cream car might sometimes be spotted swimming home along the palm-lined roads in the dusk of dawn, it was never anything but tidily driven. In other words, Mr. Jason Drinkwood was not a man of passions. And so, though there had at first been some speculation in the caravanserai of the colony as to what his intentions and inclinations might be, they were, when noted, of a very ordinary and discreet kind, and in the order of three: Female, sophisticated, *brief*.

It was something of a surprise therefore, when Jason Drinkwood was sighted with Alys Ashlin.

Miss Ashlin was a painter, partly American it was believed, and rather more than partly something else, something fey and foreign, which had afforded her a slender and unreal quality, two large and gazing eyes, and wispy ash-blonde hair. That she should be an artist was no more than one would expect, that she had some money also was, admittedly, an oddity, but since she did not "mix" very much, it was supposed she might go on as she wished. There

had, of course, been some curious rumours now and then, but it was the age of the rational, and one had only to look at the girl to know her for a hopeless romantic, who would probably drink herself to death on cocktails before she was thirty-five.

Certainly, she was not Mr. Drinkwood's type, not at all. Presumably he had met her at some gallery. Presumably her moth-like attractions had for some reason piqued a jaded palate. Whatever the cause, the colony observed that they lunched together, and took picnics to the hills in the pale car, and drank white *fine* and Russian Blushes at Co's, and danced at The Balconies, and all other fashionable spots.

Then, quite as suddenly as it had begun, the affair ended. A dark lady was seen to occupy the ice-cream chariot, and a dark lady was seen to be dining with Mr. Drinkwood at Piccaletta's. No one was in the least surprised, nor expected any more of the matter, except perhaps news of Miss Ashlin's abrupt illness in the morning gazette.

The sigh which escaped the chiselled lips of Jason Drinkwood had nothing to do with the seraphic and cloudless day, the cuisine of a just-completed breakfast, or any of the prospects before him, save only one. Putting down the small blonde card, he said, "Very well. You can bring her up here."

Thereafter Jason rose to his feet, and prepared to put another cup of coffee into his lean and graceful frame.

It was, he believed, inevitable, that this final confrontation would have to come. Unfortunately, that was the trouble with these unusual women. Though they might be entertaining for a while, they soon became merely irritating, and then, when one wanted to finish it, they simply did not know how to behave. Had he not, he now asked himself, done everything perfectly and with utter good manners? He had cancelled their last meeting giving plenty of notice, and using the most courteous and apologetic address, with just the hint of terminus he had felt necessary in Alys's case. And had he not sent her a box of white roses, three dozen of the things? What more did she want from him? But he knew only too well. She wanted a *Scene*. That was what all her tribe required.

It was true, he had met her at a gallery, her own to be precise. She had been looking very chic that day and he had mistaken her for an idler come to buy. Something in her quality had given him an urge to investigate her, and by the time he had invited her to lunch and she had accepted, it was too late to back out when he realized she was The Alys of the paintings. He knew nothing about art, had never had much time for it. He cared for pictures and ornaments as he cared for fine weather, for he liked and appreciated pleasant surroundings. Her feelings on the subject, which began to be displayed almost as soon as the entrée was brought to the table, were both alien and unalluring. However, Miss Ashlin (all those A's, S's, L's, and I-Y's seemed quite overdone), was shy. She preferred not to talk about herself, but liked to listen to him. He therefore set out to amuse her, poor little thing. Her vulnerability did rather appeal to him, even while he knew it was a mistake to like it. He could not bear stupid women, but had a deep distrust of clever ones. Alys did not fit either of these niches, though she was destined to represent both to him by the time he sloughed the liaison. Her trust and her simplicity in the matter of the male initially filled him with a desire to protect her. Later, of course, every frailty demanded of him that he pierce the weak place with a honed stiletto. Though he would not so have qualified it to himself, he was drawn to Alys Ashlin by the instincts of the tiger for the tethered lamb. Perhaps the tiger

too has moments of enjoying the lamb's charm and the music of its bleat. Perhaps, if not too terribly hungry, the tiger also will delay the ultimate seconds when he falls on his prey and tears out its entrails.

When he had caused enough damage to her, and she, trying equally to protect herself and appease him, had lain at his feet gasping: But what have I *done?* Jason had sensibly withdrawn, cancelled the next meeting — there was no fun in killing a dead sheep — and sent a box of a dozen or so white roses to mask the stench of spilled blood.

However, now, incredibly, the lamb — having already written to him on three occasions in the most aggravatingly mild of terms — had arrived at his lair. To have it out with him, he concluded with dread. To make her *Scene*.

The door opened, and she entered the sunlit room, a wisp of ashes and fainting blonde violets.

"Oh. Hallo," said Jason, with slight astonishment, as if he had been expecting anyone but she. "Will you have some coffee?"

"Thank you. I don't think so."

"Do. It's very good."

Previously, she had always done exactly as he told her. But now she said again, "I don't think coffee is appropriate."

"Really? Why ever not?"

"Jason — I may still call you that?"

"Don't be so absurd," he said, harshly.

She lowered her wild eyes — they truly were wild, as if she had come straight from the hills and the old pagan altars there, instead, plainly, from off the manicurist's couch.

"Jason . . . I'm very obtuse about these things. I'm afraid I don't understand at all. Is it that you're finished with me?"

He poured some more coffee and tried to check a not unpleasurable surge of rage.

"Well. What an ultimatum. When do

THE UNREQUITED GLOVE

the tanks arrive, and the air cover?"

"Please, be serious, Jason. I should like to know."

"Oh should you? Like to? I don't think so. Or you'd be quite well aware of the facts already."

"I see. I think I see."

"Good. Splendid." He shot her a look as he lit a cigarette. She did not smoke, she had said it affected her eyes. Certainly something had done so. They were larger than ever, and though not exactly reddened, the pre-dawn greyness of their depths was bluer and more saline. "You know really, young woman, you're making an awfully big issue out of this, aren't you? I mean."

"What do you mean?" she inquired softly. He saw with dismay that she was pulling off her mauve gloves, a signal of intended temporary permanence.

"For God's sake," he said, "we spent some time together. An interlude. It was delightful, Alice. Thank you so *very* much. But now. What can I say? I hope you won't force me to be rude."

"You mean that it is over, absolutely over. Between us."

" 'It.' What is there supposed to have been? Over? Obviously."

"Yes, obviously."

"For heaven's sake, Alice," (he had always insisted on pronouncing her name in a straightforward way, none of that *Aleez* ridiculousness), "for heaven's sake. You're acting as though we've been Romeo and Juliet. Good God, woman. Try to grow up."

"But," she said, "I love you."

He turned his back on her at once. Oh Christ, much worse than he had thought. Of course, he knew; but even she, surely, should have had the tact not to use this idiocy. After a moment he mastered himself and said, "I'm very sorry." Then, when there was only a silence, he added, "Look, I have to be over the other side of the bay in about ten minutes' time. You'll have to excuse me. I must go." He had visions of her

weeping or swooning on the sofa, being unable to rid the room of her — but when he flung round, to his genuine surprise on this occasion, he saw she was silently gone. All that remained was one of the faint violet gloves, the left one, lying *evanouissement* by the coffee pot. He fired a look of hatred at it, for she might use it as a pretext to come back. He would have to send it to her, bloody woman. But *later*. For now he was getting out.

He ran down the villa stair with a feeling of release and exultation, as if he had just won some sort of race. And for once he drove the car rather fast along the coast road.

In the small hours of the following day, when he returned, Jason noticed, vaguely, that the glove too had gone. He put this down to the tidiness of his domestics, or to a miraculous display of common sense by Miss Ashlin, in returning to retrieve her property during his absence.

About a week after these events, Gerard Caul, an intermittent friend of Jason Drinkwood's since their first meeting in the caravanserai, received a message at his hotel. Responding to it, he called Drinkwood's villa. The conversation was short: "Caul? Thank God. I'm glad. Can you come over? No, I mean now. Come to lunch. Well as soon as. Five o'clock? All right. But you'll be there. Wrong? Oh. . . . Probably nothing. No, nothing's wrong at all. Five o'clock. Till then."

Gerard, a prosaic but easy-going man, not without wealth or influence, arrived at the proper station which was, in the current parlance of colony etiquette, five minutes late. Driving up to the villa, he was rather startled to see that something was slightly amiss with its facade. His first thought was of birds, or geckos, but when next he came across the famous car, drawn up between the flower beds and an old foun-

25

tain, Gerard rejected the notion. The peculiar marks had a symmetrical nastiness about them that suggested manic human rather than faunal activity.

Presently, meeting Jason on the lower of the two terraces, Gerard waited until the drinks had been served and they were alone to remark, "Well, and who have you fallen foul of, my boy?"

At which Jason started, spilled some of his drink, and retorted with a careless laugh, "What on earth do you mean?"

"*Absit omen,*" said Gerard, and refilled Jason's glass himself. Even if he had not by now been searching for signs, he might have noticed that Jason's face appeared rather dirty, rather colourless, and that his hands had developed a nervous tremor. "Someone, patently," said Gerard, "has it in for you. The car, for example."

"That was very unfortunate," mumbled Jason. "It seems to have found a supply of something in the kitchen, I'm not sure what, some kind of molasses, or glue. . . . Very difficult, you know, to get off. I apologise for my face. That's simply writing ink. I'd forgotten how damned resistant it is to soap and water.

"Ah, yes," said Gerard. He opened his cigarette case and offered Jason the beautiful snow-white cigarettes. And watched Jason take and try to light one with his tremblous hands. "But who is this ingenious enemy, and why haven't you gone to the police? I know they can be difficult. Is that the problem?"

Jason laughed again. Dropping the cigarette, he lowered his ink-stained face into his hands and shuddered.

"My dear fellow," said Gerard, immovable.

"I'm quite all right. I shall be splendid in a moment. It's just the — frankly, the bloody hopelessness of it. I don't know what to do. At first, when it only ran about, and moved things, I tried to laugh it off. Then I thought I was going

26

mad. But I'm not the only one to see — that boy ran off, you know. Scared to death. I think the woman's caught a glimpse, too, but she just accepts it. Well, she knows *she's* safe enough. But the worst of it is, I feel such a fool. I mean, look at me. I tell you I'm afraid to go to sleep. The days are bad enough. All I can do is move out, but — I did try sleeping at — well, somewhere else, you understand. But somehow, and this is the positively horrible part, *somehow* it followed me. It must have got into the car — I don't know how, I'd been so careful — but in the morning I woke up — in this state, *patterned,* you could say, But much worse. My — companion was rather put out. One could hardly blame her. There was ink all over the sheets. She thought it was some schoolboy prank of mine."

"Yes," said Gerard. He extinguished the stub of his cigarette, folded his arms, and gazed upwards at the line of balconies above. The sun was beginning to touch them now to a languid mellowness, while the green of the oleanders shone like torches as the light drove through. It was an exquisite hour, made strangely, like the chill first dawn, always for strange revelations.

Suddenly Gerard found Jason almost at his feet, gripping him and whimpering: "You have to help me, Gerard, you have to help me —"

It was just at this moment that Gerard became aware of a different note of colour in the vine that grew about the balconies. It seemed to him the leaves contained a flower of palest mauve, or perhaps even a mauve bird, for surely it had only just appeared — but his attention was now distracted.

"Drinkwood, I'm quite prepared to do all I can. But you must tell me first —"

A large ball of mud-clay, about the consistency of setting tempera, hurtled down from the direction of the balconies. It landed on the drinks tray, splattering the soda siphon and sending Jason's glass flying. Jason gave an uncharacteristic shriek and leapt to his feet. At that instant a second mud-ball, rather larger and rather more glutinous, struck him squarely in the chest.

Instinctively the eyes of Gerard Caul had risen once more to the vine. He had the impression of a capricious nymph, casting missiles from a slender hand gloved in softest mauve. At the same time, Gerard realized and comprehended no flesh and blood nymph, however svelte or small, could hang there in the tenuous foliage. And then, *then,* he caught sight of something, something definitely mauve and capricious and definitely operating entirely alone, scrambling lightly away, up the creeper, over the balustrade and into the house.

"Whatever was that?" inquired Gerard, with the disarming fascination of a man who knows that all things have a reasonable explanation.

Jason Drinkwood, sitting in his chair with the face of ink-stained death, told him.

"Oh come now," said Gerard.

An hour and a half later, Gerard Caul took his leave. He had offered to do a great many things, but most of them had involved the summoning of doctors. Since Jason insisted, with ever-increasing hysteria, that no human agency was at work against him, Gerard was forced to concur that at least no *external* human agency was. Which left only Jason himself as the psychopathic culprit. Gerard had no desire to be included in such a fiasco, even on behalf of a friend. Besides, the atmosphere of the house was beginning to bother him. It felt positively booby-trapped. After he had explained to Jason for the twentieth time that mud might come to be near the roof and that birds had been known to drop portions of it in the past on undeserving persons below, enervation began to steal a march. The last

straw was then presented to him as Jason, now drunk, postulated a search of the house culminating in the laying of ambushes. At this juncture Gerard rose to his feet. In a weak moment he had offered Jason sanctuary at the hotel, but this had only resulted in Jason's frantic mirth and avowals that he would be "followed." Gerard left the villa. Like every true realist, he knew that in certain areas of life, all one could do for a friend was to desert him.

That Mr. Drinkwood seemed to be suffering from some form of illness of mania was quickly the talk of the colony. As the days of liquid honey spilled themselves over and over into each other, as the blue seas poured ceaselessly to and fro and the blue skies answered them with their equally ceaseless immobility, the talk rose and fell among the boulevards, over the café tables, and in the fashionable shops of the Monte d'Oro. Even at the Casino they might sometimes be heard to remark that Drinkwood was never seen there now, and the great dinner parties that splatter the turn of season with champagne corks and fireworks, also deplored his absence. It was a fact, he had been a social asset. He was so eligible and so unobtainable, so dashing, and so completely safe. What a pity it was, they said, whatever it was. But what was it, precisely? He had taken to the drink after all, they said. Or someone had thrown him over that he had cared for — no, not anyone here, some mysterious one in London, or Boston, or New York, or Paris. . . . Or it was some hereditary ailment. Or he had lost all his money. Yes, that seemed the most likely. Some kind of financial crash. These things happened constantly, even to the young and the beautiful.

Of Miss Ashlin nobody thought to ask, or to whisper. They had all forgotten her quite. As far as anybody knew she was painting somewhere, and running her petite gallery, as she had done for years. Now and then, even, a picture might be bought from her. But she did not figure in the drama of Jason Drinkwood. She had never been suited to him, wan, wispy little thing in her dilute purples and blondes. Pressed against his bronze, his vivid eyes, his white teeth and suits and car, she had been seared to cinders. But one never saw his car now, did one? There had been some sort of an accident, one thought. Those who had applied to Gerard Caul had formed the impression that Mr. Jason Drinkwood was suffering from hallucinations, and had been strongly advised to seek medical aid. Mr. Caul did not visit Mr. Drinkwood. They were not seen together in the bar at Co's, or on the tennis court at The Balconies.

It must be fairly serious, if such old friends now avoided contact. It must be rather unsavoury.

Night had fallen, and the villa lay plastered in a black stucco of darkness. At its heart sat Jason Drinkwood, drinking gin to keep awake, and to keep fear at bay. His servants had been sent forth days ago, since they had become mere witnesses to his humiliations. Besides, they facilitated disasters by those things they brought into the house in the way of foodstuffs and cleaning fluids, long after his ban on more dangerous substances. It was true, had it wanted to, his foe might already have murdered him, with one of a selection of knives, with some heavy object pushed on to his head, by fire or poison. Even the time in the car when the mauve silk hand, weightless and bodiless yet firm as flesh, had flown up at him, it was not his throat it had gone for, or even the wheel. No, it had merely perched there, on the dash, gentle and elegant, and he had stared at it, stared at every line and angle of it, every little crease in the material of its gloved life, every little stain and mark that it had

acquired in the processes of its hounding him. And, staring, he had run the car — in some ghastly evocation of a pun — off the road and into a palm. When he came to, dazed and groaning, the glove had hidden itself again. It was always shy when it had had its way with him. It would conceal itself, in a closet or a drawer, or behind a curtain. Sometimes he caught it peeping at him around a piece of furniture.

Several times, before the incident with the car, he had attempted to destroy the glove. Once he had almost got hold of it, but as he struggled to retain his grasp, it seemed to go all to nothing, not even to cloth but to air — and then he had lost it. He had lain on the polished floor where he had that time fallen, and watched it hurry upstairs, running on its finger-tips.

He had even allowed Gerard Caul's doctors to look him over. Jocund and reassuring, they had nevertheless wanted to remove him from the villa to costly nursing establishments in which they took an interest. But by then he realized the glove would follow him wherever he took refuge. Even as they tested his heart and shone lights into his eyes, he had been aware of the glove sidling round the room, now and then pausing behind the physician's back, as if to examine something, a plant or an ashtray. It was very careful with all the doctors, the glove. It never once played at revealing itself, as in the case of Gerard it had. Gerard, naturally, had refused to believe that any such thing was possible, so it had been safe to flirt with him. Even he, Jason Drinkwood, did not properly believe in the glove's animation and life, and perhaps that was what gave it its power over him. He constantly expected them to stop, the silly endless puerile awful tortures. He would constantly be thinking, on some level, that it was all nonsense, such things did not happen. And all the while the glove would be scuttling about behind the chairs, coming down from the picture-rail to tweak his hair, to upset salt into his food and dash his wine glass to the ground, to break and to despoil, or merely to flutter, sweetly as a butterfly, about him, until he broke down himself and cried like a child.

After the car, he gave up all hope.

Now he sat, with his broken wrist arrested across his chest, idly tapping the tin glass over and over against his teeth, looking sightless on darkness.

He knew the glove was near. It always was. He knew also that, if he should get up, it would pursue him. He made an experimental shift in his chair, and heard, in the huge cricket-sewn rhythm of the villa's silence, a dim slim rustle, over near the windows.

"I'll tell you what I'll do," said Jason Drinkwood coldly to the mauve glove that haunted him, "I'm going to go out now. I'm going to go out and walk across to the Monte. I'm going to go along to the gallery. Yes. Her gallery. I'm going to go straight up and knock on her door. That's what I'll do."

He wondered if the glove could actually understand words, if, as it were, it spoke English. And if that should be so, he puzzled a moment, would it try to stop him? When he got up, he flinched as he heard it lisp across the floor. But there was no assault, and by the time he stepped out on to the plains of night, he sensed that it was only going to shadow him, weaving independently along in the blue-black, avoiding the lamps, keeping under the trees, probably disappearing just before he reached his destination, the gallery on the Monte, where Alys Ashlin had her being and painted her pictures and worked her febrile magics of the night.

When he arrived at the gallery, which located itself on the oldest side of a picturesque small square, it was almost three in the morning. Yet, looking up from the street, he perceived there was a soft light in the upper storey. By using

a tiny courtyard at the back and climbing the outer stairs, he attained her studio door and jangled the bell. There was usually a porter, but he might be in bed by now. In fact, it was she who answered, appearing not at the door but on the balcony, and he gazed up at her in dismay, wondering how he could have allowed himself to be so foolish as to come here. For she was so slight a thing, so irrelevant to him, surely he had imagined it all? But then the veiled glow of the summer moon, sailing high above the hill, caught in her eyes. They were like opals, colourless, changeable, unlucky.

"Will you let me in?" he said.

"It depends what you want," she said.

"You know that," he said. He no longer felt foolish, only desperate, looking up into those cold moon-opal eyes. "I've come to tell you, to ask you — to make it — stop."

"What are you talking about?" she said.

Was she enjoying it, this power, or afraid of what he might do, maddened by all the tricks? She sounded only very tired.

He pointed to the sling which contained his wrist. He did not bother to show off his decoratively soiled clothing, the tiny holes sliced in its fabrics.

"Do you see this?"

She nodded he thought, but he was not sure. Her eyes flashed oddly as she lowered them to his arm.

"That's enough, isn't it?" he asked. "Isn't it?"

"I'm afraid I don't understand."

He found he could not speak about it directly, just as it seemed she refused to. He said lamely, "It's a bit unfair, you know. What did I do? I hardly *wronged* you, you know. For God's sake. I've had enough."

She sighed then. The sigh was like a leaf, sweetly fluttering down. The moonlight touched her hair, her white face and her slender white hands on the

balustrade, above the pots of vermilion dorisa, black by night as old blood.

"Mr. Drinkwood," she said slowly, looking past him across the roofs of the Monte to the implication of the distant bay, "I can only tell you this. Our first duty is to ourselves. To protect ourselves. There are things I must do, and obligations I must fulfill. I can't let you get in the way."

"For Christ's sake," he exploded, "what are you saying?"

"I told you once that I loved you. My emotion was very strong. You don't understand about such things, it would be fruitless to explain. But you hurt me very much, very deliberately, and there were only two things I could do. Either let the hurt eat into and perhaps destroy me, or to turn it away. Turn it back. The gift of pain you gave me, I don't want it, Mr. Drinkwood. Return to sender. If it was to be you or me, it must be you."

"You're mad," he said. He felt quite sick, and cold sweat had broken out all over him. In avalanching terror he added, in a withered, dying voice, "If I — do you want me to come back to you?"

"No thank you," she said. And then, "I'm very sorry. Good night."

"Wait, you bloody bitch!" he screamed, and a door opened sonorously in the storey below. Out into the moonlit yard stepped the porter, a large faceless obsidian shape, staring up at him. Jason was a moment stupefied, looking down at this apparition, as the balcony doors were drawn to above him. *Romeo and Juliet*. Well, he had said that.

He came down the stair unsteadily, and the porter towered in his path.

"Get out of my way," Jason mumbled. The porter obeyed him, without haste, but when Jason had negotiated the courtyard gate, he heard it being locked behind him.

He stood deflated in the alley, tears streaming down his face, in rage, in fear, in utter embarrassment and futility. As he did so, there came a soft rustling close by, like a small mauve sigh blowing through the shadows.

The letter, which was delivered by hand to Mr. Gerard Caul's suite and the Hotel Fleuris, did not especially delight him. It was in a version of Jason Drinkwood's formerly entirely readable, if slapdash, handwriting. It began, *"Dear Caul, You can still help me, if you will. I take this opportunity, since at the moment I'm not being observed, rather I do the observing, for I can see it sitting in a strawberry tree outside the window. It keeps watch on me, and I on it. Of course, how can it read? But maybe it can, by some peculiar means, do so. I can't take the chance. So, when I lose sight of it, I shall hide this letter on my person, next to my very skin."*

Getting so far, Gerard Caul was inclined to throw down the letter, but, since the remainder was brief, he resolved to finish it.

"My plan is to get out of the place — not just the villa, the whole country. The first steamer to the first homeward port. Spells don't travel over water. I remember hearing that. It may not be correct, but it's the only hope I've got. And no luggage, nothing it can stow away in. Just the garments I happen to be standing up in, and whatever essential cash and documents. And — it mustn't know what I'm up to. This is where you come in, Gerard, if you'll see me through. I won't waste your time with obvious details. You've got all the pull that's necessary. Use my funds, you know how to get at them. Just simply book me on the first boat out, with some kind of reference of your own — it may be needed. Say I've been ill, under a strain, am really quite a decent fellow, etc: I rely on you. I'm at your mercy. If you won't, I tell you I'm through, I'm lost. Yours, J.D. P.S. If you can see your way to doing this, don't telephone me, write me just one word: YES. And then, later,

date and time, only the numbers. Oh Gerard, for God's sake, do it."

Gerard Caul was offended by the whole project, but, in default of anything else, old stranglehold-ties of friendship presently forced him to pick up a pen, and write, aloofly, in a firm hand: *"Yes. G.C."*

About the middle of July, a curious occurrence overtook the passenger steamer *La Sebastienne*, as she was en route for open water.

The majority of the passengers had dispersed from their departure posts along the ship's rail, and were heading for their cabins, or the saloon. A few still at large on the landward decks were engaged to see a young man, who was in the process of removing his shoes and socks. These he then hurled away into the kohl-blue water, in the manner of offerings. They were shortly joined there by a shirt, a tie and a jacket.

The acute had already noticed that the dress of this individual young man, while of excellent material and cut, had nonetheless undergone some weird farewell rituals, prior to embarkation. These were felt, however, to be insufficient grounds for dispensing altogether with social dictates in the matter of modesty. As bit by bit, piece by — and by now intimate — piece of apparel was jettisoned, the volume of comment on the decks increased to a roar. Presently assistance was applied for. The ladies either turned their heads or did not turn their heads as a bevy of ship's personnel swarmed over the madman and bore him off. He was by this time completely naked, his face a study in triumph and anguish. Though generally it was not his mood which drew most attention.

By the cocktail hour, it was reported that the mad passenger lay sedated in his cabin, to which replacement clothing had been taken in the spirit of encouragement. It transpired that he had been rather ill, under rather a strain, that he was very sorry for his outburst, that everything was taken care of. For the remainder of the trip he was not seen again, though frequently looked for. At landfall he was smuggled ashore. The air resounded to the twang of pulled strings.

Thereafter the occurrence merely entered the lists of those travellers' anecdotes which are seldom believed and yet which tend to become the myths of other places, any places where one has never ventured, the lands of Unreal, the islands of Elsewhere.

For the sea, it swallowed Jason Drinkwood's clothes and presumably anything else that might have attached itself to them. And when the wake of *La Sebastienne* faded from the water, nothing at all was revealed there, but the sunlit currents and the ghostly palmate shapes of fish.

For his part, Gerard Caul — to whom the shipboard episode had filtered — would have been happy to hear no more of the subject which signed itself J.D. Gerard was of that estimable order of men who are able to leave behind all waste items, among them wasted friendships, with only the neat arm movement normally required in such disposals.

However, in the ensuing months, a letter arrived, a letter warm with gratitude, acidulous with proper self-mockery, and bright, ah so very bright, with relief. A letter, that is to say, from Jason Drinkwood, who, from his flat near Kensington Gardens, in the ancient city known to itself as London, now revealed that business was as usual. Indeed the letter, for all its warmth, acidity and brightness, cautiously skimmed the past, cautiously *hinted* at what would seem to have been an era of sickness, some bad dreams, an involvement with a silly and unstable female person, a revolt against summer heat and foreign climes. Only the postscript was a trifle odd. It requested that Mr. Caul would please omit to reply. Nothing, it turned out, that came from Mr. Caul's present part of the world, was being permitted access to Mr. Drinkwood's London life.

Gerard, who had not a wish on earth to reply, was gratified by obliging.

It happened a week later, that Gerard saw Alys Ashlin, as he was driving up across the Monte d'Oro. It was the swiftest viewing, a vague momentary sight, recognisable only because of Jason's agonies of description. She was standing outside one of the patisseries, buying flowers from a woman who sat there under her sunshade on the pavement. Pale violet flowers they were, the whole image a pastel, the whites, blues and lavenders of the merchandise, the dry old woman, the mild amber shade above, the contrasting blonde of the girl's hair and the little hat, the cool hands taking the clear wild mauve of the spray in a stream of blanching sun. Ah, yes, not at all displeasing. Gerard thought Miss Ashlin rather charming, a type of woman somewhat neglected now, like certain kinds of art, out of her time, delicate, fragile and too easily crushed, a gauzy thing. Then she was gone from his vision and his awareness. At no other hour of his life did he ever see her, and seldom heard of her again, and that only in the way of her work.

But it was less than a year before he heard something else of Jason Drinkwood.

"But surely, surely he must have loved her quite terribly. Oh, I do wish you'd tell me who she was."

Gerard who, if he had needed it, had used the interruption of lighting a cigarette to mask any shock he felt at the news of Jason's suicide, now answered, "My dear Cecilia. So far as I know, there was no one at all. That was just a foolish piece of gossip."

"But you're so wrong," said Mrs. Ce-

THE UNREQUITED GLOVE

cilia Hanson.

"Well, that may occasionally happen."

They were seated in the Long Room at Co's, overlooking the lawns, the bougainvillea, and the bay. The summer had come back as if it had never been gone, the distressing fire-wind of the early months was over, everything was set for another colonial season. Mrs. Hanson, whose husband had for years had business dealings with Gerard, and who, intermittently had had her own dealings with him, now continued silkily, "Of course, I know you and Jason Drinkwood lost touch — of course, you had *heard* he was dead?"

"Oh, naturally," lied Gerard.

"From the window," said Mrs. Hanson, in such a way that he suspected her of testing him. "Six floors. And the railings," added Mrs. Hanson. "Simply awful. I can never understand it. I mean, I can understand a man might feel driven to take his own life. But the method. An impulse, it must have been. He was so sunny the day before, quite himself. Not that I knew him well, ever." Her voice sharpened a little, grated a fraction, before she smoothed it over, "But Harry had just had lunch with him, at the London place, that good one. For heaven's sakes. But there you are. Brooding over this mystery woman you tell me never existed. And suddenly, unable to bear it any longer. So, the window. I blame the oranges myself."

"The oranges?" said Gerard, wondering, rather more than what she was talking about, how soon he could slip away. A vicious woman, he did not want to antagonise her unduly, but it was too hot for seduction as it was too hot for Cecilia Hanson's toiling complexion.

"Harry ordered oranges at lunch. They came from the hills here. He told me, Jason seemed quite *distrait* about it for a minute or two, then just broke out laughing, and ate two of them. But I can only conclude it was a sad reminder. Good lord. Three hours after, he flings himself from a sixth storey window."

Something tugged gently at Gerard's memory. It said: *"Don't write, my boy. Nothing from your neck of the woods, not for a while."*

"Oranges," said Gerard. He stubbed out his cigarette.

Cecilia Hanson sensuously licked the olive from her drink, a habit he disliked. There was a gleam in her eye he did not care for, and this harping on lost love. . . . Well, in the interests of fair trading with Harry, after all, he might have to take her along the coast to that dreary little shack of an hotel, chase her through the frothy waves as she giggled girlishly, overpower her in the dark room thick with scent and mosquitoes. Good manners. It did not do to offend such women.

"Now Gerard, you will tell me, won't you? Or am I going to have to do something reckless to get it out of you? What would you like?"

"Ah, Cecci. You shouldn't tempt me this way."

She snuggled closer. She wore a new perfume he liked better than the previous one, although probably, by the end of the endless afternoon, he would have come to loathe it utterly.

"Well, who was she?"

"Now, Cecci, I've said I have no idea. There was no one."

"Yes there was. Or why would he have kept her glove?"

To a man as prosaic, as easy-going, as influential, as efficient and modern and jaundiced as Gerard, his own reaction to this statement was an unwelcome, threatening thing. He turned cold, as if a wave had rushed up on him, from his feet to his skull, a cold cold icy comber from the depths of some unremembered, nonexistent sea.

"What do you mean *her glove*?"

"Well, don't snap at me for goodness' sakes. I only know what Harry told me — you know they called him and he had to — well, he said there was a glove, a woman's glove, lying there on the — right by Jason's body, under his hand. He must have been clutching it when he — as he — And Harry said it was such a pathetic little glove, all worn and torn, almost colourless, all wrinkled — it looked as if it had been through just about everything, and he must have been always wringing it in his hands or something."

Gerard's mind slipped suddenly away from Mrs. Hanson. It slipped away and saw a pale mauve fish swimming, and a pale mauve spider crawling, and then a pale mauve five-fingered wisp of silk scrambling, running on tip-toe, up rocks, over stones, through bush, through brier, over park over pale, through flood, through fire — And finally falling, fainting, from a crate of oranges. Dragging itself, poor crushed, sodden, rent and ruined fragile tinsel thing, through all the by-ways of London, and up the steps, under the door —

"Why Gerard," said Mrs. Hanson, "Gerard? Oh Gerard, I truly have missed you so."

WEIRD TALES TALKS WITH

TANITH LEE

by Darrell Schweitzer

Weird Tales: What is the greatest appeal of the out-and-out scary story?

Tanith Lee: There is a lot in the world that frightens people, and one way you can come to terms with it is by experiencing fear second hand, when you know you can put the book away or turn the TV off or walk out of the film if you have to. It's a form of practice for coping with fear, because we all experience fear in our lives. You can't avoid it. If you go through it second hand, you're practicing, and then you can face it if you have to. That's the education part. I also think people like to be frightened because it gets the adrenalin going and gives them excitement they don't always have in their own lives.

WT: Is this entirely an emotional response, or does it come in some part from an intellectual appreciation of how disconcerting reality can be?

Lee: It's a gut thing. People have always done it. The Greeks knew about it and called it catharsis, going through a whole range of emotions, not only fear, but pain and sorrow and gladness. It's something we do instinctively. I'm intellectualizing about it, but we all do it, and we all do it instinctively.

WT: Do you scare yourself when writing?

Lee: Sometimes. Yes, it happens a lot. I give myself nightmares. There's a children's book I wrote called *The Castle of Dark*, which features a kind of a vampire spirit which possesses a girl; and when I finally got the image — it appeared to me as most of my images do, as a picture in my mind — of how this thing was evolving from this girl's body like black smoke with two glowing eyes in it, I frightened the Hell out of myself, and I slept all that night with the light on.

WT: Does the fear go away when you've written the story?

Lee: Not necessarily. Sometimes when I write the story, it stirs up the feeling again. But it does go eventually.

WT: What does the writer have to do in order to make this feeling come across to the reader with undiminished force? We've all read horror stories that don't work, that don't scare us, even though the material might have seemed powerful to the author. So, what makes the one that works do so?

Lee: Good writing. The better your style is, the more you can put across. But you do get people who are lousy stylists but excellent at telling frightening stories, and you get people who write exquisitely but are very bad storytellers. If the two strengths are combined, the writer instinctively knows what to do. Also, your own reactions are a pretty good yardstick. If you scare the Hell out of yourself, you are of course going to scare a few other people.

WT: I see a common problem — I think it comes in the backwash of Lovecraft — that the writer spends the entire story building up to what the story is actually about. When he gets to what scares him, he stops. Would you agree this makes a story ineffective?

Lee: It depends on what you want to do with a story. If you really just want to scare people, there's no reason you shouldn't have stopped. That is sometimes the most disturbing element. You get to the point of terror, and then you leave everybody with this apparently insoluble problem. Of course many really satisfying horror stories do more. I'm thinking of something that really scared me, *The Day of the Triffids* by John Wyndham; I'm still scared of triffids. Admittedly it's a novel and not a short story. There he introduces a problem and there are a number of searing climaxes, but eventually the characters come to terms with the problem and deal with it the best they can. At the end of the book you are left still with the terror, but with a working solution by which they deal with it up to a point.

WT: But lots of people just build up to the premise, as if Stoker had stopped *Dracula* after four chapters, the climax being that the Count is really a vampire.

Lee: [Laughs.] Not necessarily. No, I think it's valid to end with that climax of terror, because it leaves a very nasty, frightening taste in the mouth. What do you *do*? But you're not told what to do. And if you want to, intellectually, you can go away and ask yourself what would you have done, how would you have handled that situation.

WT: Consider the story you told last night. Do you think the sequel would have been more interesting? [*Note:* The night before this interview was taped, Tanith had entertained an audience with a splendid rendition of what folklorists call a "Jump Tale." It concerned a man who gets off the train at the wrong stop late one night, in thick fog and mist. He wanders along a lonely road until he sees someone coming to-

ward him. At first he is delighted, and hurries ahead to ask directions and when the next train is due. He begins to speak, but then realizes that the stranger has no face. He runs in fright back to the station. Some while later he sees someone walking along the tracks with a lantern. It is an elderly, jolly conductor, whose presence is very reassuring. The traveler, now feeling safe, begins to wonder if his frightening experience really happened, and, somewhat embarrassed, tells his story to the conductor. "Could it really be?" he asks. "Could someone really exist without a face?" "Oh, you mean *like this*???" the conductor exclaims, ripping off his mask. Tanith made a motion of ripping off her face. The end. A good percentage of the audience duly jumped.]

Lee: It might be more interesting, but it would not have been so frightening, and that was the idea, to keep it scary.

WT: The guy might have discovered he was stranded in a whole community of faceless people and had to cope with being himself the freak.

Lee: I'm inclined to think that what would have happened after the story ended would have been that the man would have fallen to the ground in a dead faint, and when he revived the faceless man would have been standing over him, saying very apologetically, "Sorry, but that's just the way I am. I didn't *mean* to scare you."

WT: How often do you start with something funny and it comes out scary, whether intentionally or not?

Lee: Scary stories usually tell me, like everything I do, what they want to be. But there was a story called "The Third Horseman" that I sold to *Weirdbook*. It was a vampire story. Now I originally wrote this story when I was very young indeed, and when I wrote it, it was funny, *extremely* funny and very ironical. When I came to write it again, because I knew that I liked the story more than I liked its format — though I must admit it amused me — it came out as one of the most depressing and, I think, horrible stories I've ever written. But of course the thing with horror is that you've only got to tilt your perceptions very slightly and it can be *screamingly* funny. Triffids, for example, stumbling about clumsily. It could be hilarious.

WT: Is this nervous laughter, or a sense of the absurd?

Lee: I think it's a sense of the absurd. But people do giggle when they're afraid. Consider Roman Polanski's *Dance of the Vampires* [also known as *The Fearless Vampire Killers*] which is deliciously funny, and it also manages to be terribly frightening in several places, *very* depressing at the end while being funny as well. Which is very clever. It also makes a kind of definitive statement about vampires. It's very sensible in the way it deals with them. The vampires are logical. The film is very funny, so I suppose you could have a horror story that is screamingly funny and terrifying as well. Why not? Polanski did it.

WT: What is the appeal of vampires for you?

Lee: I don't know. I've been asked this before. A lot of people are fascinated by vampires. I think it's probably a wish-fulfillment: how lovely to be slim and pale and flawless. It's a bit of a drag that you can't go out in the daylight, but I suppose one could overcome that. It's a bit of a drag that you can't eat except for one thing, but I suppose you could get used to it. And there are the lovely attributes vampires have on the side, invisibility and not being seen in mirrors, and so on. One either wants to use that because it's extremely romantic in a couple of ways, or one wants to examine it and think, well, *is it true?* And if it is true, why? Which is basically a scientific approach. And if it isn't true, let's get rid of it. But vampires are just *very* appealing. They're always beautiful — not so much nowadays, but they used to be *desperately* elegant. I mean, black silk and white lace and blood-red rings and so on.

WT: When you were a child, did you ever want to grow up to be a vampire? I did for a while. I thought it would be very nice, for all I knew it was quite impossible.

Lee: Not consciously, but I think I must have done it unconsciously. I think I wanted to have vampires among my friends, but even then I had a sort of suspicion that what I liked doing best was writing. I guess it would suit my lifestyle to be a vampire. But how do you know I haven't grown up to be a vampire? This could all be a ruse.

WT: Actually, Stoker's Dracula *did* come out in broad daylight. Of course Dracula couldn't use his powers by day. He couldn't turn into a bat or a wolf . . . but then I haven't seen you do that either . . .

Lee: [Laughs.] Well, stick around. You might see something flapping over the Sheraton late . . .

WT: When did you know you wanted to be a writer? Were you born with the urge?

Lee: I didn't ever really know I wanted to be a writer. I *was* a writer. I started to write when I was nine. It became as simple to me as the act of breathing. It still is the thing I find easiest to do in the world. It isn't very hard. It's so natural for me. When I was a child I can remember being asked, "What do you want to be when you grow up?" And I said, "An actress." I suppose that was something I was wishing for, but in fact what I had to be, the only thing I could be, was a writer.

WT: How long were you writing before you started to sell?

Lee: You can't really count when I was nine, I guess, but I sold my first story, which was a children's book, in 1970. I had been writing throughout my

37

adolescence. I think one could count from about the time I was sixteen, that I was really having a go at it. I did sell fairly quickly. I wrote three children's books and they were taken by a publisher who paid for them but never published them because of a flood, and they were taken immediately afterwards by Macmillan.

WT: So you didn't have much of an apprenticeship.

Lee: One's whole life is an apprenticeship. You never learn your trade fully. You can always learn some more. I'm an apprentice now. I just happen to be a professional apprentice.

WT: Do you see specific directions in which you'd like to expand?

Lee: No, because if I wanted to do it, I'd do it. Writing is the one field where I've never had to say, "Oh, I would really like to do that. I'm going to find out how to do it." The only problem is that sometime I would certainly like to do some historical novels, and they would require a lot of research, but there would be time for that. They'd be fun to do. And I have written contemporary books, but they haven't yet been placed. But I have written them, and that's the main thing for me.

WT: Isn't it intensely frustrating to write a book which isn't published? I know that I didn't attempt to write a novel until I was selling short fiction for some years and thus was pretty sure I could sell a novel. There's this fear that all the effort will go straight into the closet.

Lee: Well I don't have a fear about it, because I'm fortunate enough to have fairly certain prospects of selling now, and also I've become aware that I must admit the commercial side of it, inasmuch as I stick out with television and so on for what I feel is due to me, because I couldn't afford to do things like that unless I get paid very well. But the big thing in my life has always been novels, and they come. If I have

to write something that isn't going to sell, I will still write it. I may be slightly concerned and think of the next payment on the house which is going to have to wait a month, and there are responsibilities such as food, and one buys things. But it's a demon that rides me. It's a very beneficial demon. It says, "You're going to do this and I'm going to nag you until you do." So you don't have a lot of choice.

WT: Do the demands of the marketplace determine what the demon is going to write? What would you do if you wanted to write something which you knew, ahead of time, was completely uncommercial. Could you tell your demon no, and work on something else?

Lee: I would write it. I'm very quick writing, normally. I came back from America and wrote a 200-page novel in under a month, and typed it in another month, and then went back to what I should have been doing. I suspect you are probably thinking of something very profound and very unlikely to find a market. That it might take longer. I would just juggle a bit with my schedule and fit it in, whereas I'll write and I won't take on certain commitments, even though they pay very well, because they won't fit into the schedule. But if I get possessive about something, I'll do it. I still would be writing other things too. Hopefully I would spend a month on the special project and go on to something else.

WT: What are your writing methods like? Do you just sit down and write, or do you outline, for example?

Lee: I did do an outline a couple of times, but it's very unusual. I always feel that the story is there. It's a matter of picking up the receiver and keeping at it until I've got it all, the entire story, as if it has a transmitter somewhere. Now maybe it has, and I am picking it up, but I just let it come, and I write it, and the characters tell me plots they think they want to do. Sometimes they have to be checked a little bit. They do terrible things like getting killed when I didn't expect them to, or not getting killed when they really ought to. The story tells me. The outline's there, but I haven't written it. It's somewhere floating in the atmosphere.

WT: Do you think the subconscious writes the story and then lets it surface?

Lee: No. I don't think it's my subconscious. I think my subconscious sometimes works out problems in plot that I'm finding difficult. Sometimes I have to hammer them out with blood, sweat, and tears, stamping around my workroom talking to myself, but I've become convinced that it isn't me. Now that's probably quite wrong, but it does feel like something's coming in, like radio waves floating in the atmosphere. It's almost as if I'm picking them up. I think it's probably fragments that one's gotten from various things, and perhaps race memories, but I don't think it can be just the subconscious. No.

WT: Do you mean race memories in the classical sense, actually remembering things our ancestors experienced?

Lee: I mean race memories. After all, we're all built of all these genes and little bits and pieces come through from the very beginning of our ancestry, and it seems quite logical that some of these genes can carry recollections. Some people are more susceptible to it than others, which means one's seen a Hell of a lot of things, the genes have, and they can pass them on to the brain, one could pick these recollections up and amalgamate a bit here and a bit there, and you'd have a story and a set of characters.

WT: In other words, a universal unconscious, to coin a phrase.

Lee: Well, one's individual universal unconscious, everything that's carried through from one's genes. Or it could

be past lives, couldn't it?

WT: Do you ever write from dreams, or base stories strongly on dreams?

Lee: I have done a couple of things, one short story which I can't recall, strangely enough, but I know I did it, and it was based solely on a dream. What usually happens is that when I'm writing, I sometimes have dreams which are loosely related to what I'm writing. I will then incorporate perhaps one or a couple of those dreams into the book, as dreams, tailoring them to fit the way the characters work. I've done that on several occasions.

WT: Do these dream images become the most vivid part of the book? What I'm suggesting is that the subconscious produces this thing which you then intellectualize into a story.

Lee: As I say, I have done it, but usually it just goes into the body of the work as a dream. I am writing a book at the moment, and while I was writing it I had a nightmare; and I realized, having woken up and gotten over the nightmare, that one of the characters in the book could well have had the same nightmare I had had. It probably was related to him. I had been thinking about him, so I gave him the nightmare, just tidying it up a little bit so that it was really his and not mine. I remember the short story, by the way. It was "The Dry Season." That was the one that was based on a dream I had when I was about fifteen.

WT: Where was it published?

Lee: I think it was in *Flashing Swords*, but I couldn't swear to it because there is some confusion in my mind about what stories have gone into what.

WT: Do you subscribe to any particular literary or aesthetic theories? Some writers have quite elaborate ones, while others just sit and write.

Lee: Such theorizing sounds idiotic to me. But that's because I know nothing about it. I certainly don't.

WT: I've always felt that theories should describe rather than dictate, but for some people they are almost ideologies. You know, movements and the like.

Lee: If one wants to do it that way, it probably works extremely well, but it wouldn't be anything that I could be successful at, because to me that would be totally alien. I wouldn't think of doing anything that way, because to me stories are alive. They have to tell me what they want, so I can't stricture them. They have to go their own way.

WT: Are you influenced by other writers, those you might once have taken as models, for example?

Lee: I'm influenced by everybody. I'm influenced by everything I see, everything I read, every rumor I pick up, every person I meet. They all influence me, and no one more than another. But of course I'm influenced, because I'm influenced by everything.

WT: Then there was no writer you took as an idol when you were younger, to be emulated?

Lee: Not to be emulated. Of course I'm quite sure that if you're madly in love with a particular writer you probably do pick up a few things. I would never set out to emulate somebody even if I admired them desperately, because we're all different, and they're doing something that is not what I'm doing. This doesn't stop me from being madly in love with them.

WT: Do you have any serious occult beliefs?

Lee: No, not really. I have practiced a very minor form of witchcraft which is based on willpower, self-fulfillment, self-desire, and positive thinking; and sometimes it's worked very well, and I think it's possible that we have the ability to do such things. Witchcraft interests me, but I don't know an awful lot about it.

WT: Part of the appeal of fantasy fiction may be that we are all believers in the supernatural under the surface. We don't believe consciously, but unconsciously is another matter.

Lee: You see, I believe in it consciously, because I think there are these powers, in ourselves mainly, which are responsible for an awful lot of the weird things that happen to us and to other people. Certainly, I'm extremely superstitious. I would never walk under a ladder because I did find that if you walk under a ladder, something pretty horrible would happen. Now I believe that was me, because I had picked up the superstition and I was afraid it would happen, and I partly made it happen. I got myself into situations in which I was nervous, where they happened, or else my will, which is quite strong, was influencing things until they turned out badly. Then I found out that if you walk under a ladder and cross your fingers and wish for something, it negates the ill luck and you have a very good chance of getting your wish to come true. In fact, the very first time I did it, I had just written to DAW books, and said, "Would you be interested in seeing a synopsis of my novel? " And they said, "Yes." Now I still firmly believe the wish under the ladder did that.

WT: I once had a witch offer to cast a spell for me. She said, "Anything you want." So I said, "Make my next story sell." I wasn't really selling yet at the time. So she did it, and the story *almost* did. The only problem was that I was supposed to take a lavender-scented bath at midnight while burning a green candle, and I declined to do this. So, while the story was accepted, the anthology never came out, and I've had this curse ever since. I wonder, if I'd done it correctly, lavender-scented bath and all . . .

Lee: Those things witches use, they're focussing agents. This is the primary importance of all those things that witches use, that are accessories to witchcraft. They are means of focussing and they are means of proving to yourself that you really are doing that thing. Had you taken the lavender-scented bath — Oh, how lovely! — while burning a green candle, however ridiculous you felt, and however ridiculous you smelled afterwards, you would have firmly fixed in your mind that you'd done it. That activates your willpower. I guess the lady knew you wouldn't do it, so she was working for you. She may have *sensed*, because she'd have to be fairly sensitive if she's a witch, that you hadn't done it, and that would negate her power. So you had the beneficial side working for you, but you negated it. I think you should duplicate those conditions sometime, and *do* it this time, and see what happens.

WT: The manuscript was already in the mail, so how would my willpower have mattered at all? It should have been the *editor's* that mattered.

Lee: You mean it was in the mail coming back to you or going out?

WT: It was going out.

Lee: But he hadn't seen it yet?

WT: I don't think he had.

Lee: That's exactly it. What you were doing in fact was you were extending your willpower because you wanted him to publish it. I would imagine that if you were a really terrible writer and had written a really awful manuscript, it probably would not have helped; but assuming you have a good manuscript, one does need luck. One does need timing. It's very hard to guess at timing. So you're throwing a protective lasso around that work. You're putting a ring of light around it, saying, "I've done this thing. I have perpetrated these acts." This bolsters it. So, when he gets the manuscript, he feels that crackle of electricity, and it probably does influence him. Do you realize that all over this country people will be taking lavender-scented baths and burning green candles and we'll have whole piles of stories being published?

WT: I suspect that the failure of the anthology was a backfiring with wide-reaching consequences. The editor in question was Lin Carter and the anthology would have come after what actually was the final anthology in the Ballantine Adult Fantasy Series. I have this feeling that because of my mishap, I wiped out the whole series. Ever after I've had a history of selling to people who go out of business.

Lee: You're going to be *so* popular. [Laughs.] You have a *lot* to answer for. What can I say? That's terrifying. But I would think not. No, that's too much of an escalation. The only thing is that maybe a lot of you were doing the same thing, failing to take baths and burn candles. Maybe a group of you could cause a thing like that. But I don't think one could.

WT: There might have been a lavender shortage.

Lee: [Laughs.] Or a shortage of green candles.

WT: The funny thing is that the curse sometimes reverses itself. If the magazine or book actually survives to publish something of mine, it usually prospers.

Lee: That sounds good.

WT: I hope I'm not the Typhoid Mary of publishing. Speaking of which, what have you published recently, or have coming out in the near future?

Lee: Well, in the past couple of years there have been *Days of Grass*, a science-fiction novel; *Sung in Shadow*, a fantasy, actually a parallel world Romeo and Juliet; three collections, *Tamastara*, which is set in India, *The Gorgon*, and the Arkham House book, *Dreams of Dark and Light*, which was nominated for the Fantasy Award. Also: *Anackire*, a sequel to *The Storm Lord*, and two further novels in the Flat Earth series, *Delirium's Mistress* and *Night's Sorceries*. Coming next year

41

(1988) is a third Vis book, *The White Serpent*, and a larger fantasy — a sort of parallel-world historical novel in an altered Europe of about 1800 — *A Heroine of the World*. Some original horror-novels will be out in England from Unwin/Hyman. The series is called *The Secret Books of Paradays*. I have also written a large fact-fiction novel on the French Revolution, but no one will touch it.

WT: What do you think of the current state of the genre?

Lee: I'm very busy. I'm in the midst of buying a new house and selling the present one, so you can imagine. I'm afraid I don't have any views particularly on the "state" of the genre. I read very little SF and fantasy.

WT: Thank you, Tanith Lee. ∎

A CAUTIONARY NOTE TO TRAVELERS THROUGH THE MUTANT RAIN FOREST

If you run deep within the gloomy fringe
where black mahoganies are upright spades
that shudder, shift and moan like ghostly shades,
be wary then of creatures fresh of tinge.
The *necrophida* moths grow huge as planes,
and feast on corpses hung in cauls of moss.
The *kongii* sloths will make the treetops toss
to shape unearthly music from the rains.
And blue *duendes* shriek along your trail,
those shadow jaguars slick and dark as oil
who'll brave a ring of fires that lick and boil
to steal your soul; you'll flee to no avail.
their stares can bristle full with spikes of light.
On them transfixed you'll spend eternal night.

— Robert Frazier

THE COMMUNAL NIGHTMARE

Fatigue has aged and lined our face's calm:
A penance paid for silence kept those years,
For staying home while friends went on to 'Nam.
We loved their wives, forgetting them as peers.
Between us moved like wine or rumored truth
This nightly dread unreeled in scenes; so spread
Like fanning stalks across the jungle roof,
We splay in waist-high thickets sprayed by lead.
At last the ambush cuts the squad bone deep
Our buddies splash and die in dreaming's mists.
We're gripped by fingers tipped with drugs of sleep,
As firm and deft as lepidopterist's.
Thus linked across this country, large in number,
We're pinned again, again in bleakest slumber.

— Robert Frazier

PROFILE: TANITH LEE

by Donald A. Wollheim

It was the Dutch publisher, Meulen-hoff, who first termed Tanith Lee "Princess Royal of Fantasy." The *Village Voice* (New York) promptly took up the title with a rave review of her works. And DAW Books has continued to so term her ever since. Nobody has challenged the title, because nobody dare claim that it is not deserved.

From the day that her novel *The Birthgrave* was first published (by DAW Books in the U.S.A), Tanith Lee has been a blazing gem in the crown of fantasy literature. She has written many novels, and varied they have been, but all have been outstanding instances of brilliant coloration, poetic conceptions, and sheer imaginative brilliance. She has written many short stories and has been sought after eagerly by the major magazines of the science fiction and fantasy fields, and yet she has appeared in semi-professional magazines and even fanzines. She has been Guest of Honor at conventions in the U.S.A., Great Britain, The Netherlands, Sweden, and elsewhere. And of course she has won awards.

But who is this whom Arkham House termed the Scheherazade of Fantasy? She is a young lady, born and raised in London, who has been writing tales since the age of nine, and who went through the usual assortment of unrewarding jobs until she broke though into the publishing world. She did two or three children's novels before her discovery by the American SF/fantasy field. Since then, she has been writing for her living with success after success:

over thirty novels, and innumerable translations and reprints, in the last fifteen years. Her stories appear all over the world. She has written episodes of serials for the B.B.C. and has had poetic dramas read over the British radio. Fantasy is her realm and she wears its crown as born to it.

As perhaps she was. When her mother was eighteen, she read the name Tanith in a book of mythology and decided that that would be the name of her daughter if she were to have one. And it did become her girl-child's name. Tanith, the Carthaginian equivalent of Ishtar, of Venus, of Aphrodite, turned out to be most fitting. There is no Tanith but Tanith . . . slightly sinister, dreamer of darkness and light, explorer of the supernatural and of the lore of ancients, who can tear aside the veil of the future and the stars, while insisting on her belief in reincarnation and its unending ties with the past, this is the stuff from which great writing flows — and continues to flow. No two stories are alike. Her world of the Flat Earth is not that of the Goddess of the Volcano nor that of the Electric Forest nor yet that of the French Revolution, but she knows them all in living color.

For me as her primary editor, the arrival of a manuscript from Tanith Lee is always an event, for who knows what wonders it will contain? Sometimes months will go by while she works on a long tale of time past or time future. And sometimes short stories will come one after another as she works that strain and her imagination bounds from one marvel to another. In 1988 there will be a short novel from Donald Grant, *Madame Two-Swords,* in a limited edition. In 1989 there will be an early start with *The Heroine of the World,* a romantic out-of-this-world novel worthy of the mainstream. We hear she is working on a new literary symphony of the Flat Earth group.

Now she has moved from the noisy city to the more rustic settings of Kent. Here we can expect new challenges and writings greater than before. "Princess Royal" . . . perhaps better the Empress of Dreams. I am reminded of Clark Ashton Smith's magnificent poem that begins (with one word changed):

Bow down: I am the empress of dreams;
I crown me with the million-coloured suns
Of secret worlds incredible, and take Their trailing skies for vestments. . .

COMING IN OUR FALL, 1988 ISSUE!

Our Special **Keith Taylor** Issue

featuring three terrific new stories by

Australia's premiere fantasist!

Men from the Plain of Lir

The Ordeal Stone

— and —

The Haunting of Mara

— also featuring —

an astonishing selection of other weird tales, including:

Still the Same Old Story
by W.T. Quick

Emma's Daughter
by Alan Rodgers

Clive Barker Interview
by Robert Morrish

Don't Risk Missing An Issue —
SUBSCRIBE TODAY!

Turn to the inside back cover for more information

TANITH LEE: A SELECTED BIBLIOGRAPHY

The Dragon Hoard (1971). Juvenile.
Animal Castle (1972). Juvenile.
Princess Hynchatti and Some Other Surprises (1973). Juvenile.
The Birthgrave (1975).
Companions on the Road (1975). Juvenile.
The Winter Players (1976). Juvenile.
Don't Bite the Sun (1976).
The Storm Lord (1976).
Drinking Sapphire Wine (1977).
Volkhavaar (1977).
East of Midnight (1977)
The Castle of the Dark (1978). Juvenile.
Vazkor, Son of Vazkor (1979).
Quest for the White Witch (1979).
Shon the Taken (1979). Juvenile.
Electric Forest (1979).
Sabella, or, The Blood Stone (1980)
Kill the Dead (1980).
Day By Night (1980).
Delusion's Master (1981)
Unsilent Night (1981). Collection.
Lycanthia (1981)
Prince on a White Horse (1982). Juvenile.
Cyrion (1982). Collection.
The Silver Metal Lover (1982).
Red as Blood, or, Tales from the Sisters Grimmer (1983). Collection.
Sung in Shadow (1983).
Anackire (1983).
Tamastara, or, The Indian Nights (1984). Collection.
Days of Grass (1985).
The Gorgon and Other Beastly Tales (1985). Collection.
Dreams of Dark and Light (1986). Collection.
Delirium's Mistress (1986).
Dark Castle, White Horse (1986).
Night's Sorceries (1987).
The White Serpent (forthcoming).
A Heroine of the World (forthcoming).
Madame Two-Swords (forthcoming).

THE INITIATE

by Ronald Anthony Cross

Prologue

Too many bright colors that all run together, like a huge watercolor painting by a madman who just didn't care. Too many sounds.

The trilling of birds, the shrill screams of the children at play, hawkers, crying their wares, old wives gossiping in the marketplace.

Too many people speaking at once in too many tongues. Oh, how they babble on in Babylon.

Amorites, Aramaeans, Elamites, Kassites, Lulubaeans, and Hittites move among the crowds chattering in little groups. Here and there a Greek or Egyptian. Babylonians speaking in their own sharp Semitic tongue. A small flock of desert Hebrews dressed in rags, sullen expressions, frightened of the big city.

Erudite priests stroll by us conversing in the ancient Sumerian tongue about matters too esoteric, no doubt, for the common language, even as the king's own soldiers, fierce little men with kinky black beards, march by, glistening in armor made of pure gold.

Too much sound and too much color.

Now and then a mysterious maiden, veiled and hidden in loose robes, glides silently through the crowd, eyes downcast as though one glance would drive a man to madness.

A covey of whores stands outside the Inn of the Red Donkey, all dressed up in brilliant-colored silks, which they occasionally throw open to reveal musky brown breasts with rosy nipples to strangers passing by.

"See, do you see, like grapes, like luscious grapes," one of them cries aloud, and they all laugh raucously like a flock of startled parrots.

The very color of the sky is too bright here, the sun hot, potent, blazing with life.

Never before a city like this one; never again a city like this one.

Move on, move on. Across a courtyard where throngs of people lounge in the shade of the imported palm trees, gazing up at a series of luxurious terraced gardens, each one higher than the next, a veritable series of jungles of vines, trees, exotic plants and birds among the rooftops, gardens hanging in the sky. Will wonders never cease.

Move on. Along the main street of the city, the sacred way, a street wide enough for thirty-five horses to trot side by side between massive blue walls with giant red-and-yellow lions glaring down ferociously from either side.

Move on until you come to the Gate of Ishtar, as tall as six tall men standing each on the other's shoulders, and taller yet.

Blue gates with a myriad of brilliantly colored sacred beasts frolicking before your eyes.

Never a city like this one, surrounded by a wall so high it appears a mountain, so wide that two men could pass each other in chariots riding along the top of it, and then a moat filled with water, and then another wall.

Behold the seven-layered tower that juts into the darkening sky, a beam of mysterious blue light glinting from the tiny room at the top. "And they said, let us build a city and a tower, whose top may reach unto heaven."

Never before such a city; never again such a city; but move on, it grows dark, and the ladies of Ishtar are beginning to stroll the streets, the thieves and cutthroats are sharpening their minds and daggers for the long night ahead.

Move on until you come to the base of the great tower, set within a series of palatial buildings to house the priests, amidst the great, richly filled storehouses, surrounded by giant fortresses with forests of towers plunging into the night sky. Move on, for it is dark and we have an appointment among the rooftops of the greatest city ever known to man.

A group of men moved laboriously across the steeply slanted roof, dressed in light robes, for it was a warm summer night. One of them, smaller than the rest and moving with astonishing agility, was dressed only in a loosely fitting pair of brown trousers tied with a string.

"Are you certain you can manage on the rooftops? It is his home, you know; he is more used to the footing here than he is to walking on the solid ground."

The three of them had halted to wait for the other two to catch up, and now the youth in brown did a strange thing in answer to their question. To everyone's astonishment he turned a series of dazzling cartwheels along the edge of the roof.

"I'm certain," he said softly, smiling as though he shared a secret knowledge between the Moon, the stars and himself. "I'm completely certain," he said again.

"The roof is slanted here; you might have fallen off; you must take care; he is an awesome opponent. I do not personally believe you can best him." He waited for an answer. When he got none

he continued compulsively. "I personally do not believe you can best him. Nobody can. His voice is powerful magic. You will topple to your doom, like all who have tried before you. He is a giant; and his voice is magic, while you are a mere stripling beside him. You spent the entire day at the gardens of Ishtar, sporting with the temple whores; and now you cavort like an acrobat along the roof's edge. What are you, a performing ferret or a seasoned warrior?"

"I am the greatest fighter the world has ever known," the youth answered in his calm, unchanging tone of voice. "Trained in the mountains of India, and by the fierce Ninevites you know so well. I have traveled the world my entire life, learning secrets of combat in cities you do not even dream exist. I have boxed with the mighty Acheans, wrestled with the tall pale riders of horses on the eastern steppes; and yes, I have trained in the schools of the monkey and the crane in the torchlit caves of the mountains that circle the city of the yellow men. Have faith, good friend; your money is well spent. I will topple this Lion-Roarer, that stalks the rooftops at night, preying upon the innocent thieves who, driven by the urgency of the moment, must take to climbing in the dark."

"He defies the Guild of Thieves. The most powerful organization in the largest city of the world. A guild a thousand years old and older. He kills and robs us when we are driven to the rooftops by the soldiers. He must be stopped."

"And so he shall, but it would help if you could tell me more of his technique. He is large; he uses no weapons; and this I can understand: the poor footing, the dark of night, a gust of wind. A man needs both hands free to balance, to grip and uproot. To clutch at the bricks should one stumble. He is correct in that. Anything held in the hand, however small, would offset the balance by a hair, among experts, a hair too much. I have decided — I will meet him empty hand to empty hand, let delicacy of balance decide the night."

"I tell you, O highly paid assassin, his voice is his weapon: with his voice alone he topples all men from the roof who cross his path."

The youth in brown shook his head, a slightly puzzled expression crossed his face like a cloud crossing the Moon. Could there be truth in this wild story, or mere superstition?

Many times in many lands he had encountered warriors of legend, mostly to find them in the light of reality revealed as clumsy oafs with little or no skill at combat. Yet there could be truth in it. He had thought of stuffing bits of cloth in his ears, but in the end was afraid it would affect his balance. No, he had made his decision. Now, come what may, he would meet Lion-Roarer on his own territory, hand to hand, without any hidden weapons or tricks.

The Moon disappeared behind a cloud and the skies grew dark. The men around him groaned.

"A bad omen, O highly paid assassin; is there anything we can do to aid you in your fearful trial?"

"Yes, you can stop calling me 'O highly paid assassin.' It gets on my nerves more than does the dying of the Moon. In many cities I am known by many names. In this great city I will be known only as Ferret. You have so named me and so it shall be. On distant isles across the sea, where the people have hair of gold, I am called Hound. In the mountains of India I am Monkey; to you I shall be Ferret. Now you must wait here for me. Come no closer until I have toppled him from the roof. Here is the purse of jewels you have given me; I will not need it if I fail. I warn you, however, should you attempt to run with it, a nightmare beside which Lion-Roarer shall be considered a pleasant memory will haunt these rooftops until the deed has been more than

paid for by the Guild of Thieves. May our Lady of Luck be with us tonight."

But the Moon hid from view as he ran lightly across the edge of the roof, and when he looked back all he could see was four indistinct shadows of men with their elbows up even with their heads.

If there had been light, you would have seen him smile. *They've got their fingers stuck in their ears,* he thought, *and they're shaking like leaves in a strong wind.*

As he moved across the rooftops alone in the dark, he felt the awe he always felt before mortal combat. It was death itself he mocked again and again, as he fought his lonely battles in the hills, in the deserts, on rooftops in great cities, and in camps of horsehide tents by the flickering light of the fire.

He paused to look over the edge into the deepening shadow and knew it was not into the street but into infinity he saw, the void that never ends.

He felt a thrill course through him in the dark. Then he felt something cold and damp touch his forehead and then his bare shoulder, a light rain.

It would be a hand-to-hand battle, in the dark, on a slippery wet rooftop, in rain.

Suddenly he began to laugh, like a whisper, a strange hissing sound, dry in the rain.

His bare feet gripped the roof; his spell of laughter passed him by; and then, as though it had always been there but never before noticed, he saw a still figure across the roof from him, standing with one leg on either side of the peak of the roof, rising into the sky at the highest point of the building like a rain god calling forth storm.

Ferret froze where he was in the shadows, his eyes fastened on the figure, his ears straining to catch some sound over the pattering of the light rain.

And though it rained still, the Moon

came out from behind a cloud; and Ferret saw a man of middle height but of powerful breadth and mighty muscles. A man with broad bones and square jaw, with a fringe of thick light hair all around his face and head, but with his upper lip shaved clean, so that he looked as though he possessed the mane of a lion. A man standing calmly relaxed with his arms folded, straddling the rooftops in an oncoming storm.

A man dressed all in gold, smiling. A man who knew that Ferret was there.

A hundred yards, Ferret thought, no more.

"Lion-Roarer, I come," he cried; and he began his charge upward across the slanted slippery roof to the peak and then along the peak in the rain, into the heart of the fight.

At first it was so subtle he didn't notice anything. He didn't hear it. It wasn't like hearing. It was like a feeling of vibration, of distances stretching out, of things slowing down. It seemed like an endless journey, that charge across the peak of the roof. It was so hard to concentrate. Then he saw it in the moonlight.

Lion-Roarer was bent over, fists clenched, loose golden clothes and beard flapping in the wind, mouth open, face contorted in a shriek.

And now he heard it and knew he had been hearing it all along, a loud vibrating wail building each moment to a higher stronger peak.

And he realized with a shock that the Moon had gone behind the clouds again and that the light with which he saw came not from the moon, but glowed mysteriously, syncopated in time somehow with the roaring of the Lion.

The first shriek ended; and he was aware that he was sitting on his knees on the peak of the roof, shaking his head aimlessly at the night sky.

Ferret sprang to his feet and began to sprint lightly down the edge, when Lion-Roarer began his second great at-

tack.

And if the first had been puzzling, dizzying; then this attack was one of stunning power.

A high-pitched, round oscillating, that brought with it a terrible light.

"Brighter than day, brighter than day," Ferret sang to himself as he tripped and stumbled along. No, as he danced; it was all, of course, a dance: as he danced along the edge into a funnel of pulsating light.

A figure waited for him at the center of the light. A figure glowing with light and warmth; he need be alone no more.

He was overwhelmed with joy. This was it. This was what he had searched the world for, wandering alone and lost among the splendor. This beautiful friendship waiting for him at the peak of the roof, in the center of the light. His eyes filled with tears.

Why was he sitting here shaking his head? He got up. He staggered. Then he forced himself to concentrate. He went on, slower this time, gritting his teeth.

My body knows what to do, no matter my mind. If I can just get my body to him it will do what it does so well, Ferret thought.

He lost track of everything as he ran — oh so slowly — down a cone of light to the figure awaiting him at the center.

There was no sound now. Lion-Roarer stood with his paws, his hands, no his paws on his waist, smiling, waiting. His mane had a golden reddish glow. His features were exaggerated, stretched. Time was stretched out. He was running forever, forever.

He was practically in reach when Lion-Roarer gave his third and most terrible cry, a short powerful blast like an explosion.

It's over, Ferret thought; *I'm not strong enough after all.*

Then light broke all about them, growing brighter and brighter while the roof began to vibrate wildly beneath his feet.

Everything is vibrating, whirling, he thought, *filled with other little things, vibrating, whirling, filled with other little things, vibrating, whirling; I can't keep track, I can't. . . .*

In the steadily increasing light, Lion-Roarer's face was etched in super clarity, but somehow things were wrong. *The beard was crimson, no it was a brilliant blue; the eyes were fire, fire; I can't keep track, I can't.*

Ferret felt the strength pour out of his knees as he closed his eyes against the light. He started to fall.

But the light didn't go away, couldn't go away. *The terrible light. Oh God, save me, whatever I am, from the terrible light, whatever that is.* Undifferentiated. Nothing but light. Nothing but light.

I thought it was dark, but it's all light. What is dark, my God, there is no dark, just light, all light.

Forever and ever, he thought. *No,* he thought, *no, I won't, I won't.*

There could be some plants in it, gently waving, nothing much. There were plants in the terrible light, gently waving, and for eons and eons of undifferentiated existence this satisfied him.

But then shadowy forms began to take place among the plants, mischievous forms. *I can run with them,* he thought; and they ran together capering among the plants in the hot desert sun, snorting and sporting, licking and kicking. It was their desire to eat the plants. They took delight in this. They tore them up and ate them up, and this was good. But then the others came, to crack their bones and eat their flesh. The terrible hunters, the slinky stalkers.

They ran. They ate and ran and killed and were killed. A forever full of running, killing, eating, being killed, being eaten, until one day, they stood on a great plain, grazing on tall grass.

There was a tree with some shade. There was a road that went beside the tree and the figure of a young woman came along the road, mysteriously veiled and dressed all in a cool blue, like the sky, like the water.

In her thick curling loose hair was pinned a silver crescent.

He watched her from among the grazing antelopes, with a strange new sensation he could not quite place.

One by one she removed her garments, until she stood naked in the shade of the tree smiling, beckoning to him.

"The time has come," she laughed; "you can run with the beasts no more."

He did not understand her words, but he felt lust rise up in him as a wave; and it was a tidal wave that swept him helplessly to the shade tree and into her arms and locked their bodies together, thrashing in the grass, in the shade beneath the tree.

And they coupled and completed, but lust rose up within him again, and later again until the Moon was high in the sky smiling down upon them, for the Moon is our Lady of Lust and Purity all at once.

"I am a virgin," she said sweetly; and he laughed because he understood her now.

"How can you be a virgin?" he said to her. "You have sported with me all day and yet you say you are a virgin."

"Look in the water," she said to him, for there was a little stream that played nearby the tree, in the tall grass among some stones and pebbles.

She dropped a handful of dirt into it, which it swept away, regaining its pure transparent quality almost at once.

"Can you soil the moving water, my friend? My essence is like the moving water, self-purifying, ever-changing. My soul is translucent blue, although my body is the body of a harlot. To me, each time is new, each man the first.

The body is made by coupling, for coupling, and true virginity is a forever-recurring miracle of life and not the stagnant withholding of oneself from the mainstream. You can no longer run with the beasts, dear friend."

Then he slept a deep sleep, fulfilled in a way of which he had not known he had been wanting. Fulfilled, but sensing that he had entered on an endless path of hunger and gluttony, winking on and off like day and night, forever. Yet he was fulfilled and he slept deeply; and when he awoke, she was gone with the night and the Moon.

He stretched himself in the light of the new day, fully contented for the time being; but when he went out to join his friends they ran from him in terror, as though he were a beast of prey.

He cried out to them aloud to come back, but now he spoke one tongue and they another. He did not understand them, and to his astonishment he realized he did not want to understand them anymore. *How could I have been content like that,* he thought. He sat down underneath the tree to think what he should do. But thinking was new to him and soon he gave it up and just sat motionless in the shade of the tree, gazing, instead of grazing, out over the vast plain before him.

Never again will I wander senselessly with the beasts. Never again will I move without a purpose, and yet I know not what to do. I will not move from beneath this tree until I find a reason to move.

Night came and then day again and then night, and he did not move. But on the third day, just as the sunlight began to break through the darkness, he suddenly got to his feet. *If I don't have a purpose to move, why then I must move in search of a purpose,* he thought. *How simple it is.* He began to wander, aimlessly as before on the surface; but inside of himself he was alert and questioning. As he traveled he read each

rock, and each tree and each star. And yet he found in them nothing of himself, for he knew not how to look.

After a while the Sun went out and he entered a land of inner night.

So dark, he thought. *Nothing but dark.* And yet he traveled on. Gradually, he began to make out different shapes in the darkness. He felt himself forming yet another universe within his mind's eye.

One lone star was born, and then he saw by the light of the first new star a scene of delicate enchantment.

Seven other stars broke out encircling the first and lit up a cool meadow covered with short green grass. One purple mountain cut the night sky as sharp and clean as a distant pyramid. One tree, on which a red bird perched and now called once, a raucous lonely cry.

A young woman with long soft hair knelt in the starlight.

At first he thought she had come to gather water from the pond, in the two ornate vessels she held in her hands. But then he saw that she was pouring water out of the vessels, one into the pond, and one onto the grass. As he approached, she smiled up at him with an expression of open joy.

"Why do you pour your water out," he asked her, "instead of carrying it to your home?"

"This is my soul and the soul of this plane and of this light. This is done so that the minds of men will flower, later on, in the full light of the Sun."

Looking into her eyes he saw they were the same cool blue as the water she poured. He knew instinctively that everything was safe here and free from all strife and loneliness.

"You wear no clothes."

"There are no clothes here," she said, and he saw that he also was naked in the starlight.

"I want to give up searching, striving, struggling," he said; "all of it. I just want to stay here with you," he said. He touched her soft hair.

"No one can ever make you leave," she said.

"I want to make love to you forever," he said.

"Here you can do anything you want to do," she said, "and no one can ever make you leave."

So he lived in starlight, with the beautiful young water-bearer in the cool meadow. Here no time passed and nothing ugly ever entered in. He was never hungry and he was never cold. A deep sense of peace settled over him like a blanket; and when he was not willing her otherwise, he watched her pour her waters out and listened to the lonely call of the lonely bird from the distant tree. Little by little he forgot everything else, until all he knew was the meadow, the girl and the star.

"There was never anything else. There will never be anything else," he said.

"So be it," she answered. But even as she spoke, a figure appeared in the meadow, of colossal buffoonery.

"How did that clown get in here?" he asked her indignantly.

"You let him in yourself," she answered.

An acrobat clown, he was. He turned a series of comic somersaults and rolled up to a stop at their feet.

"You dare to wear clothes in the sacred valley?"

"Fools needn't follow rules," the clown said. His voice was as raucous as his manner. "I travel the paths of the myriad worlds, all of them, every one of them, all the same in the long run. I go everywhere and I wear everything."

"How sad to travel all of the time, poor clown. The maid and myself live here in this quiet starlit valley, completely at peace. But since you are here, tell me about the wayside, the dusty road, the journey without end."

The clown got to his feet and made a grandiose gesture with his hand. "Ta," he imitated the fanfare of a trumpet. "Some of the paths are like this." He began a series of cartwheels. "And some are like this." He began to hop awkwardly on one foot. "Some like this and others like this," he handsprang, he crawled laboriously, "all the same and yet I travel them all."

"But why do you travel if it's all the same?"

"Because our purpose is to travel those paths however we can, happy or unhappy, awkwardly or with grace, to perfect them ceaselessly, to finish and finish and finish that which can never be finished. To climb up, fall down, climb up, fall down [he illustrated this], climb up, fall down. Through the endless sea of pain and pleasure, ecstacy and grief, clear through to the end, where we find ourselves like children, only at the beginning.

"We travel because we are travel, and we complete what can never end."

The clown's eyes were wild, crazy. They didn't belong in that gentle starlight.

Suddenly Ferret began to tremble; his body was swept with a wild burning sensation. "I've left something undone," he said.

"Of course," the fool replied, and disappeared.

"Something terrible, unpleasant, and filled with strife," Ferret said. The valley began to fade. The water maid knelt down and began pouring out her waters for the minds of men.

"Of course," he said, echoing the fool. The valley sped away until it was only a tiny blue dot in the black sea of his consciousness. He opened his eyes.

The roof rushed up at him and he realized he was falling. He curled in his head, somersaulted, and catapulted up on his feet. With a thrill he realized he had closed with the Lion after all, and now he threw a sudden fusillade of straight snapping blows, each of which the Lion struck sharply aside, followed by a terrible right-handed blow stopped at the wrist. But as the blow stopped at the wrist the Ferret's body came on, the elbow folded and whipped into the left side of the Lion's head, once, twice; the wounded Lion, body frozen, mind dazed, clinging to Ferret's wrist, striving senselessly to twist away from the elbow, too late, oh much too late. And Ferret, still curling in closer, twisted around in a circle, following his elbow, and threw a high spinning kick with his left leg that came around from behind and caught the Lion a third time on the left side of his head, snapping loose his futile wrist hold, and causing him suddenly to do a loose staggering fool's dance, frantically, hopelessly trying to regain his balance, in the rain, on the slanted roof. But the Ferret snapped to him like a ball on a string; and now he struck the loosening, already-falling form another quick, stiff blow; and simultaneously catching with his free hand one of the loose stumbling feet, he hurled Lion-Roarer from the rooftops into the void that never ends.

He stood there dazed, trying to recreate what happened, trying to understand an inexplicable sense of loss, of futility he had not felt before.

When the cheering, clowning group of men had made its laborious way, crawling across the rooftop to him, he was yet standing silent.

"Fantastic," one of them said, "we saw it all: you stumbled; you seemed to go unconscious and fall; you catapulted up raining blows, so fast and strong; the Moon came out in the rain to watch.

You are the greatest fighter in the world; you can go no farther."

"And yet," he said, still trying to remember something that had come and gone in the blinking of an eye, "and yet, it means nothing to me; and somehow I feel I am only at the beginning of some indescribable road, gazing into endless possibilities.

"Lion-Roarer was a great fighter. Come," he smiled. "I'll treat you all to drinks."

Epilogue

A figure in loose white robes rushed down a dark tunnel which opened into a room lit by candles.

"You are all here. Good," she said, "blessed be. I have grave news. I have wondrous news. The Lion has fallen. He has abandoned his form, it lies empty in the streets, and this is grave news indeed."

Moans of anguish filled the air of the hidden room.

"I have wondrous news. He has initiated a new member into the sacred mysteries. He has done so without the conscious knowledge of the boy himself, but that is neither here nor there. A new member has taken the endless path."

Deep vibrations of bliss filled the room.

"He is just a boy," she said, "a lonely boy." She smiled. Her eyes were the transparent blue of a clear mountain lake.

■

PRINCESS

by Morgan Llywelyn

One of them heard someone call her princess and after that they all called her Princess, thinking it was her name. They did not understand the sarcasm implied in princess or honey or baby, applied to a tired woman in middle years with an aching back and work-reddened hands.

They would come trooping in close to closing time, chattering among themselves, and crowd close to the bar demanding drinks. "Orange bitters, Princess," or "Whiskey, plenty of whiskey. In a big glass, Princess." The tops of their heads hardly reached the level of the bar, and when she brought the drinks they would jump up, their wrinkled grey faces and bald skulls flashing into her vision as they caught glimpses of the glasses. Then a scaly hand would come over the lip of the bar and seize the drink. Out of sight there were gurglings and the smacking of lips, then the hand deposited the empty glass back on the polished wood.

Feet pattered toward the door. "Good night, Princess!" one of them always remembered to call.

A pile of coins glittered in payment for the drinks.

She neither laughed at them nor shrank away from them as the other townspeople did. Who was she to laugh at anyone? Homely old maid eking out a thin living in a rundown bar on the wrong side of a dying town. Her looks had always been a magnet for caustic comments, so she could feel a certain empathy with the ones who came in just before closing time, because the bar was emptiest then.

Every night she polished the glasses on her apron and rearranged the bottles and jugs behind the bar, glancing through the smeared window from time to time as if she were waiting for someone special. But there was no someone special, never had been.

She polished and waited as the smoke got thicker and thicker in the room, then what patrons she had began to straggle out, back to shabby houses and depressing flats not very different from her own. Gray lives.

At last the door swung inward instead of out and she felt the cold air blow in with them. If there were any people left in the bar, they always left then. No one seemed to want to stay.

People whispered that they had a mine of some sort up in the hills. Whatever it was, they made enough to pay for their drinks, though they never left any extra for a tip. But in time she noticed that the windows of the bar sparkled in the morning when she came down from the seedy apartment on the floor above, and the step in front was swept clean. Sometimes a jug of wild flowers waited for her just outside the door. One night it rained and she had forgotten to bring in the laundry, her threadbare clothes and stained towels. In the morning she found them neatly folded and stacked under the overhang of the eaves, safe and dry.

One night one of the few regulars had too much to drink and said ugly things to her. He wasn't a mean man, but his tongue was rough. She would have cried if her tears had not all dried up long ago. Then the door swung inward;

from behind the bar she could not see who entered, but the townman did. He started to get up and then his face changed color and he sat down again, hard, on the barstool. She could hear the broken vinyl creak on the seat cushion. A thin thread of saliva dropped onto the man's chest from his parted lips. He drained his glass quickly and staggered out.

No one said ugly things to her after that.

Sometimes, lying on her narrow bed above the bar, she dreamed of a handsome man coming for her, driving up in front one day with a screech of tires. He would carry her away in a big car that smelled new inside, and she would never look back.

She knew it was a dream. But she still glanced out the window, sometimes. The few cars she saw were battered and dusty, like everything else in the town.

Still, she felt strangely content. Not happy, because she had never been happy and could not have identified the feeling if it crept up on her. But her life began to seem full and she had companionship of a sort.

"Princess," one of them would say out of her sight, over the edge of the bar, "you look nice tonight." They could not possibly see her, and she did not try to lean across and look down at them; it was better if you didn't look at them. But she would smile to herself and give her thinning hair a pat.

"Make me something hot to drink," the voice would say. "The night is cold; it's frozen the flanges of my nose."

Small titters from his companions. Not laughter; they did not laugh like people. They laughed as squirrels might, fast and shrill.

When they were in the bar no new customers entered. What business there was fell off. In time it was safe for them to come in the afternoon; there was no one in the room anyway to stare at

them. The business, always shaky, should have failed completely. But it didn't. There always seemed to be just as much money in the register at the end of the day as there had been when townspeople came. And she liked it better, not having to put up with the problems townfolk brought.

She was standing on the other side of the bar one day, down at the end with her back toward the door, trying to repair the broken vinyl on the barstool with a piece of tape. She was holding her lower lip between her teeth and a wisp of hair kept falling down in her eyes. She was so preoccupied she didn't hear them come in. She thought she was alone until she felt the touch.

It was as light as cobweb, trailing up her leg. Under her skirt. Not attacking, not even invading. Just . . . exploring, with a gentle and innocent curiosity, like that of a blind person touching the face of a stranger.

She froze.

No one had ever touched her there before.

But an unaccustomed feeling of warmth permeated the core of her being, a feeling with a color — rose-gold — and a fragrance, the scent of honeysuckle blooming. She closed her eyes and stood immobile.

At last the touch ceased. The colors faded, the fragrance too. When she opened her eyes the bar was empty. But she knew something wonderful had come to her.

The next time the liquor wholesaler called on her she bought better brands of whiskey and some imported beers. She had never ordered good stuff before. The townspeople only drank the cheapest and wouldn't have known the difference. But the first time she poured the good liquor the stack of coins left on the counter afterwards was higher.

In fact, there seemed to be more money altogether, though she couldn't have explained how. When she added up her receipts she found she could afford to replace the seats on the barstools — not that anyone used them anymore. The only customers she had now were too short to climb up on them. She thought of ordering shorter barstools, then decided that would be vaguely ridiculous. No one was complaining.

Instead she went to the town's only emporium, which featured dead flies lying feet-up in the windows, and bought herself a new blouse. Soft, pretty, a sort of rosy-gold color. She got a little bottle of perfume, too. One that smelled like honeysuckle to her.

When she asked the salesgirl for face cream she was rewarded with a strange look, but the other woman didn't dare say anything. No one made any smart cracks about her anymore.

She rubbed the cream into her skin every night, in the flat above the bar. When she peered into the mirror she couldn't see that it made any difference, but her skin felt better. The wind off the desert had dried it out; now it was soft to the touch. She ran her fingertips across her cheek wonderingly.

The next night one of them put coins into the old jukebox in the corner that had been dead for fifteen years. It came to life with a shudder and a screech, and a baritone voice began celebrating, "The Way You Look Tonight."

The seasons passed; the town finished dying. There were no battered cars left to park on the streets, which were abandoned to blowing dust and an occasional tumbleweed, rolling along like a spidery bouquet. She didn't go out for food. There was always something in the pantry when she went to look for it. And when she emptied a bottle for her customers she began finding a full one behind it on the mirrored shelves back of the bar. Everything she needed was already there.

On the lazy afternoons and in the long, blue evenings there were only eight of them in the bar, the seven little creatures and the hunchbacked albino woman. But it was enough. ∎

BAD LANDS

by Nancy Springer

"It is not good to go there," he said across the rim of a Budweiser. "They are called bad lands for a reason."

I said, "I am bad, too."

I looked hard at him over my own beer without really seeing him, just seeing some sort of Indian drinking too much, the hooded eyes, the black hair stringing down to the dirty shirt. I don't remember which tribe. To me, one Indian was pretty much the same as another. Just like one white guy, red hair, red neck, blue jeans, was pretty much the same as another to him.

Or maybe it bothers me that I ought to know what tribe he was and I don't. Seemed like there were always two people fighting inside me, back then before I died.

I demanded, "You gonna guide me or not?"

"What you want to see wild horses for?"

"None of your business."

Kicking around the dust states all my life, close to forty years, doing dirt-eating jobs to get by, trucking, highway work, construction work, cattle herding, holding my own on the jobs and in the bars, I guessed I'd learned how to handle Indians. I was offering good money for a guide, and he should take it or leave it. All the money I had in the world, in fact. I'd sold my gear, cleaned out my savings and I didn't care. Wasn't thinking of my old age. Guess I knew even then I wouldn't have any.

He just looked at me in that damn flat-faced Indian way, and the other guy inside me, fighting me as always, made me say, "Nothing illegal."

It was against the law by then to kill wild horses. Instead, there were government roundups. People could take mustangs home with them. Adoption, they called it. But plenty of wild horses still went to rustlers, to feed somebody's dogs.

The Indian's dark face didn't show anything when he made up his mind, but he said, "What's your name?"

"Just call me Jake."

Without even a shrug he downed the rest of his beer, took the money I gave him and went off to buy the transportation and supplies. His name was Charlie Broken Arrow. I knew that from the other Indians, the ones who had refused to guide me. They had sent me to him. He was the only one was drunk or reckless or desperate enough to do what I wanted.

Just call me Jake, I had told him, not quite knowing why. It was my half-breed grandfather's name. Jake the gypsy. That taint in my blood never let me feel white as other white men. Maybe it accounted for the hidden idiot inside me who had sent me here. Which was the reason I wasn't about to tell this Indian my real name. I was a crazy damn fool on a damn fool errand, and I needed a guide.

The next morning, on fourth-hand ATVs loaded down with plastic jugs of water but not much else, we started.

Even in springtime the bad lands were a gypsum-colored hell, like the

crazy ridges knifing into the sky were made of nothing but weather-stained spackling, like the buttes were lumps of dumped concrete left over from some project where the contractor had done a better job than he did here. The ground felt like concrete underfoot, but chalky dust came up from it to coat us. After a few hours we looked like ghosts out of the gray-white hell. Somewhere in this huge hole made of gullies and gulches and draws, buttes and bottoms and clay-colored mesas and dry white tablelands, two thousand square miles of purgatory, part Indian reservation, part public land and all sheer hellhole — somewhere in these bad lands, somebody had told me, the last of the true Spanish mustangs roamed. Barb mustangs, wild since the days the conquistadors rode their thick-necked granddaddies north out of Mexico. Stunted now from hiding in hellholes like this one, but proud and tough, still wild and free after four hundred years of —

I shook my head to shake away the thought. Maybe Charlie thought I was trying to shake the dust out of my hair, like a foolish white man, always fighting the world. The gray-white dust would stick no matter what, crawl into our lungs and our pores. With his dark skin showing gray under the powder, Charlie Broken Arrow looked like a white man's corpse roaring along on a corpse-white three-wheeler, swigging whiskey as he went. This was the guide I had hired to take me to the mustangs. I had an idea that he was as no-good a specimen of his race as I was of mine.

Charlie knew where to find the mustangs because he knew his way through this muddle of white ridges and dusty ravines and dry canyons, this moonscape, to the few water holes. Even Spanish mustangs need a little water.

I looked at his flat face as seldom as I could. He gave me the uneasy feeling, this Indian guide, that he knew the

hellhole landscape of my soul, that he knew how my bad thoughts were sending me into the bad lands.

Bull, I told myself. Of course he had to have thoughts of what I wanted with the mustangs. But he could not possibly have guessed the truth.

We came to a water hole before dark, and caught sight of them as we roared in, the wild horses, a few hammerheaded, broom-tailed broncs in the sundown light, running away, gone in an eyeblink.

We stowed the hot machines in the nearest gulch and sat on the flank of a bone-white ridge in the dusk, waiting for them to come back. They might or they might not. Depended on how wise they were, and how thirsty.

The bad lands seemed to glow like a huge fungus against the darkening sky. Somewhere a coyote cried. A shadow startled me: an owl flying close by.

Charlie Broken Arrow said to me, "What do you want with the wild horses, white man?" The tone of his voice, ugly. He was drunk.

"I told you, none of your business!"

I meant to shut him up, but it didn't work. He said, "Have you come to look on what you have done, white man? To look at the few you have left, here in this place fit only for reptiles, while your cattle fatten on the good grasslands?"

I barked out a laugh. "I ain't got no cattle," I said. But he went on as if he hadn't heard me.

"Only a few years ago my people kept many wild ponies. And the cattlemen came and said to get the horses off the land where they wished to graze their cattle. Our chief told them that the land belonged to us and to the wild horses as much as it did to them. Perhaps more. And the men came in airplanes and shot the horses, shot them all in a single day. Were you one of those killers, white man?"

I said, "Shut up. There ain't never no horses going to come drink while you're yapping."

He spat, and looked at me flat and hard, and did not shut up. "White man," he said, ugly.

I said, "I told you my name. Call me Jake."

"White man," he taunted, "You come to look at what you have done, the way the white men come to look on the Indians?"

"No," I said. He was damn close, but not right entirely. I had come to — to — I did not know the words for what I wanted of the mustangs.

He sat looking at me, and when he spoke again he sounded quieter. "You are full of what my ancestors called bad medicine. I ought to go and leave you here."

"You are full of shit!" I did not know the way out. The bad lands would kill me slowly if he left me there. "It would be the same as murder."

"No murder. You came here meaning to stay."

That scared me, though his ugliness had not. Drunk Indians I had handled before, but not — not this. How could he know it about me? Know what I had not yet admitted to myself?

I couldn't think of a fucking thing to say, and I couldn't seem to talk, anyway. I sat. Charlie Broken Arrow sat looking at me, and after a couple minutes he said in a peculiar, soft voice, almost a whisper, or maybe a snake hiss, "I will help you, white man."

That voice, as flat as his face. I couldn't tell if he was mocking me again. Louder than I meant to I snapped, "What the hell do you mean?"

In that same odd ghost of a voice he said, "Shaman's blood runs strong in me. I will help you to your desire."

Scared, I swore at him, and then I demanded, "What the Hell you talking about!" But he seemed not to hear me at all.

He sat. He stared straight ahead, and then he started to chant.

Nothing I could understand. He muttered and droned and hissed in what might have been the language of his own people, and his voice blended with the voice of the night wind bellying over the ridges, and I thought of taking the whiskey bottle from his slack hand and knocking him over the head with it, and stood up to do it, then stopped, wondering why I was terrified of the mumblings of a drunk Indian. . . .

And then the vengeance struck.

Down out of the night sky it curled like a panther's scream, shivering my spine. In all my no-good life I had never felt anything like it. Felt, not heard. It was not a sound. It was a storm in the air and in me, bone-deep, fit to shake me to my soul if I still had one left after what I had done in my time.

"It is the dead horses," said Charlie Broken Arrow, triumphant, out of the darkness next to me.

Damn crazy Indian. "Whatcha mean?" I yelled at him. "It's a sandstorm!" Though I knew he was right. I felt stallion scream and thud of hooves. My sweat ran cold, trickling down, leaving trails in the ghost-white dust on my face.

"All of them," he said. "All the dead mustangs." His voice sounded calm and happy, singsong but not at all slurred by the whiskey any longer. "The ones you shot, sent over the cliffs, ran to death."

White men, he had to mean. Not me.

"The trampled foals, the panicked mares tangled in barbed wire. The stallions choked with ropes. All of them."

In the darkness I felt hot breath, and fury. I seemed to glimpse a pair of eyes red as fire — and I shut my own eyes, but the red ones still gleamed in the night inside my own skull. I fell; I lay curled on the nostril-clogging ground, trying to cover my head with my hands, and it seemed to me that I could not

61

breathe, that trampling hooves were knocking the breath and life out of me, that one well-placed kick would splatter my brains pinkish-gray on the gray dust of the bad lands. Many times in my life I had been scared before, but never in the same way. I was soul-scared. And in the night I could hear Charlie laughing. He sounded very far away, but I knew he was sitting right next to me —

Laughing.

None of it was happening to him, the terror, the pain. And in a distant way I knew that it was all a trick of his, that the thudding hooves were not real, they had not raised blood or even bruises on me, and I jumped up — I wanted to kill him. But even worse I wanted to get away.

I ran blind with agony in the night, stumbling. My three-wheeler, not far ahead — I staggered the small distance to it, gunned it and took off across the night, not caring if I ran it over a cliff. But after a minute, the pain eased and I realized I could see. A moon had come out of someplace, and the chalk-white bad lands cast black shadows underneath it. About the same time I realized I was not alone. Charlie Broken Arrow on his ATV was roaring along right beside me. And not far behind us both, eyes flamed. Eyes red as fire. The mustangs ran there.

I could see them.

They were not real. I knew real mustangs, and these were mustangs, wild as the bad lands, but not real. They were running toward us, not away. The stark, black shadows of the sawtooth ridges showed through their bodies, through the deep chests where their big, pumping hearts should have been, through the heavy bones of their heads. Blue fire played around their flying manes. They were not real. But I could see them.

My wrist spasmed and twisted back, sending me shooting forward at full throttle. The ATV took wild leaps over dips and gullies, hit like lead, flew again. I must have been going sixty. No bronc could move that fast. I knew that, because —

I knew because I had once herded wild horses from machines as fast as this one.

But the ghost herd running in the moonlight surged forward without effort, like a hundred broadwing hawks on the wind. They surrounded me. These mustangs did not run on the ground; they skimmed it, and their hooves did not send up any puffs of dust. There must have been thousands of them, all colors in the moonlight: bay, paint, sorrel, blue grullo, every kind of gray and dun and splash-marked, speckled roan. Maybe all the mustangs that — that men like me had ever killed. The herd of them seemed to fill the bad lands, and it seemed to me that I saw pools of blood in the flared nostrils of the closest ones.

I swerved, trying to get away from them, and nearly crashed against the Indian. "Go away!" I screamed at him. The bastard, I thought I had left him behind. But there he was, his black eyes narrowed to slits while mine, I knew, rolled wide and white and frightened.

The dead mustangs were herding us. And I knew in my gut that they moved on legs that might as well have been piston-driven steel. They would run us to exhaustion, as I had once helped to run them.

Charlie Broken Arrow shouted at me across engine roar, "What have you done?"

I looked at him, at his flat, fighter-nosed face ghost-white with dust.

I slowed down enough to stay alive a while longer and yelled at him, "You maggot, make them go away!"

He shook his head. Somehow the gesture let me know he was not refusing me, but — somehow he was caught up in this craziness with me, and he was afraid.

I barked, "You mean to tell me you can't?"

"I — they are too strong for me!" The spirits he had summoned had gotten out of hand. He made as good a shaman as I did a white man.

He yelled at me again, "What have you done? Are you a murderer?" And because he was there, I told him the truth.

I shouted back, "I was a mustanger."

Another dirt-eating job, a way to get by. Round up the broncs off the public land. A white man knew the world was put there for cattle and sheep to graze on, and horses were to break and use, and a man did a good thing by rounding up the useless horses and putting them to work as glue and fertilizer. A white man didn't mind hurting a useless horse before he killed it, either.

Charlie Broken Arrow shouted at me, "What have you come here for?"

I couldn't put it in words. I wanted — I wanted — I wanted to stand up in shame. I wanted to look a mustang in the eye and find something there. Maybe — myself.

I was no proper white man. The God-damn gypsy in me —

A memory, hidden away somewhere in the bad lands of my mind, like a bronc holed up in a canyon. A voice, my grandfather's, talking about — the spirits, I couldn't remember the gypsy name for them, the angry spirits that used to come and shake the wagons at night. They were the ghosts of — children, all the children who had died because they were neglected or beaten or unwanted, stillborn, aborted, abandoned, unnamed. . . . And my grandfather had told how his grandmother had lost her voice, one such night, so that she was never able to speak aloud again, because all night she had shouted into the angry wind, taking the dead children, one by one, to her heart. Adopting them. Naming them.

And something came out of hiding in my mind, and something more than half-crazy in me understood, because I knew that somewhere a kid was standing outside a government pen, looking into a chosen pair of wild eyes and saying to her mustang, I'll name you Stormy.

A stud the color of dark steel ran beside me, his eyes and nostrils glinting red. He surged nearer, snaked his head toward me, ears laid back, teeth bared to attack. Huskily I called to him, "Stormy!"

The red rage in his eyes faded away. He tossed his long head as if to neigh, and sparks flew from his mane, and he was gone.

"Jake!" shouted Charlie Broken Arrow.

I turned my head to look into his narrow eyes. His face was stirring, its chalky mask cracking.

"How did you know what I'd forgot?"

I stared back at him. I felt jerked around by my own insides and tired enough to die, I couldn't answer, I couldn't think. But the look must have told him something. He turned away, slowed down his three-wheeler and started naming names.

Beautiful names, some in English, some in the language of his people. They floated off his drunken tongue like a shaman's chant. Dakota Sky Fox, Medicine Hat, Wise Falcon, Talisman. "Ho," he said to a big gray mare who ran near him, the bad lands showing through her body and the blue fire in her mane and on her hooves, "ho, my sister. I see you, I know you, Flying Dove. Go, brave one, be at peace. Go to where the happy herds run, Flying Dove." His voice sounded quiet, even above his engine's yammering.

Like a blue candle flame flickering out, the gray bronc was gone.

I had slowed my three-wheeler to stay with Charlie Broken Arrow, and heard the names, and the gypsy in me

63

started to sing, and I was no longer tired. I said aloud, "Cayuse, Señora, Doña María. Prairie Pride, Vixen, Conquistador. Paladin. Renegade. Shenandoah." It wasn't because I was afraid of what they might do to me. I could not have pulled those names out of fear. But they were so beautiful running in the moonlight, the wild horses, I wanted to name them, I wanted to adopt them all. I loved them with a hurting heart, the way once, long ago, I had loved things that flew, eagles on the wind. I was a thousand kids saying, I'll call you Lightning. I'll call you Wildfire.

"Blue Thunder," said Charlie Broken Arrow by my side. "Desert Rain." We had slowed our three-wheelers to a crawl, without much thinking about it; the motors muttered low as we drifted along a dry riverbed, and the dead wild horses, walking, or seeming to walk, floated around us with the bright badland stars showing through their heads, their forelocks. There were fewer of them than there had been before. The ones who were left looked at us with big, dark eyes, their ears pricked forward, hopeful. I didn't want to fail any of them. I started to study them one by one.

"Warrior," I named a young stud splash-marked in three colors, and he dipped his head and disappeared, leaving the bad lands for some better place.

And then the herd stallion came.

Driving, driving, snaking his head almost to the ground he came, his ears laid back and his teeth bared and a strange white fire, white as the stars, white as the bad lands in the moonlight, burning in his eyes. He seemed twice as big as any other mustang there, though he stood no taller than any of them. The ghost herd swirled like smoke away from in front of his charge and scattered in all directions, into the bad lands, into sky, up the dark gulches between the stars. Quicker than smoke in a strong wind the mustangs were all gone but him, the stallion.

He was black, a clear, shining black, like the stone they call Apache tear, with starlight darting through him like fury. And he saw us, or me. His white-fire eyes blazed at me. He charged — he had never stopped charging, but his long head came up, his heavy neck arched because I was a man, not a horse. A white man. And I wanted to send my ATV up to sixty again. But what had I come here for, except to meet him? He was — was —

I stopped my three-wheeler dead and cut the motor. I stood up. Charlie Broken Arrow, the damn fool, cut his motor as well. Suddenly I could hear the night, and the hoofbeats as the black mustang bore down on me. He raised no dust, but from the sound I knew those hooves were real enough to do — what I wanted them to do.

"Get out of here," I told Charlie.

Instead he said to the stallion, "Ho, my brother. I know you." His voice came out thin as the stuff these broncs were made of. "You are wild as wind, proud as the eagle on the wind. Black Eagle, be at peace, give up the rage that burns your heart. Go where the happy herds run."

In pure scorn the black mustang swirled to a stop and stood a galloping stride away from me, tossing his head, his eyes blazing at Charlie. He stood untouched by the name, and I saw his proud Barb profile, heavy, hawklike, with the moon lighting it up like black rock crystal.

"Magic Eagle," Charlie tried again, "Star Magic, Starwind, Night Storm, be at peace."

The child inside me said, I'll call you Apache Tear. But it was a long time since I had been a child. I was a man, I had done the things men do.

"Black Wind," Charlie was saying, "Ravenwing," and the black stud snaked his head and neck toward him, threatening. White-ember eyes smoldered. The stallion's anger was for Charlie, now, as well as for me.

"Stop it," I said to Charlie. "Jackass, you can't name him. He's all those things."

He was everything. Wind, night, storm, black wildfire, all the wild horses, all the things that can't be tamed, broke, used. He reared, and blue flames sprang from his mane. His hooves shone gunmetal blue; in half a heartbeat they would crash down on me and trample me into the bad lands until I lay part of the dust. I did not move. I had come here for this. But hands grabbed me and jerked me back. Charlie.

I fought loose from him. "Get out of here!" I yelled at him.

"This is not right!" he yelled back. "You have strong medicine now. Use it! Name him!"

The black mustang whammed to his feet not more than an arm's length in front of me, flung back his great head and shrilled out a screech, part wild wind rising, part wolf, part mountain cat, part madwoman. A sound like no other sound anyone had ever heard, even in that lonesome place. It shivered off the ghost-white cliffs and canyons of the bad lands, sobbed back to me. It foretold my death.

"Apache Tear," I said to the black vengeance in the night, "hold on just a minute, while I explain to this stupid Indian."

Apache Tear was not his name, not any more than any of the others were. Not any more than my name was Jake. But it gave us a sort of understanding. He waited. He tossed his black head, and pawed the white ground, white as old bones, but he waited.

I said to Charlie Broken Arrow, "There were fifty-three broncs in the herd we rounded up, me and five other guys trying to make a buck. It was winter. We ran them with snowmobiles. There were some new foals that couldn't keep up. They fell behind, and we left them there in the snow to starve or be killed by coyotes.

"We ran the herd until they were staggering and they never gave in to us or gave up trying to get away. We could barely handle them. We tried to take them up a canyon and got into a bad place. Seven of the horses went off the cliff. A pregnant mare got her foot caught in rocks under the snow and couldn't get loose. She was blocking the trail. We slit her throat and took her leg off with the chain saw so we could heave her body out of the way."

The black stallion of the dead mustangs remembered her. He knew her name and the name of the unborn foal. I remembered her, too. She was a sorrel. I could see her frightened eyes and blond forelock, her shaggy body, ribby from sparse eating. If I thought about her, I would know her name.

I did not think about her any longer than I had to, and I did not look at the black stallion as I talked. I looked at the blank, flat face of the Indian.

"It was a four-day drive to where the pen and the truck was. All the way the wild horses never gave up fighting us. We roped them and forced wire through their nostrils to slow them down. Some broke their necks fighting the ropes. Some wore themselves out and died on the way. Some were trampled in the pen or bashed their brains out against the top of the truck, rearing up."

I couldn't say any more, but I couldn't stop thinking about it. Less than half the wild horses had made it to the slaughterhouse. And the death waiting there for them was not much gentler than I had been, taking them to it. I still smelled hot blood on my hands.

White men did the things I had done. The men I knew had no use for sissies. But nothing had been right for me during the years since then. Nothing made me happy. Food tasted like dust. Women had left me.

I remembered the wild horses better than I did the women.

"So your medicine went bad," said Charlie Broken Arrow, "and you came here to beg pardon of the mustangs."

"No. I came to get back my soul."

I turned, then, and looked into the white-hot eyes of the wild horse-spirit facing me, and I knew I had come to the right place.

"Get out of here," I told the Indian without looking away from the black mustang, "or he'll take you, too."

Beside me, Charlie spoke to the stallion as if to a god. "Great one, is that true?" he asked. "I have a choice?"

But I was the one who answered him. "Shit! Of course you do!" I barked. "You didn't have to come this far with me. You didn't have to run with me when the herd came down. Why are you here at all?"

He said, "I am your guide."

Something in his voice made me steal a look at him. His face didn't show much, but I knew I had been right about him. He was more than half-crazy. A no-good, like me.

"Jake," said Charlie Broken Arrow, "may you find your soul soon. You have given mine back to me. I thank you."

The white-fire eyes we both faced made me sure of what I told the Indian. "You will be a great shaman among your people. Go in peace."

He lifted a hand to me in a gesture like a priest's before he rode away.

I think Charlie watched from the mesa, saw what happened. I think he went back to become a wise man and a maker of songs in his tribe, and in one of his songs he called me Jake.

Because men still call me Jake. My hooves are hard and real, my hide rust-red as my hair once was and scarred from many battles. I run the bad lands, I try to protect my mares. I must always be alert; I seldom graze, even when grazing is to be found. Life is as hard as my hooves. My head hangs heavy on my lank neck, my ribs show. Sagebrush tangles my mane and tail, rips them short. I shiver with longing at the scent of water. In winter, cold freezes the blood; sometimes the foals and old mares lie dead come morning. Wolves threaten. Life is cold ache, hunger pinch, stallion fights, wolf-fear, panther-fear, the fear of humans.

Humans. They are the worst. Men come often, despite the laws. My soul is my own; I defy them. I would rather die of thirst on the bone-dry mesas than approach them where they wait by the waterholes. I have learned many ways to avoid and escape and defeat them. They talk about me among themselves; they call me Red Devil, Gypsy Jake, Whirlwind. None of them will ever own me, no matter what they name me. I know humans too well ever to trust any. If they ever trap me, I will die before I submit to them.

With every colt I save, every mare I guide away from men, I make up for my past life. Perhaps after I die I will come back as something better than a man. I run, with my herd I run in the wind, and it is good, but I long to soar, to be a flying thing.

■

IMPROBABLE BESTIARY: THE GHOUL

The Ghoul, as a rule, is unlikely to drool
Over puddings or porridge or gravy or gruel.
His diet is strict, his reserve never softens:
The meats that he eats
Must come *packaged in coffins!*
The meals that he steals
May be short, tall, or hairy,
Their flavours may change, and their colourings vary,
But nothing will *ever* go down his esophagus
Unless it's been kept in a tasteful sarcophagus
(He's quite anthropophagous.)

The Ghoul, as a rule, is impassive and cool
Over raspberry trifle and gooseberry fool.
For only one menu can nourish his avarice:
The stews that he chews
Must be freshly cadaverous!
And this leads to one other delicate matter
Regarding the Ghoul, and the lunch on his platter:

Although he's a glutton, he never steals mutton.
Although he's a thief, he will never take beef.
He'll never be found to impound a ground round,
And he won't even purloin a sirloin.
He's now coming closer; he's
Dragging his groceries
Swiftly behind him: at midnight, you'll find him
Where nightshade is blooming —
That greedy old sinner
The Ghoul is consuming
A seven-corpse dinner.

— F. Gwynplaine MacIntyre

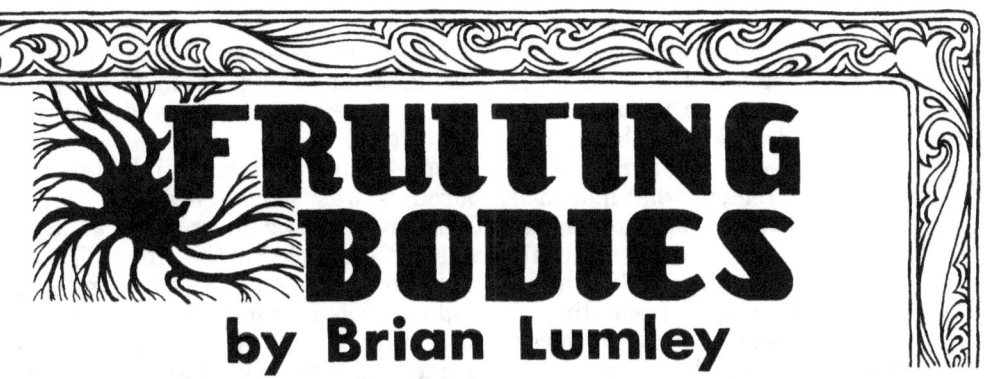

FRUITING BODIES
by Brian Lumley

My great-grandparents, and my grandparents after them, had been Easingham people; in all likelihood my parents would have been, too, but the old village had been falling into the sea for three hundred years and hadn't much looked like stopping, and so I was born in Durham City instead. My grandparents, both sets, had been among the last of the village people to move out, buying new homes out of a government-funded disaster grant. Since when, as a kid, I had been back to Easingham only once.

My father had taken me there one spring when the tides were high. I remember how there was still some black, crusty snow lying in odd corners of the fields, coloured by soot and smoke, as all things were in those days in the Northeast. We'd gone to Easingham because the unusually high tides had been at it again, chewing away at the shale cliffs, reducing shoreline and derelict village both as the North Sea's breakers crashed again and again on the shuddering land.

And of course we had hoped (as had the two hundred or so other sightseers gathered there that day) to see a house

or two go down in smoking ruin, into the sea and the foaming spray. We witnessed no such spectacle; after an hour, cold and wet from the salt moisture in the air, we piled back into the family car and returned to Durham. Easingham's main street, or what had once been the main street, was teetering on the brink as we left. But by nightfall that street was no more. We'd missed it: a further twenty feet of coastline, a bite one street deep and a few yards more than one street long, had been undermined, toppled, and gobbled up by the sea.

That had been that. Bit by bit, in the quarter-century between then and now, the rest of Easingham had also succumbed. Now only a house or two remained — no more than a handful in all — and all falling into decay, while the closest lived-in buildings were those of a farm all of a mile inland from the cliffs. Oh, and of course there was one other inhabitant: Old Garth Bentham, who'd been demolishing the old houses by hand and selling bricks and timbers from the village for years. But I'll get to him shortly.

So there I was last summer, back in the Northeast again, and when my business was done of course I dropped in and stayed overnight with the Old Folks at their Durham cottage. Once a year at least I made a point of seeing them, but last year in particular I noticed how time was creeping up on them. The "Old Folks"; well, now I saw that they really were old, and I determined that I must start to see a lot more of them.

Later, starting in on my long drive back down to London, I remembered that time when the Old Man had taken me to Easingham to see the houses tottering on the cliffs. And probably because the place was on my mind, I inadvertently turned off my route and in a little while found myself heading for the coast. I could have turned round

right there and then — indeed, I intended to do so — but I'd got to wondering about Easingham and how little would be left of it now, and before I knew it . . .

Once I'd made up my mind, Middlesborough was soon behind me, then Guisborough, and in no time at all I was on the old road to the village. There had only ever been one way in and out, and this was it: a narrow road, its surface starting to crack now, with tall hedgerows broken here and there, letting you look through to where fields rolled down to the cliffs. A beautiful day, with seagulls wheeling overhead, a salt tang coming in through the wound-down windows, and a blue sky coming down to merge with . . . with the blue-grey of the North Sea itself! For cresting a rise, suddenly I was there.

An old, leaning wooden signpost said "Easingh—", for the tail had been broken off or rotted away, and "the village" lay at the end of the road. But right there, blocking the way, a metal barrier was set in massive concrete posts and carried a sign bearing the following warning:

DANGER!
Severe Cliff Subsidence.
No Vehicles Beyond This Point . . .

I turned off the car's motor, got out, leaned on the barrier. Before me the road went on — and disappeared only thirty yards ahead. And there stretched the new rim of the cliffs. Of the village, Easingham itself — forget it! On this side of the cliffs, reaching back on both sides of the road behind overgrown gardens, weedy paths and driveways, here stood the empty shells of what had once been residences of the "posh" folks of Easingham. Now, even on a day as lovely as this one, they were morose in their desolation.

The windows of these derelicts, where

there were windows, seemed to gaze gauntly down on approaching doom, like old men in twin rows of deathbeds. Brambles and ivy were rank; the whole place seemed despairing as the cries of the gulls rising on the warm air; Easingham was a place no more.

Not that there had ever been a lot of it. Three streets lengthwise with a few shops; two more, shorter streets cutting through the three at right angles and going down to the cliffs and the vertiginous wooden steps that used to climb down to the beach, the bay, the old harbour and fish market; and standing over the bay, a methodist church on a jutting promontory, which in the old times had also served as a lighthouse. But now —

No streets, no promontory or church, no harbour, fish market, rickety steps. No Easingham.

"Gone, all of it," said a wheezy, tired old voice from directly behind me, causing me to start. "Gone forever, to the Devil and the deep blue sea!"

I turned, formed words, said something barely coherent to the leathery old scarecrow of a man I found standing there.

"Eh? Eh?" he said. "Did I startle you? I have to say you startled me! First car I've seen in a three-month! After bricks, are you? Cheap bricks? Timber?"

"No, no," I told him, finding my voice. "I'm — well, sightseeing, I suppose." I shrugged. "I just came to see how the old village was getting on. I didn't live here, but a long line of my people did. I just thought I'd like to see how much was left — while it *was* left! Except it seems I'm too late."

"Oh, aye, too late," he nodded. "Three or four years too late. That was when the last of the old fishing houses went down: four years ago. Sea took 'em. Takes six or seven feet of cliff every year. Aye, and if I lived long enough it would take me too. But it won't 'cos I'm getting on a bit." And he grinned and

nodded, as if to say: so that's that! "Well, well, sightseeing! Not much to see, though, not now. Do you fancy a coffee?"

Before I could answer he put his fingers to his mouth and blew a piercing whistle, then paused and waited, shook his head in puzzlement. "Ben," he explained. "My old dog. He's not been himself lately and I don't like him to stray too far. He was out all night, was Ben. Still, it's summer, and there may have been a bitch about. . . ."

While he had talked I'd looked him over and decided that I liked him. He reminded me of my own grandfather, what little I could remember of him. Grandad had been a miner in one of the colliery villages farther north, retiring here to doze and dry up and die — only to find himself denied the choice. The sea's incursion had put paid to that when it finally made the place untenable. I fancied this old lad had been a miner, too. Certainly he bore the scars, the *stigmata*, of the miner: the dark, leathery skin with black specks bedded in; the bad, bowed legs; the shortness of breath, making for short sentences. A generally gritty appearance overall, though I'd no doubt he was clean as fresh-scrubbed.

"Coffee would be fine," I told him, holding out my hand. "Greg's my name — Greg Lane."

He took my hand, shook it warmly and nodded. "Garth Bentham," he said. And then he set off stiffly back up the crumbling road some two or three houses, turning right into an overgrown garden through a fancy wooden gate recently painted white. "I'd intended doing the whole place up," he said, as I followed close behind. "Did the gate, part of the fence, ran out of paint!"

Before letting us into the dim interior of the house, he paused and whistled again for Ben, then worriedly shook his head in something of concern. "After

71

rats in the old timber yard again, I suppose. But God knows I wish he'd stay out of there!"

Then we were inside the tiny cloakroom, where the sun filtered through fly-specked windows and probed golden searchlights on a few fairly dilapidated furnishings and the brassy face of an old grandfather clock that clucked like a mechanical hen. Dust motes drifted like tiny planets in a cosmos of faery, eddying round my host where he guided me through a door and into his living-room. Where the dust had settled on the occasional ledge, I noticed that it was tinged red, like rust.

"I cleaned the windows in here," Garth informed, "so's to see the sea. I like to know what it's up to!"

"Making sure it won't creep up on you," I nodded.

His eyes twinkled. "Nah, just joking," he said, tapping on the side of his blue-veined nose. "No, it'll be ten or even twenty years before all this goes, but I don't have that long. Five if I'm lucky. I'm sixty-eight, after all!"

Sixty-eight! Was that really to be as old as all that? But he was probably right: a lot of old-timers from the mines didn't even last *that* long, not entirely mobile and coherent, anyway. "Retiring at sixty-five doesn't leave a lot, does it?" I said. "Of time, I mean."

He went into his kitchen, called back: "Me, I've been here a ten-year. Didn't retire, quit! Stuff your pension, I told 'em. I'd rather have my lungs, what's left of 'em. So I came here, got this place for a song, take care of myself and my old dog, and no one to tip my hat to and no one to bother me. I get a letter once a fortnight from my sister in Dunbar, and one of these days the postman will find me stretched out in here and he'll think: 'Well, I needn't come out here anymore.'"

He wasn't bemoaning his fate, but I felt sorry for him anyway. I settled myself on a dusty settee, looked out of

the window down across his garden of brambles to the sea's horizon. A great curved millpond — for the time being. "Didn't you have any savings?" I could have bitten my tongue off the moment I'd said it, for that was to imply he hadn't done very well for himself.

Cups rattled in the kitchen. "Savings? Lad, when I was a young 'un I had three things: my lamp, my helmet, and a pack of cards. If it wasn't pitch-'n-toss with weighted pennies on the beach banks, it was three-card brag in the back room of the pub. Oh, I was a game gambler, right enough, but a bad one. In my blood, like my Old Man before me. My mother never did see a penny; nor did my wife, I'm ashamed to say, before we moved out here — God bless her! Savings? That's a laugh. But out here there's no bookie's runner, and you'd be damned hard put to find a card school in Easingham these days! What the Hell," he shrugged as he stuck his head back into the room, "it was a life. . . ."

We sipped our coffee. After a while I said, "Have you been on your own very long? I mean . . . your wife?"

"Lily-Anne?" he glanced at me, blinked, and suddenly there was a peculiar expression on his face. "On my own, you say. . . ." He straightened his shoulders, took a deep breath. "Well, I *am* on my own in a way, and in a way I'm not. I have Ben — or would have if he'd get done with what he's doing and come home — and Lily-Anne's not all that far away. In fact, sometimes I suspect she's sort of watching over me, keeping me company, so to speak. You know, when I'm feeling especially lonely."

"Oh?"

"Well," he shrugged again. "I mean she *is* here, now isn't she." It was a statement, not a question.

"Here?" I was starting to have my doubts about Garth Bentham.

"I had her buried here," he nodded,

which explained what he'd said and produced a certain sensation of relief in me. "There was a Methodist church here once over, with its own burying ground. The church went a donkey's years ago, of course, but the old graveyard was still here when Lily-Anne died."

"Was?" Our conversation was getting one-sided.

"Well, it still is — but right on the edge, so to speak. It wasn't so bad then, though, and so I got permission to have a service done here, and down she went where I could go and see her. I still do go to see her, of course, now and then. But in another year or two . . . the sea. . . ." He shrugged again. "Time and the tides, they wait for no man."

We finished our coffee. I was going to have to be on my way soon, and suddenly I didn't like the idea of leaving him. Already I could feel the loneliness creeping in. Perhaps he sensed my restlessness or something. Certainly I could see that he didn't want me to go just yet. In any case, he said:

"Maybe you'd like to walk down with me past the old timber yard, visit her grave. Oh, it's safe enough, you don't have to worry. We may even come across old Ben down there. He sometimes visits her, too."

"Ah, well I'm not too sure about that," I answered. "The time, you know?" But by the time we got down the path to the gate I was asking: "How far is the churchyard, anyway?" Who could tell, maybe I'd find some long-lost Lanes in there! "Are there any old markers left standing?"

Garth chuckled and took my elbow. "It makes a change to have some company," he said. "Come on, it's this way."

He led the way back to the barrier where it spanned the road, bent his back and ducked groaning under it, then turned left up an overgrown communal path between gardens where the houses had been stepped down the declining gradient. The detached bungalow on our right — one of a pair still standing, while a third slumped on the raw edge of oblivion — had decayed almost to the point where it was collapsing inwards. Brambles luxuriated everywhere in its garden, completely enclosing it. The roof sagged and a chimney threatened to topple, making the whole structure seem highly suspect and more than a little dangerous.

"Partly subsidence, because of the undercutting action of the sea," Garth explained, "but mainly the rot. There was a lot of wood in these places, but it's all being eaten away. I made myself a living, barely, out of the old bricks and timber in Easingham, but now I have to be careful. Doesn't do to sell stuff with the rot in it."

"The rot?"

He paused for breath, leaned a hand on one hip, nodded and frowned. "Dry rot," he said. "Or *Merulius lacrymans* as they call it in the books. It's been bad these last three years. Very bad! But when the last of these old houses are gone, and what's left of the timber yard, then it'll be gone, too."

"It?" We were getting back to single-word questions again. "The dry rot, you mean? I'm afraid I don't know very much about it."

"Places on the coast are prone to it," he told me. "Whitby, Scarborough, places like that. All the damp sea spray and the bad plumbing, the rains that come in and the inadequate drainage. That's how it starts. It's a fungus, needs a lot of moisture — to get started, anyway. You don't know much about it? Heck, I used to think I knew *quite* a bit about it, but now I'm not so sure!"

By then I'd remembered something. "A friend of mine in London did mention to me how he was having to have his flat treated for it," I said, a little lamely. "Expensive, apparently."

Garth nodded, straightened up. "Hard to kill," he said. "And when it's active, moves like the plague! It's active here, now! Too late for Easingham, and who gives a damn anyway? But you tell that friend of yours to sort out his exterior maintenance first: the guttering and the drainage. Get rid of the water spillage, then deal with the rot. If a place is dry and airy, it's OK. Damp and musty spells danger!"

I nodded. "Thanks, I will tell him."

"Want to see something?" said Garth. "I'll show you what old *Merulius* can do. See here, these old paving flags? See if you can lever one up a bit." I found a piece of rusting iron stave and dragged it out of the ground where it supported a rotting fence, then forced the sharp end into a crack between the overgrown flags. And while I worked to loosen the paving stone, old Garth stood watching and carried on talking.

"Actually, there's a story attached, if you care to hear it," he said. "Probably all coincidental or circumstantial, or some other big word like that — but queer the way it came about all the same."

He was losing me again. I paused in my levering to look bemused (and maybe to wonder what on Earth I was doing here), then grunted, and sweated, gave one more heave and flipped the flag over onto its back. Underneath was hard-packed sand. I looked at it, shrugged, looked at Garth.

He nodded in that way of his, grinned, said: "Look. Now tell me what you make of this!"

He got down on one knee, scooped a little of the sand away. Just under the surface his hands met some soft obstruction. Garth wrinkled his nose and grimaced, got his face down close to the earth, blew until his weakened lungs started him coughing. Then he sat back and rested. Where he'd scraped and blown the sand away, I made out what appeared to be a grey fibrous mass running at right angles right under the pathway. It was maybe six inches thick,

looked like tightly-packed cotton wool. It might easily have been glass fiber lagging for some pipe or other, and I said as much.

"But it isn't," Garth cocntradicted me. "It's a root, a feeler, a tentacle. It's old man cancer himself — timber cancer — on the move and looking for a new victim. Oh, you won't see him moving," that strange look was back on his face, "or at least you shouldn't — but he's at it anyway. He finished those houses there," he nodded at the derelicts stepping down toward the new cliffs, "and now he's gone into this one on the left here. Another couple of summers like this 'un and he'll be through the entire row to my place. Except maybe I'll burn him out first."

"You mean this stuff — this fiber — is dry rot?" I said. I stuck my hand into the stuff and tore a clump out. It made a soft tearing sound, like damp chipboard, except it was dry as old paper. "How do you mean, you'll 'burn him out?' "

"I mean like I say," said Garth. "I'll search out and dig up all these threads — mycelium, they're called — and set fire to 'em. They smoulder right through to a fine white ash. And God — it *stinks*! Then I'll look for the fruiting bodies, and —"

"The what?" His words had conjured up something vaguely obscene in my mind. "Fruiting bodies?"

"Lord, yes!" he said. "You want to see? Just follow me."

Leaving the path, he stepped over a low brick wall to struggle through the undergrowth of the garden on our left. Taking care not to get tangled up in the brambles, I followed him. The house seemed pretty much intact, but a bay window in the ground floor had been broken and all the glass tapped out of the frame. "My winter preparations," Garth explained. "I burn wood, see? So before winter comes, I get into a house like this one, rip out all the wooden fixings and break 'em down ready for burning. The wood just stays where I stack it, all prepared and waiting for the bad weather to come in. I knocked this window out last week, but I've not been inside yet. I could smell it, see?" he tapped his nose. "And I didn't much care for all those spores on my lungs."

He stepped up on a pile of bricks, got one leg over the sill and stuck his head inside. Then, turning his head in all directions, he systematically sniffed the air. Finally he seemed satisfied and disappeared inside. I followed him. "Spores?" I said. "What sort of spores?"

He looked at me, wiped his hand along the window ledge, held it up so that I could see the red dust accumulated on his fingers and palm. "*These* spores," he said. "Dry rot spores, of course! Haven't you been listening?"

"I *have* been listening, yes," I answered sharply. "But I ask you: spores, mycelium, fruiting bodies? I mean, I thought dry rot was just, well, rotting wood!"

"It's a fungus," he told me, a little impatiently. "Like a mushroom, and it spreads in much the same way. Except it's destructive, and once it gets started it's bloody hard to stop!"

"And you, an ex-coal miner," I stared at him in the gloom of the house we'd invaded, "you're an expert on it, right? How come, Garth?"

Again there was that troubled expression on his face, and in the dim interior of the house he didn't try too hard to mask it. Maybe it had something to do with that story he'd promised to tell me, but doubtless he'd be as circuitous about that as he seemed to be about everything else. "Because I've read it up in books, that's how," he finally broke into my thoughts. "To occupy my time. When it first started to spread out of the old timber yard, I looked it up. It's —" He gave a sort of grimace. "— it's interesting, that's all."

By now I was wishing I was on my way again. But by that I mustn't be misunderstood: I'm an able-bodied man and I wasn't afraid of anything — and certainly not of Garth himself, who was just a lonely, canny old-timer — but all of this really was getting to be a waste of my time. I had just made my mind up to go back out through the window when he caught my arm.

"Oh, *yes!*" he said. "This place is really ripe with it! Can't you smell it? Even with the window bust wide open like this, and the place nicely dried out in the summer heat, still it's stinking the place out. Now just you come over here and you'll see what you'll see."

Despite myself, I was interested. And indeed I could smell . . . something. A cloying mustiness? A mushroomy taint? But not the nutty smell of fresh field mushrooms. More a sort of vile stagnation. Something dead might smell like this, long after the actual corruption has ceased. . . .

Our eyes had grown somewhat accustomed to the gloom. We looked about the room. "Careful how you go," said Garth. "See the spores there? Try not to stir them up too much. They're worse than snuff, believe me!" He was right: the red dust lay fairly thick on just about everything. By "everything" I mean a few old sticks of furniture, the worn carpet under our feet, the skirting-board and various shelves and ledges. Whichever family had moved out of here, they hadn't left a deal of stuff behind them.

The skirting was of the heavy, old-fashioned variety: an inch and a half thick, nine inches deep, with a fancy moulding along the top edge; they hadn't spared the wood in those days. Garth peered suspiciously at the skirting-board, followed it away from the bay window and paused every pace to scrape the toe of his boot down its face. And eventually when he did this — suddenly the board crumbled to dust under the pressure of his toe!

It was literally as dramatic as that: the white paint cracked away and the timber underneath fell into a heap of black, smoking dust. Another pace and Garth kicked again, with the same result. He quickly exposed a ten-foot length of naked wall, on which even the plaster was loose and flaky, and showed me where strands of the cotton-wool mycelium had come up between the brickwork and the plaster from below. "It sucks the cellulose right out of wood," he said. "Gets right into brickwork, too. Now look here," and he pointed at the old carpet under his feet. The threadbare weave showed a sort of raised floral blossom or stain, like a blotch or blister, spreading outward away from the wall.

Garth got down on his hands and knees. "Just look at this," he said. He tore up the carpet and carefully laid it back. Underneath, the floorboards were warped, dark-stained, shrivelled so as to leave wide gaps between them. And up through the gaps came those white, etiolated threads, spreading themselves along the underside of the carpet.

I wrinkled my nose in disgust. "It's like a disease," I said.

"It *is* a disease!" he corrected me. "It's a cancer, and houses die of it!" Then he inhaled noisily, pulled a face of his own, said: "Here. Right here." He pointed at the warped, rotting floorboards. "The very heart of it. Give me a hand." He got his fingers down between a pair of boards and gave a tug, and it was at once apparent that he wouldn't be needing any help from me. What had once been a stout wooden floorboard a full inch thick was now brittle as dry bark. It cracked upwards, flew apart, revealed the dark cavities between the floor joists. Garth tossed bits of crumbling wood aside, tore up more boards; and at last "the very heart of it" lay open to our inspection.

"There!" said Garth with a sort of grim satisfaction. He stood back and wiped his hands down his trousers. "Now *that* is what you call a fruiting body!"

It was roughly the size of a football, if not exactly that shape. Suspended between two joists in a cradle of fibers, and adhering to one of the joists as if partly flattened to it, the thing might have been a great, too-ripe tomato. It was bright yellow at its centre, banded in various shades of yellow from the middle out. It looked freakishly weird, like a bad joke: this lump of . . . of *stuff* — never a mushroom — just nestling there between the joists.

Garth touched my arm and I jumped a foot. He said: "You want to know where all the moisture goes — out of this wood, I mean? Well, just touch it."

"Touch . . . that?"

"Heck, it can't bite you! It's just a fungus."

"All the same, I'd rather not," I told him.

He took up a piece of floorboard and prodded the thing — and it squelched. The splintered point of the wood sank into it like jelly. Its heart was mainly liquid, porous as a sponge. "Like a huge egg yolk, isn't it?" he said, his voice very quiet. He was plainly fascinated.

Suddenly I felt nauseous. The heat, the oppressive closeness of the room, the spore-laden air. I stepped dizzily backward and stumbled against an old armchair. The rot had been there, too, for the chair just fragmented into a dozen pieces that puffed red dust all over the place. My foot sank right down through the carpet and mushy boards into darkness and stench — and in another moment I'd panicked.

Somehow I tumbled myself back out through the window, and ended up on my back in the brambles. Then Garth was standing over me, shaking his head and tut-tutting. "Told you not to stir up the dust," he said. "It chokes your air and stifles you. Worse than being down a pit. Are you all right?"

FRUITING BODIES

My heart stopped hammering and I was, of course, all right. I got up. "A touch of claustrophobia," I told him. "I suffer from it at times. Anyway, I think I've taken up enough of your time, Garth. I should be getting on my way."

"What?" he protested. "A lovely day like this and you want to be driving off somewhere? And besides, there were things I wanted to tell you, and others I'd ask you — and we haven't been down to Lily-Anne's grave." He looked disappointed. "Anyway, you shouldn't be driving if you're feeling all shaken up. . . ."

He was right about that part of it, anyway: I did feel shaky, not to mention foolish! And perhaps more importantly, I was still very much aware of the old man's loneliness. What if it was my mother who'd died, and my father had been left on his own up in Durham? "Very well," I said, at the same time damning myself for a weak fool, "let's go and see Lily-Anne's grave."

"Good!" Garth slapped my back. "And no more diversions — we go straight there."

Following the paved path as before and climbing a gentle rise, we started walking. We angled a little inland from the unseen cliffs where the green, rolling fields came to an abrupt end and fell down to the sea; and as we went I gave a little thought to the chain of incidents in which I'd found myself involved through the last hour or so.

Now, I'd be a liar if I said that nothing had struck me as strange in Easingham, for quite a bit had. Not least the dry rot: its apparent profusion and migration through the place, and old Garth's peculiar knowledge and understanding of the stuff. His — affinity? — with it. "You said there was a story attached," I reminded him. ". . . To that horrible fungus, I mean."

He looked at me sideways, and I sensed he was on the point of telling me

something. But at that moment we crested the rise and the view just took my breath away. We could see for miles up and down the coast: to the slow, white breakers rolling in on some beach way to the north, and southwards to a distance-misted seaside town which might even be Whitby. And we paused to fill our lungs with good air blowing fresh off the sea.

"There," said Garth. "And how's this for freedom? Just me and old Ben and the gulls for miles and miles, and I'm not so sure but that this is the way I like it. Now wasn't it worth it to come up here? All this open space and the great curve of the horizon. . . ." Then the look of satisfaction slipped from his face to be replaced by a more serious expression. "There's old Easingham's cemetery — what's left of it."

He pointed down toward the cliffs, where a badly weathered stone wall formed part of a square whose sides would have been maybe fifty yards long in the old days. But in those days there'd also been a stubby promontory, and a church. Now only one wall, running parallel with the path, stood complete — beyond which two-thirds of the churchyard had been claimed by the sea. Its occupants, too, I supposed.

"See that half-timbered shack," said Garth, pointing, "at this end of the cemetery? That's what's left of Johnson's Mill. Johnson's sawmill, that is. That shack used to be Old Man Johnson's office. A long line of Johnsons ran a couple of farms that enclosed all the fields round here right down to the cliffs. Pasture, mostly, with lots of fine animals grazing right here. But as the fields got eaten away and the buildings themselves started to be threatened, that's when half the Johnsons moved out and the rest bought a big house in the village. They gave up farming and started the mill, working timber for the local building trade. . . .

"Folks round here said it was a sin,

all that noise of sawing and planing, right next door to a churchyard. But . . . it was Old Man Johnson's land after all. Well, the sawmill business kept going 'til a time some seven years ago, when a really bad blow took a huge bite right out of the bay one night. The seaward wall of the graveyard went, and half of the timber yard, too, and that closed old Johnson down. He sold what machinery he had left, plus a few stacks of good oak that hadn't suffered, and moved out lock, stock and barrel. Just as well, for the very next spring his big house and two others close to the edge of the cliffs got taken. The sea gets 'em all in the end.

"Before then, though — at a time when just about everybody else was moving out of Easingham — Lily-Anne and me had moved in! As I told you, we got our bungalow for a song, and of course we picked ourselves a house standing well back from the brink. We were getting on a bit; another twenty years or so should see us out; after that the sea could do its worst. But . . . well, it didn't quite work out that way."

While he talked, Garth had led the way down across the open fields to the graveyard wall. The breeze was blustery here and fluttered his words back into my face:

"So you see, within just a couple of years of our settling here, the village was derelict, and all that remained of people was us and a handful of Johnsons still working the mill. Then Lily-Anne came down with something and died, and I had her put down in the ground here in Easingham — so's I'd be near her, you know?

"That's where the coincidences start to come in, for she went only a couple of months after the shipwreck. Now I don't suppose you'd remember that; it wasn't much, just an old Portuguese freighter that foundered in a storm. Lifeboats took the crew off, and she'd already unloaded her cargo somewhere up the coast, so the incident didn't create much of a to-do in the newspapers. But she'd carried a fair bit of hardwood ballast, that old ship, and balks of the stuff would keep drifting ashore: great long twelve-by-twelves of it. Of course, Old Man Johnson wasn't one to miss out on a bit of good timber like that, not when it was being washed up right on his doorstep, so to speak. . . .

"Anyway, when Lily-Anne died I made the proper arrangements, and I went down to see old Johnson who told me he'd make me a coffin out of this Haitian hardwood."

"Haitian?" maybe my voice showed something of my surprise.

"That's right," said Garth, more slowly. He looked at me wonderingly. "Anything wrong with that?"

I shrugged, shook my head. "Rather romantic, I thought," I said. "Timber from a tropical isle."

"I thought so, too," he agreed. And after a while he continued: "Well, despite having been in the sea, the stuff could still be cut into fine, heavy panels, and it still French polished to a beautiful finish. So that was that: Lily-Anne got a lovely coffin. Except —"

"Yes?" I prompted him.

He pursed his lips. "Except I got to thinking — later, you know — as to how maybe the rot came here in that wood. God knows it's a damn funny variety of fungus after all. But then this Haiti — well, apparently it's a damned funny place. They call it 'the Voodoo Island,' you know?"

"Black magic?" I smiled. "I think we've advanced a bit beyond thinking such as that, Garth."

"Maybe and maybe not," he answered. "But voodoo or no voodoo, it's still a funny place, that Haiti. Far away and exotic. . . ."

By now we'd found a gap in the old stone wall and climbed over the tumbled stones into the graveyard proper. From where we stood, another twenty paces would take us right to the raw edge of the cliff where it sheared dead straight through the overgrown, badly neglected plots and headstones. "So here it is," said Garth, pointing. "Lily-Anne's grave, secure for now in what little is left of Easingham's old cemetery." His voice fell a little, grew ragged: "But you know, the fact is I wish I'd never put her down here in the first place. And I'd give anything that I hadn't buried her in that coffin built of Old Man Johnson's ballast wood."

The plot was a neat oblong picked out in oval pebbles. It had been weeded round its border, and from its bottom edge to the foot of the simple headstone it was decked in flowers, some wild and others cut from Easingham's deserted gardens. It was deep in flowers, and the ones underneath were withered and had been compressed by those on top. Obviously Garth came here more often than just "now and then". It was the only plot in sight that had been paid any sort of attention, but in the circumstances that wasn't surprising.

"You're wondering why there are so many flowers, eh?" Garth sat down on a raised slab close by.

I shook my head, sat down beside him. "No, I know why. You must have thought the world of her."

"You don't know why," he answered. "I did think the world of her, but that's not why. It's not the only reason, anyway. I'll show you."

He got down on his knees beside the grave, began laying aside the flowers. Right down to the marble chips he went, then scooped an amount of the polished gravel to one side. He made a small mound of it. Whatever I had expected to see in the small excavation, it wasn't the cylindrical, fibrous surface — like the upper section of a lagged pipe — which came into view. I sucked in my breath sharply.

There were tears in Garth's eyes as he flattened the marble chips back into

place. "The flowers are so I won't see it if it ever breaks the surface," he said. "See, I can't bear the thought of that filthy stuff in her coffin. I mean, what if it's like what you saw under the floorboards in that house back there?" He sat down again, and his hands trembled as he took out an old wallet, and removed a photograph to give it to me. "That's Lily-Anne," he said. "But God! — I don't like the idea of that stuff fruiting on her. . . ."

Aghast at the thoughts his words conjured, I looked at the photograph. A homely woman in her late fifties, seated in a chair beside a fence in a garden I recognized as Garth's. Except the garden had been well-tended then. One shoulder seemed slumped a little, and though she smiled, still I could sense the pain in her face. "Just a few weeks before she died," said Garth. "It was her lungs. Funny that I worked in the pit all those years, and it was her lungs gave out. And now she's here, and so's this stuff."

I had to say something. "But . . . where did it come from. I mean, how did it come, well, here? I don't know much about dry rot, no, but I would have thought it confined itself to houses."

"That's what I was telling you," he said, taking back the photograph. "The British variety does. But not this stuff. It's weird and different! That's why I think it might have come here with that ballast wood. As to how it got into the churchyard: that's easy. Come and see for yourself."

I followed him where he made his way between the weedy plots toward the leaning, half-timbered shack. "Is that the source? Johnson's timber-yard?"

He nodded. "For sure. But look here."

I looked where he pointed. We were still in the graveyard, approaching the tumble-down end wall, beyond which stood the derelict shack. Running in a parallel series along the dry ground, from the mill and into the graveyard, deep cracks showed through the tangled brambles, briars and grasses. One of these cracks, wider than the others, had actually split a heavy horizontal marble slab right down its length. Garth grunted. "That wasn't done last time I was here." he said.

"The sea's been at it again," I nodded. "Undermining the cliffs. Maybe we're not as safe here as you think."

He glanced at me. "Not the sea this time," he said, very definitely. "Something else entirely. See, there's been no rain for weeks. Everything's dry. And *it* gets thirsty same as we do. Give me a hand."

He stood beside the broken slab and got his fingers into the crack. It was obvious that he intended to open up the tomb. "Garth," I cautioned him. "Isn't this a little ghoulish? Do you really intend to desecrate this grave?"

"See the date?" he said. "1847. Heck,

I don't think he'd mind, whoever he is. Desecration? Why, he might even thank us for a little sweet sunlight! What are you afraid of ? There can only be dust and bones down there now."

Full of guilt, I looked all about while Garth struggled with the fractured slab. It was a safe bet that there wasn't a living soul for miles around, but I checked anyway. Opening graves isn't my sort of thing. But having discovered him for a stubborn old man, I knew that if I didn't help him he'd find a way to do it by himself anyway; and so I applied myself to the task. Between the two of us we wrestled one of the two halves to the edge of its base, finally toppled it over. A choking fungus reek at once rushed out to engulf us! Or maybe the smell was of something else and I'd simply smelled what I "expected" to.

Garth pulled a sour face. "*Ugh!*" was his only comment.

The air cleared and we looked into

the tomb. In there, a coffin just a little over three feet long, and the broken sarcophagus around it filled with dust, cobwebs and a few leaves. Garth glanced at me out of the corner of his eye. "So now you think I'm wrong, eh?"

"About what?" I answered. "It's just a child's coffin."

"Just a little 'un, aye," he nodded. "And his little coffin looks intact, doesn't it? *But is it?*" Before I could reply he reached down and rapped with his horny knuckles on the wooden lid.

And despite the fact that the sun was shining down on us, and for all that the seagulls cried and the world seemed at peace, still my hair stood on end at what happened next. For the coffin lid collapsed like a puff-ball and fell into dusty debris, and — God help me — *something in the box gave a grunt and puffed itself up into view!*

I'm not a coward, but there are times when my limbs have a will of their own. Once when a drunk insulted my wife, I struck him without consciously knowing I'd done it. It was that fast, the reaction that instinctive. And the same now. I didn't pause to draw breath until I'd cleared the wall and was half-way up the field to the paved path; and even then I probably wouldn't have stopped, except I tripped and fell flat, and knocked all the wind out of myself.

By the time I stopped shaking and sat up, Garth was puffing and panting up the slope toward me. "It's all right," he was gasping. "It was nothing. Just the rot. It had grown in there and crammed itself so tight, so confined, that when the coffin caved-in. . . ."

He was right and I knew it. I *had* known it even with my flesh crawling, my legs, heart and lungs pumping. But even so: "There were . . . *bones* in it!" I said, contrary to common sense. "A skull."

He drew close, sank down beside me gulping at the air. "The little un's bones," he panted, "caught up in the fibers. I just wanted to show you the extent of the thing. Didn't want to scare you to death!"

"I know, I know," I patted his hand. "But when it moved —"

"It was just the effect of the box collapsing," he explained, logically. "Natural expansion. Set free, it unwound like a jack-in-the-box. And the noise it made —"

"— That was the sound of its scraping against the rotten timber, amplified by the sarcophagus," I nodded. "I know all that. It shocked me, that's all. In fact, two hours in your bloody Easingham have given me enough shocks to last a lifetime!"

"But you see what I mean about the rot?" We stood up, both of us still a little shaky.

"Oh, yes, I see what you mean. I don't understand your obsession, that's all. Why don't you just leave the damned stuff alone?"

He shrugged but made no answer, and so we made our way back toward his home. On our way the silence between us was broken only once. "There!" said Garth, looking back toward the brow of the hill. "You see him?"

I looked back, saw the dark outline of an Alsatian dog silhouetted against the rise. "Ben?" Even as I spoke the name, so the dog disappeared into the long grass beside the path.

"Ben!" Garth called, and blew his piercing whistle. But with no result. The old man worriedly shook his head. "Can't think what's come over him," he said. "Then again, I'm more his friend than his master. We've always pretty much looked after ourselves. At least I know that he hasn't run off. . . ."

Then we were back at Garth's house, but I didn't go in. His offer of another coffee couldn't tempt me. It was time I was on my way again. "If ever you're back this way —" he said as I got into the car.

I nodded, leaned out of my window.

"Garth, why the Hell don't you get out of here? I mean, there's nothing here for you now. Why don't you take Ben and just clear out."

He smiled, shook his head, then shook my hand. "Where'd we go?" he asked. "And anyway,Lily-Anne's still here. Sometimes in the night, when it's hot and I have trouble sleeping, I can feel she's very close to me. Anyway, I know you mean well."

That was that. I turned the car round and drove off, acknowledged his final wave by lifting my hand briefly, so that he'd see it.

Then, driving round a gentle bend and as the old man side-slipped out of my rearview mirror, I saw Ben. He was crossing the road in front of me. I applied my brakes, let him get out of the way. It could only be Ben, I supposed: a big Alsatian, shaggy, yellow-eyed. And yet I caught only a glimpse; I was more interested in controlling the car, in being sure that he was safely out of the way.

It was only after he'd gone through the hedge and out of sight into a field that an after-image of the dog surfaced in my mind: the way he'd seemed to limp — his belly hairs, so long as to hang down and trail on the ground, even though he wasn't slinking — a bright splash of yellow on his side, as if he'd brushed up against something freshly painted.

Perhaps understandably, peculiar images bothered me all the way back to London; yes, and for quite a long time after. . .

Before I knew it a year had gone by, then eighteen months, and memories of those strange hours spent in Easingham were fast receding. Faded with them was that promise I had myself to visit my parents more frequently. Then I got a letter to say my mother hadn't been feeling too well, and another right on its heels to say

she was dead. She'd gone in her sleep, nice and easy. This last was from a neighbour of theirs: my father wasn't much up to writing right now, or much of anything else for that matter; the funeral would be on . . . at . . . etc, etc.

God! — how guilty I felt driving up there, and more guilty with every mile that flashed by under my car's wheels. And all I could do was choke the guilt and the tears back and drive, and feel the dull, empty ache in my heart that I knew my father would be feeling in his. And of course that was when I remembered old Garth Bentham in Easingham, and my "advice" that he should get out of that place. It had been a cold sort of thing to say to him. Even cruel. But I hadn't known that then. I hadn't thought.

We laid Ma to rest and I stayed with the Old Man for a few days, but he really didn't want me around. I thought about saying: "Why don't you sell up, come and live with us in London." We had plenty of room. But then I thought of Garth again and kept my mouth shut. Dad would work it out for himself in the fullness of time.

It was late on a cold Wednesday afternoon when I started out for London again, and I kept thinking how lonely it must be in old Easingham. I found myself wondering if Garth ever took a belt or filled a pipe, if he could even afford to, and . . . I'd promised him that if I was ever back up this way I'd look him up, hadn't I? I stopped at an off-license, bought a bottle of half-decent whisky and some pipe and rolling baccy, and a carton of two hundred cigarettes and a few cigars. Whatever was his pleasure, I'd probably covered it. And if he didn't smoke, well I could always give the tobacco goods to someone who did.

My plan was to spend just an hour with Garth, then head for the motorway and drive to London in darkness. I don't mind driving in the dark, when the weather and visibility are good and the driving lanes all but empty, and the night music comes sharp and clear out of the radio to keep me awake.

But approaching Easingham down that neglected cul-de-sac of a road, I saw that I wasn't going to have any such easy time of it. A storm was gathering out to sea, piling up the thunderheads like beetling black brows all along the twilight horizon. I could see continuous flashes of lightning out there, and even before I reached my destination I could hear the high seas thundering against the cliffs. When I did get there —

Well, I held back from driving quite as far as the barrier, because only a little way beyond it my headlights had picked out black, empty space. Of the three houses which had stood closest to the cliffs only one was left, and that one slumped right on the rim. So I stopped directly opposite Garth's place, gave a honk on my horn, then switched off and got out of the car with my carrier-bag full of gifts. Making my way to the house, the rush and roar of the sea was perfectly audible, transferring itself physically through the earth to my feet. Indeed the bleak, unforgiving ocean seemed to be working itself up into a real fury.

Then, in a moment, the sky darkened over and the rain came on out of nowhere, bitter-cold and squally, and I found myself running up the overgrown garden path to Garth's door. Which was when I began to feel really foolish. There was no sign of life behind the grimy windows; neither a glimmer of light showing, nor a puff of smoke from the chimney. Maybe Garth had taken my advice and got out of it after all.

Calling his name over the rattle of distant thunder, I knocked on the door. After a long minute there was still no answer. But this was no good; I was getting wet and angry with myself; I tried the doorknob, and the door swung open. I stepped inside, into deep gloom, and groped on the wall near the door for a light switch. I found it, but the light wasn't working. Of course it wasn't: there was no electricity! this was a ghost town, derelict, forgotten. And the last time I was here it had been in broad daylight.

But . . . Garth had made coffee for me. On a gas-ring? It must have been.

Standing there in the small cloakroom shaking rain off myself, my eyes were growing more accustomed to the gloom. The cloakroom seemed just as I remembered it: several pieces of tall, dark furniture, pine-panelled inner walls, the old grandfather clock standing in one corner. Except that this time . . . the clock wasn't clucking. The pendulum was still, a vertical bar of brassy fire where lightning suddenly brought the room to life. Then it was dark again — if anything even darker than before — and the windows rattled as thunder came down in a rolling, receding drumbeat.

"Garth!" I called again, my voice echoing through the old house. "It's me, Greg Lane. I said I'd drop in some time. . . ?" No answer, just the *hiss* of the rain outside, the feel of my collar damp against my neck, and the thick, rising smell of . . . of what? And suddenly I remembered very clearly the details of my last visit here.

"Garth!" I tried one last time, and I stepped to the door of his living-room and pushed it open. As I did so there came a lull in the beating rain. I heard the floorboards creak under my feet, but I also heard . . . a groan? My sensitivity at once rose by several degrees. Was that Garth? Was he hurt? *My God!* What had he said to me that time? "One of these days the postman will find me stretched out in here, and he'll think: 'well, I needn't come out here anymore.'

I had to have light. There'd be matches in the kitchen, maybe even a torch. In the absence of a mains supply, Garth would surely have to have a torch. Making my way shufflingly, very cautiously across the dark room toward the kitchen, I was conscious that the smell was more concentrated here. Was it just the smell of an old, derelict house, or was it something worse? Then, outside, lightning flashed again, and briefly the room was lit up in a white glare. Before the darkness fell once more, I saw someone slumped on the old settee where Garth had served me coffee . . .

"Garth?" the word came out half-strangled. I hadn't wanted to say it; it had just gurgled from my tongue. For though I'd seen only a silhouette, outlined by the split-second flash, it hadn't looked like Garth at all. It had been much more like someone else I'd once seen — in a photograph. That drooping right shoulder.

My skin prickled as I stepped on shivery feet through the open door into the kitchen. I forced myself to draw breath, to think clearly. *If* I'd seen anyone or anything at all back there (it could have been old boxes piled on the settee, or a roll of carpet leaning there), then it most probably had been Garth, which would explain that groan. It *was* him, of course it was. But in the storm, and remembering what I did of this place, my mind was playing morbid tricks with me. No, it was Garth, and he could well be in serious trouble. I got a grip of myself, quickly looked all around.

A little light came into the kitchen through a high back window. There was a two-ring gas cooker, a sink and drainer-board with a drawer under the sink. I pulled open the drawer and felt about inside it. My nervous hand struck what was unmistakably a large box of matches, and — yes, the smooth heavy cylinder of a hand torch!

And all the time I was aware that someone was or might be slumped on a settee just a few swift paces away through the door to the living-room. With my hand still inside the drawer,

I pressed the stud of the torch and was rewarded when a weak beam probed out to turn my fingers pink. Well, it wasn't a powerful beam, but any sort of light had to be better than total darkness.

Armed with the torch, which felt about as good as a weapon in my hand, I forced myself to move back into the living-room and directed my beam at the settee. But oh, Jesus — all that sat there was a monstrous grey mushroom! It was a great fibrous mass, growing out of and welded with mycelium strands to the settee, and in its centre an obscene yellow fruiting body. But for God's sake, it had the shape and outline and *look* of an old woman, and it had Lily-Anne's deflated chest and slumped shoulder!

I don't know how I held onto the torch, how I kept from screaming out loud, why I simply didn't fall unconscious. That's the sort of shock I experienced. But I did none of these things. Instead, on nerveless legs, I backed away, backed right into an old wardrobe or Welsh-dresser. At least, I backed into what had once *been* a piece of furniture. But now it was something else.

Soft as sponge, the thing collapsed and sent me sprawling. Dust and (I imagined) dark red spores rose up everywhere, and I skidded on my back in shards of crumbling wood and matted webs of fiber. And lolling out of the darkness behind where the dresser had stood — bloating out like some loathsome puppet or dummy — a second fungoid figure leaned toward me. And this time it was a caricature of Ben!

He lolled there, held up on four fiber legs, muzzle snarling soundlessly, for all the world tensed to spring — and all he was was a harmless fungous thing. And yet this time I did scream. Or I think I did, but the thunder came to drown me out.

Then I was on my feet, and my feet were through the rotten floorboards, and I didn't care except I had to get out of there, out of that choking, stinking, collapsing —

I stumbled, *crumbled* my way into the tiny cloakroom, tripped and crashed into the clock where it stood in the corner. It was like a nightmare chain-reaction which I'd started and couldn't stop; the old grandfather just crumpled up on itself, its metal parts clanging together as the wood disintegrated around them. And all the furniture following suit, and the very wall panelling smoking into ruin where I fell against it.

And there where that infected timber had been, there he stood — old Garth himself! He leaned half out of the wall like a great nodding manikin, his entire head a livid yellow blotch, his arm and hand making a noise like a huge puff-ball bursting underfoot where they separated from his side to point floppingly toward the open door. I needed no more urging.

"God! Yes! *I'm going!*" I told him, as I plunged out into the storm . . .

* * *

After that . . . nothing, not for some time. I came to in a hospital in Stokesley about noon the next day. Apparently I'd run off the road on the outskirts of some village or other, and they'd dragged me out of my car where it lay upside-down in a ditch. I was banged-up and so couldn't do much talking, which is probably as well.

But in the newspapers I read how what was left of Easingham had gone into the sea in the night. The churchyard, Haitian timber, terrible dry rot fungus, the whole thing, sliding down into the sea and washed away forever on the tides.

And yet now I sometimes think:

Where did all that wood *go* that Garth had been selling for years? And what of all those spores I'd breathed and touched and rolled around in? And sometimes when I think things like that it makes me feel quite ill.

I suppose I shall just have to wait and see. . . .

∎

BECAUSE

Outside shining windows, snow is falling;
warmth pervades the peaceful quiet rooms
as firelight flickers on the polished hearth —
so why does he pace across the rug, down
the hall, through a door and back again?
Again and again, as the fresh snow falls,
till the failing embers shift to ash
and the room grows cold?

Because the snow brings memories,
because he is haunted by the life
he never wholly lived.

Because he is old.

— **Joseph Payne Brennan**

85

AFTER THE LAST ELF IS DEAD

by Harry Turtledove

The city of Lerellim burned. Valsak reckoned a good omen the scarlet flames and black smoke mounting to the sky: black and scarlet were the colors of the Dark Brother the high captain served.

An ogre came up to Valsak, savage head bent in salute while it waited for him to notice it. "Lord, the quarter by the river is taken," it reported.

The man nodded. "Good. Only the citadel left, then." His eyes narrowed as he studied the great stone pile ahead. Atop the tallest tower, the Green Star still flew, the proud banner snapping defiance in the breeze. Men and elves shot from the battlements at the Dark Brother's ring of troops as it tightened around them.

Valsak rubbed his chin. The citadel would be expensive to take. The high captain's mouth widened in a tight-lipped smile. He knew the difference between expensive and impossible.

Thunderbolts lashed out from the fortress, spears of green light. Valsak swore, and had to wait for his vision to clear to see what damage the enemy's magic had done. He smiled again: almost none. The Dark Brother put forth all his might now, to end once for all the pretensions of these bandits who had for so long presumed to style themselves High Kings in his despite.

Valsak turned to his lieutenant. "Gather a storming party, Gersner. We will go in through the main gate, once our wizards have thrown it down."

"It shall be done, high captain." Gersner was small, thin, and quiet; anyone who did not known him would have had trouble imagining him as any kind of soldier. Valsak knew him, and knew his worth. Within minutes, men and ogres began gathering before the main gate. A proper murderous crew, Valsak thought, almost fondly. The warriors brandished swords, spears, maces. Whatever the butcher's bill they would have to pay, they knew they stood on the edge of victory.

Two black-robed wizards, one with a bandage on his head, made their way through the storming party. Soldiers stepped back fearfully, letting them pass. They in turn bowed before Valsak. To wield their magic, they had to stand high in the Dark Brother's favor. He stood higher, and they knew it.

He pointed. "Take out the gates."

They bowed again, and stayed bowed, gathering their strength. Then they straightened. Crimson rays shot from their fingertips; crimson fire smote the metal at the top of the gates and ran dripping down them, as if it were some thick liquid. Where the fire stuck and clung, the metal was no more.

Then the clingfire slowed, nearly stopped. The bandaged wizard staggered, groaned, gave back a pace.

"Counterspell!" his comrade gasped hoarsely. He cried out a Word of power so terrible even Valsak frowned. That Word was plenty to occupy the men or elvish wizards trapped in the citadel. With them distracted thus, the other black-robe recovered himself, stepped up to stand by his colleague again. The fire began to advance once more, faster and faster.

Soon the gates were burned away. The harsh smoke from them made Val-

sak cough. He drew his sword, picked up his shield. "Forward!" he shouted. He charged with his warriors. No officer could make troops dare anything they thought him unwilling to risk himself.

Archers appeared in the blasted doorway. Elf-shot shafts flew far, fast, and straight. Men and ogres behind Valsak fell. An arrow thudded against his buckler. The shield was thin and looked flimsy, but the magic in it gave better protection than any weight of wood or metal. Not even elf-arrows would pierce it, not today.

The archers saw they were too few to break up Valsak's attack. Those his own bowmen had not slain darted aside, to be replaced by heavily armored men and elves.

"If their gates can't hold us out, their damned soldiers won't!" Valsak yelled. His storming column's cheers rose to the skies, along with the smoke from falling Lerellim.

Recognizing the high captain as his foes' commander, an elflord sprang out to meet him in single combat. The elf was tall and fair, after the fashion of his kind, with gold hair streaming from beneath his shining silvered helm. Not a hint of fear sullied his noble features; more than anything else, he seemed sorrowful as he swung up his long straight blade. Even in mail, he moved gracefully as a hunting cat.

Valsak killed him.

Cunning alone had not raised the high captain to his rank. As happened often in the Dark Brother's armies, he had climbed over the bodies of rivals, many of them slain by his own hand. And in the wars against the High Kings and their elvish allies, he fought always at the fore.

He would never be so fluid a warrior as the elflord he faced, nor quite as quick. But he was strong and clever, clever enough to turn his awkwardness to advantage. What seemed a stumble

88

was not. His shield turned the elf's blow; his own sword leaped out to punch through gorget and throat alike.

The elflord's fine mouth twisted in pain. His eyes, blue as the sky had been before the fires started, misted over. As his foe crumpled, Valsak felt something sigh past him: the elf's soul, bound for the Isle of Forever in the Utmost West. *Flee while you can,* the high captain thought — *one day the Dark Brother may hunt you even there.*

The fall of their leader threw the gateway's defenders into deeper despair than had been theirs before. With some, that increased their fury, so they fought without regard for their own safety and were sooner killed than might otherwise have been true. Others, unmanned, thought of flight, weakening the stand still more. Soon Valsak and his warriors were loose in the citadel.

He knew where he wanted to take them. "The throneroom!" he cried. "Those who cast down the last of this rebel line surely will earn great rewards from our master!" The cheers of men and ogres echoed down the corridors ahead of them as they stormed after Valsak. Some might have dreamed of lordships under the Dark Brother, some of loot beyond counting; some of women there for the taking; the ogres, perhaps, just of hot manflesh to eat. All their dreams might turn real now, and they knew it.

There was plenty more fighting on the way. Desperate parties of men and elves flung themselves at Valsak's band. The high captain got a slash on his cheek, and never remembered when or how. But the defenders were too few, with too many threats to meet: not only was the gate riven, but by this time the Dark Brother's armies had to have flung ladders and towers against the citadel's walls. Like the city outside, it was falling.

"Ha! We are the first!" Gersner called

when the invaders burst past the silver doors of the throneroom and saw none of the Dark Brother's other minions had come so far so fast.

In front of the guards around the High King's throne, a white-robed, white-bearded wizard still incanted, calling on the Light. "Fool! The Light has failed!" Valsak shouted. The wizard paid no heed. Valsak turned to Gersner. "Slay him."

"Aye." The smaller man sprang forward. The wizard tried to fling lightning at him, but the levinbolt shriveled before it was well begun. Laughing, Gersner sworded the old man down.

Valsak's warriors flung themselves on the guards. The high captain saw they had the numbers and fury to prevail. That left only the High King. His sword was drawn, but he still sat on the throne, as if while his fundament rested there he remained ruler of the Western Realm.

Maybe that sort of mystic tie had existed once, but the Dark Brother's rise broke all such asunder. Watching his guards, men and elves, die for him, the high King must have realized that. He sprang to his feet, crying to Valsak, "I'll not live, for you, filthy master, to make sport of !"

To Valsak's disappointment, the High King did fight so fiercely he made his foes kill him. "Miserable bastard," Gersner muttered, a hand to his ribs; one of the High King's slashes had almost pierced his mailshirt and the leather beneath it, and must have left a tremendous bruise. By then, though, the last guards were down, the men and ogres taking turns shoving steel into the corpse as it lay sprawled on the steps before the throne.

Above the royal seat, the air began to shimmer and twist, as if being kneaded by unseen hands. Then the Dark Brother, in all his dreadful majesty, assumed the throne he had coveted through the five ages since the

First Beginning. His warriors bent the knee before him as, smiling, he surveyed the carnage in the throneroom.

He spoke then, and Valsak knew his words echoed from the Frozen Waste in the north to the deserts and steaming jungles of the Hotlands. "The world is mine!" he said.

"The world may be the Dark Brother's, but some folk have yet to believe it," Valsak said sourly as his long column of horsemen and footsoldiers moved slowly toward the mountains looming ahead. His backside ached from a week in the saddle.

Gersner frowned. "Our job is to teach them," he said, a touch of reproof in his voice.

"Aye," Valsak said. "Teach them we do." His eyes went to the fields to one side of the road. Bands of marauders wearing the Dark Brother's black surcoats were plundering the farms there. Some farmers must have been resisting from one stout building, for several raiders were working toward it with torches.

Valsak swung up a mailed hand. "Column left!" he called, and trotted toward the farm building. Riders followed. "Nock arrows," he added, and fit his own action to word.

The Dark Brother's irregulars cheered to see reinforcements riding to their aid. But Valsak led his troopers to cordon the farm building away from the raiders, and his men faced out, not in.

The marauders' leader, a man with features so dark and heavy he might have been a quarter ogre, angrily rushed up to Valsak. "Who do you think you are, and what in the name of the Dark Brother's dungeons are you playing at?" he shouted.

"I am the high captain Valsak, and if you invoke the Dark Brother's dungeons in my hearing again, you will earn the chance to see what you have called upon," Valsak said. He sat quiet upon his horse, coldly staring down as the fellow in front of him wilted. Then he went on, "I will give you back the second part of your question: what are you playing at here?"

"Just having a bit of sport," the other said. "We won, after all; why not take the chance to enjoy it?"

"Because if you go about burning farms, we will all be hungry by and by. I have fought for the Dark Brother more years than you have lived" — a guess, but a good one, and one calculated to put the marauder in fear, for Valsak looked no older than he — "and I have never known his soldiers to be exempt from the need to eat. The war we fought took out enough farms on its own. I do not think the Dark Brother would thank you for wantonly destroying more of what is his."

He expected that to finish demoralizing the irregular, but the fellow had more to him than Valsak had expected. He put hands on hips and said, "Hoity-toity! You talk like that, why weren't you on the other side at Lerellim? You —"

He never got farther than that. Valsak nodded to the archer at his left. A bowstring thrummed. The irregular clutched at the arrow that suddenly sprouted in his chest. Still wearing a look of outraged disbelief, he toppled.

"Does anyone else care to question my loyalty?" Valsak asked quietly. No one did. "Good. I suggest you move on then, and if you want a bit of sport, try a brothel." The irregulars, outnumbered and outfaced, perforce moved on. Their leader lay where he had fallen.

One of the farmers came out of the stronghouse, looked from the corpse to Valsak and back again. "I thank you," he said at last.

"I did not do it for your sake," the high captain answered, "but for the Dark Brother's. You and yours are his, to be used as he sees fit, and not to be despoiled by the first band of armed men that happens by."

"I don't care why you did it. I thank you anyway," the farmer said. " 'Twas nobly done."

Valsak scowled. In his rude way, and no doubt all ignorant of what he meant, the rustic was saying the same thing the marauder had. Nobility! Valsak knew where his loyalty lay, and that was that. He jerked a thumb at the raider's body. "Bury this carrion," he told the farmer, then turned back to his troop. "Ride on!"

Gersner knew better than to question his commander in front of the men. But when they camped that night, he waited till most of them were in their bedrolls, then asked, "Did you really feel you had to set on our own? After the war we fought against the cursed High Kings, that may not sit well."

" 'After' is the word, Gersner," Valsak said, as patiently as he could. "Except for mopping-up jobs like this one we're on, the war is over. This is not enemy territory, to be ravaged to hurt the foe. It *belongs* to the Dark Brother now."

Gersner grunted. "And if he chooses to send it to ruin?"

"Then his will be done. But it is not done, as you and I know, through a band of small-time bandits who happen to have coats the same color as ours. Or do you think otherwise?"

"Put that way, no." Gersner let it drop. He did not seem altogether happy, but Valsak wasted no time fretting over whether subordinates were happy. He wanted them to obey. Gersner had never given him cause to worry there.

The mountain keep looked strong enough. Before the war was won, it might have held up Valsak and his forces for weeks or even months. Now, with the Western Realm's heart torn out, he knew he could take it. It would still cost. Valsak had spent lives lavishly to take the citadel of Lerellim. He was not, however, a wasteful man. The need had been great then. Now it was less. And so, while Gersner and the troopers waited behind him and carefully said nothing, he rode forward alone, to parley.

The sentry above the gate shouted, "Go back, black-coat! My lord Oldivor has taken oath by the Light never to yield to wickedness, or let it set foot here."

"They swore that same oath in Lerellim, and the Dark Brother sits on the throne there. What has your precious lord to say to that? Will he speak with me now, or shall I pull his castle down around his ears and then see what he has to say? Now fetch him" — Valsak let some iron come into his voice — "or I will make a point of remembering *your* face as well."

The sentry disappeared fast enough to satisfy even the high captain.

The man who came to peer down from the gray stone walls at Valsak was tall and fair and, the high captain guessed, badly frightened: had he been in the other's boots, he would have been. The local lord made a game try at not showing it, though, shouting, "Begone, in the name of the High King!"

"The High King is dead," Valsak told him.

"Aye, you'd say that, wouldn't you, black-coat, to make us lose heart. Well, your tricks and lies are worthless here." Several men on the battlements shouted agreement.

"There are no tricks or lies. Along with others here, I was one of those who killed him. Should you care to share that honor with him, I daresay it can be arranged."

Appalled silence fell in the castle. Valsak let it stretch. Fear worked only for the Dark Brother. When Oldivor spoke again, he sounded less bold. "What would you have of me?"

"Yield up your fortress. You have not yet fought against the Dark Brother's servants, so no offense exists save failing to leave here when the High King, ah, died. I am high captain of the Dark Brother; I have the power to forgive that small trespass if you make it good now. You and yours may even keep your swords. All you need do is swear your submission to the Dark Brother, and you shall depart in peace. In his name I avow it."

"Swear submission to evil, you mean," the man on the battlements said slowly.

"The Dark Brother rules now. You *will* submit to him, sir, whether or not you swear the oath. The choice is doing it before your castle is sacked and you yourself — if you are lucky — slain." Valsak paused. "Do you need time to consider your decision? I will give it to you, if you like."

Oldivor stood suddenly straighter. "I need no time. I will stand by my first oath, and will not be forsworn. If the High King and his line have failed, then one day, with the aid of the elves, a new line will rise up to fight again for freedom."

"The elves are dead," Valsak said. "If you have anyone in your keep with the least skill at magic, you will know I tell no lies."

That knocked some of the new-come spirit out of the noble on the walls above the high captain. "So Velethol was right," he said. Valsak thought he was talking more to himself than to anyone else. But then Oldivor gathered himself again. "I will fight regardless, for my honor's sake," he said loudly. He had the backing of his men, if nothing else: they cheered his defiance.

Valsak shrugged. "You have made your choice. You will regret it." He rode back to his own line.

"A waste of time?" Gersner asked.

"A waste of time." Valsak turned to the lesser of the two wizards who had seared away the gates of Lerellim's citadel. "Open the keep for us."

The wizard bowed. "It shall be done,

high captain." He summoned his powers, sent them darting forth. This mountain keep's gates were not elf-silver, only iron-faced wood. They caught at once, and kept on burning despite the water and sand the defenders poured on them from the murder-holes above. Soon the gateway stood naked for Valsak's warriors.

As at the citadel, warriors rushed to fill the breach in the fortifications. "Shall I burn them down, high captain?" the wizard asked. "They have scant sorcery to ward them."

Valsak rubbed his chin. "Burn a couple, but only a couple — enough to drive the others away from the portal," he said judiciously. "If we take some alive, the Dark Brother's army will be better for it. These are no cowards we face."

The wizard sniffed, but at Valsak's scowl he said, "It shall be as you wish, of course." It was also as Valsak guessed: after two men turned to shrieking fireballs, the rest drew back. The high captain's warriors had no trouble forcing an entrance.

Once inside the keep, Valsak spied Oldivor not far away, still leading what defense he could make. "Now will you yield?" the high captain shouted. "Your men have fought well enough to satisfy any man's honor. The Dark Brother would smile to gain the loyalty you show now for a cause that is dead."

Afterwards, he realized he should not have mentioned his master's name. His foe's haggard face twisted into a terrible grimace. "So long as we live and fight, the cause is not dead!" he shouted. "But you soon will be!" He came rushing toward Valsak, hewing down one of the high captain's men who stood in his way.

Valsak soon took his foe's measure; as a warrior who had slain an elf, he was in scant danger from this petty border lord, who had ferocity but no great skill. Still, the high captain looked to beat him as quickly as he could. He was not the sort of man to toy with any opponent — who could say when the fellow might get lucky?

And indeed, luck intervened, but not on Oldivor's side. When Valsak's sword struck his, the blow sent the blade spinning out of his sweaty hand. "Take him alive!" Valsak shouted. Three black-coated soldiers sprang on the castle lord's back and bore him to the ground.

After that, resistance faded rapidly. Only Oldivor's will had kept the fortress' warriors fighting once the gates went down. As they gave in, Valsak's troops gathered them into a disgruntled crowd in the courtyard.

"Shall we slaughter them?" Gersner asked. "That will make the next holding we come to think twice about fighting us."

"Or make it fight to the death," Valsak said. "Let's see first if we can spend fewer of our own troopers than we would on that path."

His lieutenant sighed. "As you wish. What then?"

Valsak strode up to the prisoners. "You, you, you, you, and you." He beckoned. None of the five men at whom he had pointed came forward willingly. His soldiers shoved them out. Fear on their faces, they eyed the captain, waiting for his decree.

"You are free," he told them. "Go on; get out of here. Go where you will."

Now both they and his own followers were gaping at him. Gersner, he saw out of the corner of his eye, looked about ready to explode. "What's the catch?" asked one of the five. "The Dark Brother and his never give anything for free — we know that." The others nodded.

"Who does?" Valsak retorted. "Here, though, the price is small. Wherever you go, tell the folk you meet that so long as they raise no insurrection and obey the Dark Brother's officers, they'll have no trouble. If they plot and connive and resist, they will suffer what they deserve. Anything else? No? Then leave, before I think twice of my own softness."

The five soldiers wasted no time. They ran for the gates. Valsak's warriors stood aside to let them pass. They might doubt the high captain, but they feared him.

"What about the rest of us?" a prisoner called. Gersner, who had been talking quietly with the wizard, looked up at the question.

"You have resisted in arms the Dark Brother, the overlord of all the world," Valsak said in a voice like ice. "You will serve him henceforward in the mines, fit punishment for your betrayal." He turned to his lieutenant. "Tell off a section to bind them and guard them on their journey to the mines."

"Aye, my lord." Gersner sounded happier than he had since the beginning of the campaign. Mine slaves seldom lasted long. Gersner chose a junior officer and his small command. They hurried up to begin chaining the captives in long lines.

Valsak held up a hand. "A moment. I want them first to hear my judgment for their leader." Oldivor lay before him, trussed up like a chicken. "Let him be brought before the Dark Brother's throne, to be dealt with as our master thinks proper. That is as it should be, for it was the Dark Brother himself he treacherously opposed here, after twice being offered the opportunity to yield."

A sigh ran through all the warriors in the courtyard, from winners and losers alike. The Dark Brother's revenge might last years, and even then leave its victim alive for more suffering.

"I betrayed no one, offered treachery to no one!" Oldivor shouted. "I stood by the loyalties I have always held."

"They are the wrong ones," Valsak said, "especially now."

"I hold to them, even so. What would you have done, were our positions reversed?"

"I chose the winning side, so the problem does not arise." The high captain turned to his warriors. "Take this stubborn blockhead away."

Pass by pass, castle by castle, raider band by raider band, Valsak scoured the mountain country clean. With the Dark Brother and his power immanent in the world, the fighting was never hard. But it came, again and again: no matter how hopeless the struggle, few yielded tamely to the new order of things.

"Strange," Valsak mused after yet another keep had fallen to his magician and his soldiers. "They know they cannot prevail against us, yet they will try, time after time." He watched another line of prisoners, many wounded, trudge off into captivity.

Gersner made a dismissive gesture. "They are fools."

"*Can* they be such fools as that? Truly, I doubt it. I tell you, Gersner, I begin to admire them. They cling to their dead cause, never caring about the cost. The Dark Brother would cherish such steadfastness, would they only direct it toward him."

"You've wasted enough time, trying to convince them of that," his lieutenant said.

Valsak frowned. Gersner's tongue was running rather free these days. "They too are possessions of the Dark Brother, could they be made to see it. Wantonly slaying troops of such potential wastes his substance. I will not do that without exploring other choices first, as I have said, lest I anger him by my omission."

"As you have said, sir," Gersner agreed. The high captain nodded to himself. Yes, that had the proper tone of respect to it.

The last prisoners limped by. Valsak shook his head. Such a shame that soldiers of such bravery could not — or rather, would not — see sense. When

93

the campaign began, he had thought Oldivor an aberration. Since then, he had seen too many warriors stubborn unto death to believe that any longer.

Obstinacy, however, sufficed no more than courage. The campaigning season had some weeks left when Valsak told the wizard, "Send word to our master the Dark Brother that I have subjected all this country to his rule, and have stamped out the last embers of rebellion that lingered here."

The wizard bowed, supple as a snake. "It shall be as you desire."

"Come over here a moment, wizard," Gersner called from beside his tent. "I too have a message for you to give our master."

The wizard's hooded eyes went to Valsak. The high captain nodded permission.

Valsak set garrisons in some of the fortresses his troops had not damaged too badly. Then, with the balance of the army, he turned back toward Lerellim. "A triumphant procession will be in order, I dare say," he told Gersner. "We have earned it."

"I am sure, my lord, the Dark Brother will reward you as you deserve," his lieutenant said.

A day and a half outside what had been the High Kings' capital and was now the Dark Brother's, a pair of riders on matched black stallions came up to the approaching army. One of them displayed the Dark Brother's sigil; the red axe glowed, as if aflame, on a field of jet. "High captain," the messenger said, "you are bidden to precede your host, that the Dark Brother may learn from you of your deeds."

"I obey," was all Valsak replied. He turned to Gersner. "I will see you in Lerellim. Care well for the army till then, as if you were high captain."

"Rest assured I shall," Gersner said.

Valsak urged his horse ahead, trotting with the two riders toward the city. He gratefully sucked in cool, clean air.

"A relief to be away from the dust and stinks of the army," he remarked to one of the messengers.

"Aye, my lord, it must be," the fellow agreed. His comrade leaned over to touch the Dark Brother's sigil to the back of Valsak's neck. Instantly the high captain lost all control of his limbs. He tumbled to the ground in a heap. The messengers dismounted, picked him up and slung him over his horse's back like a sack of beans, then took chains from their saddlebags and bound his wrists to his ankles under the beast's belly.

His mouth was still his. "What are you doing?" he shouted, trying to show anger rather than fear.

"Obeying the Dark Brother's command," one of the men said stolidly. After that, the terror was there. Valsak knew it would never leave him for whatever was left of his life. He still tried not to show it. If Oldivor could go to his fate still shouting defiance, Valsak's pride demanded no less of him.

Unfortunately, he knew more than the fortress commander. That made a bold front harder to maintain before these underlings. Before the Dark Brother, no front would hold, not for long.

It was midafternoon the next day when the messengers dropped him, still chained, in front of the Dark Brother's throne. Those terrible yellow eyes pierced him like a spear.

"I — am yours, my master," he stammered.

"Of course you are mine, worm beneath my feet." The soundless voice echoed in his skull like the tolling of a great bronze bell. "The world is mine."

"But I am yours willingly, my master, as I have always been." Had he not been telling perfect truth, Valsak would never have dared protest.

"Are you indeed?" Valsak felt mental hands riffling through his mind. He cried out in torment; who was there to beg the Dark Brother to be gentle? After some while that might have been forever or might have been a heartbeat, the Dark Brother's voice resounded once more: "Aye, you are. It is not enough."

"My master?" Valsak cried in anguish, though his anguish, he saw, was just beginning.

"Fool!" The Dark Brother flayed him with words. "Do you think I rooted out nobility in my foes only to see it grow among those who are my own? So you admire the doomed rebels you beat for holding so stubbornly to their worthless cause, do you?"

"They thought they were right." Now that Valsak realized nothing would save him, he spoke without concealment.

"And so they opposed me." Infinite scorn rode the Dark Brother's voice. "What idiocy would you essay, simply for the sake of doing what you thought was right?"

"My master, I —" Valsak had to stop then, for the Dark Brother squeezed his mind for truth like a man squeezing an orange for juice. "— I do not know," was what came out of his mouth, and what, he knew, sealed his fate.

"Nor do I," the Dark Brother rumbled, "and I have no wish to be unpleasantly surprised. Gersner will make a good high captain — he thinks only of his own advantage, which lies with me alone. Thus he betrayed you. A mind like that I can understand and use. As for you —" The Dark Brother paused a while in thought. Then he laughed, and his laughter was more wounding even than his speech. "I have it! The very thing!"

Valsak found himself gone from the throneroom, in a space that was not a place. Yet the Dark Brother's eyes were on him still, and the torment he had known in his interrogation was as nothing beside what he felt now. It went on and on and on. In that torment, he took some little while to notice he was not alone.

Next to him, twisting in that notplace, was Oldivor. Their eyes met. Valsak saw the satisfaction that filled the other's face. So did the Dark Brother. Satisfaction was not why the castle lord was here. An instant later, his anguish matched Valsak's again.

They watched each other hurt a long, long time.

HAUNTED HOUSE

On these worn and splintered floors
unremembered dead once walked.
Broken tables, shattered chairs,
lie forgotten by the sagging stairs.

The only language spoken here
is more than silence, less than speech.
Shadows in the dusty halls
deepen as the darkness falls.

The house is empty, yet something seems
to stir its mote-filled, mildewed air —
something struggling to be heard
without a mouth to form a word.

— Joseph Payne Brennan

When I say I understand
I don't,
not really.
I know what you're thinking,
TELEPATHY
would come in handy here,
except for the broaching
of everyone's privacy.
Would you *really* like
to share every nasty little thought,
every crochet and nuance,
would you?
Really?
Ah yes,
I know what you're thinking.

— Janet Fox

THANATOPSIS

(in the combined styles of
James Witcomb Riley & T.S. Eliot)

It takes a heap o' dyin'
Jes' t' make a grave a tomb,
But a li'l bit embalmin'
Will make the corpses bloom.

— a napkin poem by **Marvin Kaye**

MY MOTHER'S PURSE

by Ken Wisman

All parents are magical. Parental magic manifests itself in a terrifying ability to read minds, oracular powers to predict and ward off future disasters, incredible feats of strength, unearthly command of mystic languages — and so on down the list of estimable accomplishments in the supernatural arts.

And, as each child knows, there are secret nooks or objects in which parents hide away their mysteries, dark crannies that hold the source of all parental power. A closet, for instance. A cellar. A jewelry box. All wrapped in magic words and spells meant to instill fear and trepidation.

Such a secret object was my mother's purse.

That purse would whisper to me at night from the next room. And it was a matter of the mirror that she talked with and the pictures
> and
>> other
>>> magical
>>>> mystical
>>>>> things.

Now there was the tale of Suneby Jones, a child hero who it was said burnt his courageous toes on the sun while swinging the highest height ever attained on a swing. And the story of Scooza Fascianado who once caught a glimpse of the real Santa, whereupon Scooza promptly turned to chocolate. (Her statue can be seen in Cheddarwicke museum.)

And of these heroes and heroines my childhood mind was full, and of great feats that would live forever in the annals of childhood. So I was obsessed with the possession of mother's purse and the deepest delving into its infinite mysteries — no matter what the consequence, no matter what dark secrets I would uncover.

Family legend has it that from the first moment that I could crawl I made a beeline for my mother's purse. Yes, and all my ambulatory successes — from crawling to walking to running — were secondary, merely means to the end of obtaining The Pocketbook.

Naturally, since mother and father could read my mind, they were always thwarting my intentions. And yet there were times when I actually wrapped my pudgy hands around the strap, grasped the silver clasp, felt the leather, whose silken, exotic feel bespoke its unusual origins — no animal of this ordinary Earth had been sacrificed for its construction.

Ah, but did I ever get to truly look into the purse's recesses? Did I ever get to pull forth its treasures? Oh, yes. And yes again. But to what terrible end? And the gain of such terrifying knowledge?

I was age seven. Mother and father were preparing to go out, moving about the room and dressing. I was on the bed, busy with some toy or other. And the purse was on a bureau safely on the other side of the room.

Mother had taken her watch from the purse and had it in her hand for some reason. It was a special watch and I had seen her use it before. The watch had seven numerals with the number 14 at the top, the number 12 following, the number 10 next and around to 8, 6, 4 and 2 — somewhat like this:

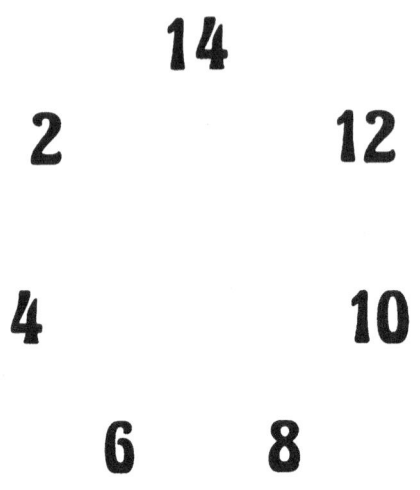

14

2   **12**

4   **10**

6   **8**

The purpose of that chronometer was to stop time for fourteen minutes. And mother, absentminded with the gold bangles she was slipping around her right wrist, let the watch drop onto the bed.

When her back was turned I grabbed the watch and pushed in the button as I had seen her do. She and father froze in time. I made a beeline for the purse and threw it upon the bed.

Savoring the moment, I drew my hands gently over the sides of the purse and allowed my cheek to touch it. Then I snapped it open with a vengeance.

And, oh, what a sweet wind wafted from therein. The whispering that I had heard of a night became laughter. I heard singing. And so I inserted my hand into the warmth of that container, which made my fingers tingle and my body thrill.

I pulled forth a mirror. It was about the size of a woman's hand, and woven around the edges were two snakes, one gold and one silver, each with a tiny ruby eye.

I looked into the mirror and my re-

flection spoke. "Have you ever heard of Pandora's Box?"

"No," I replied.

"Pity," said the mirror. "The analogy would be wasted."

I propped the mirror against a pillow, where it kept up an annoying chatter about "danger" and "dire straits" and "possible harm to a tender, developing psyche."

As I prepared to dip my hand in once again, I noticed movement out of the corner of my eye. I had forgotten that the watch worked at two-minute intervals. But I had the device at the ready and pressed the button at the side and halted mother's and father's hasty advance.

Thus unchallenged, I dipped my hand once more into the purse and this time I pulled forth a package of Juicy Fruit gum, then a box of Chiclets. I had struck paydirt.

My hand grabbed packages of Dentyne, rolls of mints, boxes of Smith Brothers cough drops. I piled them on the bed. I dipped again, grasping handfuls of Sugarless gum, Sen-Sen, Lifesavers.

The piles spilled onto the floor. The room filled to the wallsockets with sugar treats, rolls of mints, and wrapped toffees. Indeed, I would have drowned in these sweets, the cornucopia outlasting my childish greed — except the second interval was up and the movement of my mother and father broke my momentum.

I pushed the watch's button, the hands wound round to the 8, and I was free once more to indulge in my obsession.

"You'll note that you are getting in deeper and deeper," the mirror said.

It was accurate. When I pulled forth the mirror, my hand went only as far as my wrist. When I yanked out the candy, my arm went midway up my forearm. And when I put my hand in the third time my arm went in up to

MY MOTHER'S PURSE

my elbow.

Unmindful, I pulled out a stack of oval objects. These were mother's faces. The pretty one she put on when she went out to parties with father. The attractive one she put on when the boss came for dinner. The sexy one for when she went behind closed doors.

I peeled off each one of these faces, which were as thin as crepe, and arranged them around the bed. I chose one of my favorites — mother's pretty face, her eating-out-at-restaurants demeanor with subdued, red lipstick, eye shadow and powder carefully applied.

I took the face and pressed it against my own, trying it on much as any child tries on articles of his parents' clothing. I looked into the mirror for the effect. It was a bizarre juxtaposition, a boyish/feminine clown of exaggerated dimensions — the mouth pursed and sensual, the eyes heavy lidded.

I was frightened. I didn't like the face at all. But when I went to tear the thing off it stuck. I panicked, thinking that I might have to spend my life with rouged cheeks and long eyelashes. I rolled desperately across the bed, clawing at my face.

"There is a tab just below the chin," the mirror said matter-of-factly. "Pull it."

I pulled the tab and the face peeled away like paper between two slices of cheese.

"You know, the mirror is right," the face said as it hung limp and harmless in my hand. "This may only be an inkling of what you could be in for."

But my parents' movement distracted me, and they were halfway to the bed before I could set the watch again.

This time when I plumbed the depths of the purse, I pulled forth a tiny bottle of cut crystal and took out the stopper.

The most exquisite scent I had heretofore or ever smelled wafted from the depths of that tiny phial. It arose in visible vapors like the stylized waves of seas depicted in children's books. The perfume caressed me, stroked me, wrapped around me with a heat and sensuality.

Something awoke inside of me. Something beyond my mere seven years. I rose on the bed and looked in the mirror, which elongated to full length. I watched with surprise as my body grew before my eyes.

My muscles expanded to ludicrous size, my chest filled with a forest of hair, my eyes shone back from a face full-bearded and gone to near bestiality with the sensuality awakened by the perfume.

"Is that how I'll look?" I asked the mirror.

"No," the mirror replied. "That's how you will feel."

With that my parents came unfrozen and rushed toward the bed. But a mere click of my watch, which was at the ready in my right hand, halted their advance.

And so I went to the purse a fourth time and went down full to my shoulder to pull up a red velvet change purse. Inside were all manner of coins:

a penny
  a nickel
    a dime
      a quarter
        a silver dollar
          a Susan B. Anthony
            a 20 dollar gold piece

The reliefs of Lincoln, Roosevelt, Washington, and Susan B. were all singing. They sounded like a choir chanting spiritual chants, though what they sang was anything but religious:

funnymoneyfunnymoneyfunny-moneyfunnymoneyfunnymoney
  funnymoneyfunnymoneyfunny-moneyfunnymoneyfunnymoney

And when I put them in a row upon the bed they rolled this way and that, round and round like the wheels on a train. Then they began to reproduce. One begat two. Two begat four. Four begat eight, and eight sixteen.

They rose in stacks. The stacks tipped with tinkling sounds of silver, copper and gold. And the spilled coins became more stacks that rolled round and round and chanted.

funnymoneyfunnymoneyfunny-
moneyfunnymoneyfunnymoney
funnymoneyfunnymoneyfunny-
moneyfunnymoneyfunnymoney

The coins spilled off the bed in gold and silver falls. Coins covered the floor and furniture, the gum and mints. I watched in fascination as the coins rose in a flood to the very top of the bed.

Then the watch ticked off the final seconds, unfreezing mother and father who had to swim their foot closer to the bed. I quickly hit the button, then grabbed the seven original coins and dropped them back into the red velvet change purse.

"You really should cease and desist," the mirror informed me. "You are getting into depths you'll find difficult to handle."

But I turned the mirror against the bedspread. And reaching into the purse, I stretched to my chest to see what I could see. Thus I pulled forth a leather wallet. It held a plastic foldout filled with photos of family and mother's and father's friends.

I greeted each photo and they replied in like.

Then I found a photo of mother's brother, my Uncle Waring. He had died when I was three, and I barely remembered him.

"What's it like to be dead?" I asked him.

He replied in somber tones: "Cold. Colder than the coldest winter ever in the North or South. And dark. Darker than the darkest day when all the stars wink out. Lonely. Lonelier than being the only one left on Earth . . ."

As Uncle Waring continued this depressing litany, his face changed. I saw his flesh turn green, his eyes dry up and fall out. A mold grew on his flesh which ate it up and dried it and crumbled it like dust. And soon his skull was only speaking through a death grin.

I watched all this with horror. And then the watch ticked round to the last two seconds. Mother and father drew to the very bed itself, their arms and hands poised over me and the purse, before I could reset the watch.

And what drove me now? I had had wonders enough and those not very pleasant. Was it a childish pride that controlled me or envy for truths reserved for my "elders"?

"Both," the mirror said, its surface muffled by the bedspread. "Beware."

But I wouldn't listen. Oh, no. I went to that well one more time, though the smell coming forth from the purse was no longer of mints and lipsticks and perfumes. No. It was dank and sulfuric, and the laughter I had heard was now vaguely demonic.

When I reached in, I went clear up to my chest and found to my surprise that I could poke in my head as well. Inside a wind whipped around me and there was a blinding fire.

And lo, what did I see but a figure of my father and a figure of my mother — but in a guise heretofore never seen. Both stood naked, their flesh a bright blood-red, their faces twisted in wicked, toothy smiles. Their feet were hooves, and a pair of black horns rose from their foreheads.

Father ran up and pulled my arm so that I fell deeper into the purse.

"You're not my parents!" I screamed.

"Oh, but we are," father said wickedly. "We're the ones that lie just below the masks."

"Yes," my mother seconded. "Always ready to pop out at your provocation."

"Come down and join us," father said. He pulled a bit harder, but my feet were jammed tightly on the lip of the purse.

"Yes, do," said mother. "Come see our toys and instruments of discipline."

I was shown row on row of whips and switches, belts and paddles.

"Let us introduce you to our allies in the art of acceptable behavior," said father.

A vision of every bogey and boogeyman that any parent had ever threatened a child appeared. Things that hid beneath beds, inside closets — shadow, swamp and sewer things snapped and clicked and grinned and drove in a whirlpool all around my hanging form. And I felt myself slipping slowly, down to the claws and nails and yellow fangs . . .

And suddenly something strong had hold of my feet and was pulling me up. Then a crew of the bogeys hopped up and grabbed my arms.

A tug of war transpired — between whatever benign force had grabbed me above and all the forces of Hell below. It ended with a pop as I exploded forth from the purse and sprawled with my parents on the floor.

"We can't trust you alone for a min-ute," my mother said, smoothing her evening gown. "Just look at the mess you've made." She indicated the articles scattered around the bed and room.

"We all have limits, you know," my father said.

Yes, I knew. And I could see that red and horned physiognomy spitting and clawing just below the surface of his face.

"Forgive me, mother and father, it will never happen again," I began and made one of the longest and most placating speeches of my life until my parents stood open-mouthed and dumbfounded. So shocked were they, they forgot to assign a proper punishment.

And me? What of me in the aftermath?

My fame rose in the secret annals of heroes that children tell of. I was right up there with Carnaby Flatte, who once left the safety of his yard and fell off the edge of the world. And next to Angel Bloom, who jumped from a seven-story window and flew into outer space.

And what price did I pay? My innocence. My youth. For I now know of all those sins and sad and secret things reserved for adults.

Such are the wages of truth. ∎

The Kingdoms of the Air

by Tanith Lee

— Who is he, that Knight riding by?

— His name is Cedrevir. He has been Questing.

— Pale as death, and his eyes looked blind. I thought, a good thing the horse knows its way. I thought, there is one wounded by unseen arrows.

— They are an ancient Fellowship, these Knights. It is in their vows to invite the Quest, whatever it may be, whatever its peril or strangeness. But many return home as you have seen.

— This Cedrevir: What Quest then was his? Do you know it?

— Yes, and I will tell it you.

At the Midsummer Feast they met, as it is usual for them to do, this Fellowship of Knights, up there in the Castle of Towers.

In the Castle's heart there is a great hidden hall, the entrances to which are known only to an Initiate. The hall is built as a perfect circle, its floor and walls paved with blocks of polished stone. From the high dome of the roof hang down the thousand swords and shields, banners and devices, of all the Knights who are and have been of the Fellowship. High on the walls the torches burn in iron cages of curious

shape, so they resemble the heads of serpents and monsters which breathe fire. In the floor is set, in fine mosaic, a huge round sun-disc, and on the rayed rim of it stand the Knights, repeating the circle of power a third time, in flesh and steel.

For each man comes to that place fully armed and in mail, though each surcote is of undyed and unembroidered linen, and the vizor of each helm lowered, and though every man carries in his gauntleted hand a sword, it has no mark.

(There are ways of knowing a man, even under these circumstances. From his height and build, his voice, his manner, or by some expression in his eyes.)

There they stood, then, at this Midsummer near to midnight, in the dark light of the dragon-torches. They performed their rites, and reaffirmed their vows. In turn they confessed any of their transgressions against God, Man, or the Fellowship. They told, in turn, of their feats, and furnished proofs, which might be anything, from a lady's scarf to the severed hand of an enemy.

There is one further property in that hall. On a tall stand to the east is a clock, in the form of a golden sword and a marble heart on water. As the liquid drips down through the basin, the weights go up, and all morning the golden sword lifts slowly, until, at noon, it strikes a golden chiming apple in the summit of the clock. Then, as the water gradually refills the basin, the weights sink, the marble heart floats up and the sword descends, until at midnight its yellow blade pierces through the heart, which gives out a long singing note.

Shortly before midnight at Midsummer, when the sword is just grazing the marble, an Invocation is spoken by all the Knights of the circle. There are those that say a certain wine is then drunk, a wafer eaten and an incense burned. Every man bows his head and awaits what will come to him.

Then the sword enters the marble heart, and the heart sweetly cries.

Cedrevir heard the note of the heart, as he had previously heard it, twelve times in all, for he had been six years a Knight of the circle. At first he had been strung, expectant and eager, but year by year these emotions dulled to patience. He had undertaken betweenwhiles many adventures, all successful. As a warrior he was valiant and accomplished, and as a priest — for the Initiate of the Fellowship is both — he was equally, chaste, and passionate. He had done no wrong, he had fought with honour and skill, but yet nothing had come to him at midnight of Midsummer, or in the dark Midwinter either.

Now however, as the note faded from the water-clock, Cedrevir began to hear another sound so like, that for a moment he thought the heart cried out a second time. Then he became aware that what he heard was the voice of a maiden, singing. Her tones were pure and thin as beaten silver, and her words were these:

Primo dolens lancea est
Corona dolor de Dominus
Est secundo et tertio
Gradalis cruenta fulgero

The voice rang all round the hollow chamber, and in the hollows of helm and skull it rang.

Cedrevir raised his head, sure that every other Knight did in like fashion, and looked with wide grey eyes. There, at the centre of the mosaic sunburst, a column of light so sheer and bright it dimmed the torches rose up from floor to roof. Even as Cedrevir stared into this radiance, half dazzled, uncannily half not, he began to make out objects moving, there within the column. For a moment he did not know what these things were. Then, though never before having seen them, he recognized each, and a low faint groan burst from him.

He fell to his knees, and wild bells began to ring, and mildly, terribly, the aching voices sang *Primo dolens lancea est corona dolor de Dominus est secundo et tertio gradalis cruenta fulgero.* And down the pillar of white fire came drifting like a cobweb a spear of silver with a burning tip that shone even more fiercely than the light, and from it fell ceaselessly petals of crimson that became butterflies as they faded. And after the burning bleeding spear, a garland of fiery thorns which also bled, and as the drops burst from it they changed to roses of gold that opened on hearts like the moon and stars themselves. Lastly there weightlessly fell a chalice of a deep clear flaming green, a colour whose depths seemed bottomless as the sea. And from the lip of the chalice there ran a stream of blood, but the blood was like liquid gold and it blazed brighter than the sun.

Then, another voice spoke at the Knight's right shoulder. It seemed to him it was the voice of a man, but before them, on the ground, a glowing shadow showed with folded wings. "Seek then these things, Cedrevir. The Lance of Pain, the Sorrowing Crown, the Cup of the Life's Blood. That is your Quest, and may you be true to it."

After that came darkness on the wide grey eyes of Cedrevir.

C edrevir knew well enough what he had had revealed to him in the vision. And when he came to himself in the Castle of Towers, and recounted what he had seen — for no other but himself had been made witness to it — no man of the Fellowship was in ignorance.

In the great light had passed the three holy relics of the Sacrifice of Christ: The Spear that had pierced His side, the Thorn-Crown that had garlanded His brows, the Chalice in which had been shared the sacred blood-wine of the Last Supper, and in which the true blood of His wounds had subsequently been caught.

These articles, long reverenced as aspects of the Martyrdom, are, we say, supposed to have remained on Earth. Indeed, their whereabouts, as you may hear, are known, though not by situation. A fortress, called the Castle of the Jewel of Goodness (which is, Carba Bonem), that is where they are lodged, and tended there by mysterious guardians. All about Carba Bonem stretches a vast waste that has no seasons in it save only heat or cold, but that is named, for its looks and barrenness, the Winterlands. And in the waste is a dead forest as old as the world, which is named the Wood of the Savage Hart. But the way to it, the forest, the wasteland, the secret Castle of the Jewel of Goodness, they lie off the edge of any map, beyond the memory of any traveller. It is not possible to come to them either by accident or by design. And so the quiet priests told Cedrevir as he kneeled before them, with his dark head bowed and beautiful hands upon the hilt of the sword which bore his device, a couched *sarpafex.*

For many days then he fasted and watched, and kept by himself or with these learned ones from whom he sought counsel. All this while, the images of the vision stayed clear before him as if he had seen them only a moment ago, and in his ears the voices sang *Dolens lancea. Corona dolor. Gradalis cruenta fulgero.* And the last voice told him, waking and sleeping and watching, *This is your quest. Be true to it.*

Then at last there came an hour just before sunrise, when the birds piped over the meadows, and the sky was pale as a shell. And Cedrevir came from the Castle of Towers.

He rode as if to a battle, sword, shield, and lance at their stations, clad in mail of steel. Both he and the blond horse

105

were trapped and clad in his colour, the blue-grey of distances. And worked on the saddle-cloth, and enamelled on the shield and sword-hilt, the snake-lynx of his blazon, silver and blue and gilt.

In the fields, where the women and boys were labouring, they raised their heads among the tall corn, to watch Cedrevir go by. There is a Knight of the Fellowship, they said, he goes Questing. For the look of setting forth is, though unlike, as unmistakable as that other look with which, often, they return.

So he rode across the Near Lands, towards the North, for north lies the House of Winter, and in the North there are mountains, the high places. And that was all the guide he had to find a spot that is of the Earth but not on the Earth; a spot that some wise men say is a myth, although also a certain truth.

Beyond the Near Lands lie others less known, but all were wrapped in the late richness of summer, and it may be supposed that human tasks went on there much as they do everywhere. In the orchards, vineyards and fields they would be making ready for harvest, toiling on into evening under the wide golden skies. At the streams and wells the women gathered with their washing and their buckets, and by the rivers they cut reeds. Where the castles stood up on the hills, or some massive tower thrust from the woods, the sentries would remark a riding Knight. Some challenge or greeting might be offered him. And now and then, at a lonely chapel, the priest would render lodging, blessing, bread and wine, most frequently in silence.

Perhaps two months Cedrevir traveled, going always northwards, questioning on the way those he met, where it seemed the sign of knowledge was on them, here a hermit in his cell, there an old peasant woman, or a little child even, with a freckle like a star on its forehead. Otherwise, sometimes, the Knight himself would be petitioned for his help, and so would fight, a champion against some wrong. And then again there were those who sought to tempt him aside, to view a wonder, which might be a mysterious flower that grew in a ruined pagan temple, a thing which would work miracles, or a fountain that gushed from a rock at the striking of his fist. Or there were, from time to time, those who desired to corrupt, such as a white-shouldered woman in a red gown, who leaned from her window so her long hair, scented with a strange spice, brushed the face of Cedrevir as he rode by. But for her he did not stay.

One dusk, when the light still hung like a dome of crystal high up in the vault of heaven though all the landscape darkened, Cedrevir came on a broken tower beside a lake. Through the windows of the tower the shining afterglow ran like spears, and the lake itself lay like a great pool of sky fallen on the Earth. Not a breeze stirred and not a cloud marred the surface of air or water. Then the stars began to dew and daisy out, and one lit more brightly than the rest upon the strand against the lake. It was a torch, that burned in a cage of bronze before a pavilion. And as Cedrevir rode close, other lights bloomed in the pavilion's heart, and turned it to a bulb of softest fire.

Presently two Knights stepped from the pavilion. They were of another fellowship, and on the shield of one was the device of a falcon, and on the other a white bull with wings.

"Where are you going, Knight-at-Arms?" said he of the falcon-shield.

"Northward," replied Cedrevir. "It is a Vowed Journey."

There is not a fellowship, they say, that does not honour the Quest, or the bond of it.

The two Knights nodded. He of the bull-shield spoke next.

"We guard here the Lady Marismë, our sister."

"I do not challenge that, nor offer any threat to her."

"No. But she is a seeress, trained in the Luminous Arts," said the falcon-shield Knight.

"If you would confer with this lady, our sister, I believe she will do her best to help you," said the bull-shield Knight. "Only this morning, by her art, she descried you, and said, 'Here we will linger and await a traveller from the South. He seeks a key to his Quest, which I, maybe, shall find for him.'"

Now the two Knights stood in shadow beyond the torch, and their faces were hidden under their glistening and dark helms. It came to Cedrevir that he did not credit all that they had said to him, and yet they had spoken no lie. It was the deep shadow of occult things on them, but not of wickedness, as it was only night had darkened the lake.

Just then, the draperies of the pavilion parted with a flutter, and a woman came out. On her the torch shone full, and she was young, and fair, with clear wild eyes. Her white gown was bordered with gems like water-drops, and on her dim hair drifted a net like silver spray.

She said nothing to Cedrevir, and her eyes looked into him and through him. It was a terrible gaze, for she seemed to see his very birth and death, and all other matters that might come between. Then she beckoned, only once, and drew back into the pavilion.

"Follow her," said the falcon-shield Knight. "She is honourable, as are you. And if you were not, she is well able to protect herself. Besides, we are here."

So Cedrevir, in a sort of trance, for her eyes had curiously affected him, dismounted and entered the tent after the lady.

There was a woven carpet on the

107

ground within the tent, and the lamps hung in clusters from posts of bronze. But the lady stood in the centre of the pavilion where there was a pedestal of carved wood. And on the pedestal before her, a golden bowl filled with water.

"Come here and see," said the Lady Marismë.

Cedrevir went to the pedestal, and looked down with her into the bowl.

At first there was only the clarity of the water over the gold. Then there came a turbulence that was in the water and not in it, and a veil seemed to be torn away. There in the bowl, as if miles off, a great host was fighting in the sky. It was a gorgeous and a fearsome battle, for a setting sun, and also bolts of lightning, flashed upon the gems and metals of the warriors, caught upon swords that blazed with inlay, and catching the crests and banners showed devices so mystic and so strange they were not at once understandable. But the sun was going down and the clouds, amethyst and purple and scarlet as the trappings of the Knights, began to lower and smother the scene. Then a trumpet sounded, unheard — but perfectly to be viewed — a long line of fire as from some comet. At the signal, through the cloud-mass there came riding two mighty lords, and all the host drew back away from them to give them room. And this was very dreadful, for it was plain at once that these two Knights were brothers. Each was golden, each as clearly beautiful and as sparkling as something made of the sun itself, and as hard to look on. But one was clad all in gold and white, and on his helm was a crest like stars, and on his shield a device for which there was no name at all, it might not be expressed or written, yet Cedrevir, glimpsing it, was filled by joy and terror. The other Knight was arrayed in the colours of heat and fire, and in his crest burned a green jewel so marvellous the eye seemed to drink at it. His

shield had no device, but on his banner, that one bore behind him, were embroidered the words: *Non Serviam.*

They met with a clash, these two, that shook the sky; their lances splintered and the pieces rained down like blood and lava on the world. Each sword came from its scabbard like a lightning stroke that lit all heaven. And as they dashed once more upon each other, the last of the red sun fell, and on a cloth of gold, dead black yet shining bright, they fought, on and on, as the moon rose under their chargers' feet.

There was no telling how long the combat lasted; time had no meaning there. Cedrevir watched with awe and misgiving, in pity and dread and triumph. It was the First Battle, when the angels of God had fought together. The golden Knight was the Archangel Michael. He clothed like fire, whose banner proclaimed his rebellion — *I will not serve* — was Lucifer, before his fall.

When the final blow sang home, ever expected, ever impossible, needful and terrible for all that, the sky seemed to crack from end to end. Cedrevir did not behold the fall of him, Prince Lucifer, yet he saw flung out from the clouds a green shooting-star. It smoked and flamed, tearing downward to the earth. Over hills and heights it ripped its path, and there the ocean spread, glittering and unresting in the moon's sway. And here, in the sea, the emerald meteor went down, hissing. It was the jewel from the helm of Lucifer, the Prince of Hell, quenched in water.

But it was only the clear water in the seeress' bowl that Cedrevir now saw, and the Lady Marismë standing on the other side of it, who spoke to him.

"That spiritual jewel was the green ruby, his pride and pleasure. It lay in the sea, lost to him, as all else had been lost, until, with the centuries, it was washed ashore. Men, seeing it a stone beyond price, fashioned therefore a chalice. So to the lords of the Earth it passed, after the fire, the air and the water. Solomon the Wise drank from it. And through a line of kings it entered the possession of the Prince of All, Jesus, the Christ. You are seeking His Grail. In the world or out of the world."

"Lady, I am. And have always wondered at the tale, that the ornament of Satan, the Evil One, should become the holy Cup of the Christ."

"But is He not," said Marismë, "called the Redeemer?"

Cedrevir bowed his head. "But," he said, "do you know the road to Carba Bonem?"

"I shall tell you its name," she said. "This road is called *I will*."

Cedrevir sighed. Then, surprised a little, he saw the lamps had burned away and that the soft light in the tent was dawn coming in from without. The moments of the magical revelation had consumed an entire night.

"If you wish," said the Lady Marismë, "you may now accompany us to our kingdom."

Then she spoke a word, and the whole pavilion lifted as a ball of thistledown lifts. It blew up into the air, and all its appurtenances and furnishings with it, and vanished quite. There they were, then, on the strand of the lake, and nearby the lady's Knights leaning on their shields, while on the hill-slope under the old tower the blond horse cropped the grasses.

At this minute the sun rose between two eastern hills, and threw down its rosy sword point-foremost straight across the lake. And out of the sun's glory, there might be seen a slender raft with a transparent sail coming slowly towards them, guided by no agency that Cedrevir could discern.

As Cedrevir stood pondering, the Knight of the winged-bull approached him and said, "Your horse is safely penned within an ancient wall, no longer visible, for this was the stronghold of magicians, and power remains. Come now with us, if you will."

Then the raft drew against the shore. The lady stepped on it, and after her the two Knight-brothers, and the three stayed, waiting courteously. So Cedrevir went after them, onto the raft, which hardly looked stout enough to uphold the lady alone. But when he was on it, it began to move again, its sail turning to the morning breeze, and went back the way it had come.

The lady was foremost of the craft, with the sunlight on her, and she said to Cedrevir, "You must know that in time past, we dwelled on shore, where the tower leans, which is all that remains of a great castle. One season, the waters of the lake rose and overwhelmed the land. We, swept away, outlasted the catastrophe. And now, live there."

"Where is that, lady?"

"Beneath your feet, bold Knight. Under the water."

The raft had reached the middle of the lake, and suddenly it stopped, with only its swan-white wake fading behind it.

Then Marismë laughed, and she went out, on to the very water, and after her her two brothers. And the liquid of the lake buoyantly held them up, and then gently drew them in. And as she slowly sank, Marismë called to Cedrevir. "Bold Knight, will you make bold to follow? We are your protectors in this. I, by the Arts called Luminous, will ensure you against harm. But you must be trustful, fearless, and swift. Follow now or do not follow."

Then Cedrevir also laughed aloud. "Say then I will," said he. (But his eyes, by turns, were black or blazing.)

Blithely as they, or so it seemed, he stepped onto the water, which held him upright with only a little motion, just such as the raft had, then gradually began to take him in, in company with the other three. Thus they sank together under the mirror of the lake.

This was the curious property either of the lake, or of the lady's magic, that there was no sensation of wetness, only of a silken levity, and that Cedrevir found himself enabled, as did his hosts, freely to breathe the water. Also, that he might hear and see, touch and taste, and in every other way respond and act as if he were above the surface on dry land. Yet everything was, too, transmuted and different. All speech, for example, now sounded to him like the sweetest singing. (And he heard besides the songs of the fish which darted here and there like linnets, as he descended.) As for vision, a dark radiance hung over all things, and proceeding through the kingdom beneath the lake, every movement was swathed in the sleeves, robes and veils of silver eddies.

Under the water was a land that, in many ways, resembled the country of the Earth. There was a road there, which led to a castle on a hill, but the road was paved with great round pebbles washed smooth and lucent as glass, and above, the castle glimmered green as peridot. All about the road were orchards and groves, where fruit grew shining, like apples of milky gold. The fish sat singing in the branches of the trees, whose foliage was fine and etiolate as strands of a girl's hair. Under the castle clustered a town of stone, and sometimes men and women passed to and fro. Seeing the Lady Marismë, these persons bowed to her. There was also something shadow-like about them, and it seemed to Cedrevir that here, too, though nothing was hidden, all was not shown.

As they neared the castle, the doors of the building opened and a Knight rode forth. He was clad in black, even

to the plumes of his helm's high crest. The horse he sat was black and thin, but it was armoured all over, and its legs braced by black iron. And when they climbed and came up with the Black Knight, he turned his head to look at them, and he had no face, only a skull.

"It is Death," said Marismë, and she saluted him, and her brothers with her.

Death nodded, and made to pass on. Then, apparently noting Cedrevir, he spoke to him.

"I shall meet again with you, in another place," said Death. "But that is many years hence."

Cedrevir crossed himself. But he would not be shamed, and looked long on Death, and it began to seem to him that behind the skull, there was a man's face, and two somber eyes that regarded him. No sooner did he think this, than the apparition raised his hand and lowered the black vizor of his helm. Death rode away down the hill on the iron horse.

"Do not be concerned," said Marismë. "Our kind, though we live, are also numbered with the drowned. He has some rights over us, being in part our king." And in the open doorway of the castle, she turned to Cedrevir and said, "There are three mighty citadels of Powers. The Powers of the Water, which are inconstant and eternal. The Powers of Earth and Fire, which mingle, and are of the passions, and by which most wrongdoing is invoked. The Powers of the Air, whereof there are many kingdoms, for they lie closest to God — not in that they are in the sky, but in their permeation of everything, and their invisibility like breath, and life itself."

When she had said this, she went forward into the castle, entering a huge hall there that had looked empty and dark before, but lit up at her coming.

Presently, as it would happen in a sort of dream, Cedrevir found himself seated on a dais at the Lady's right hand, before a board draped with damask. On this every delicacy that might be got from the dry world, or that might be found in fresh water, was displayed on dishes of gold and silver, while servers processed ceaselessly through the hall bearing jewelled trenchers and long-necked ewers of wine. And in that ambience of water, not a morsel of food was lost, or a drop of liquor spilled out or mixed in the currents of the lake, but flowed from beaker to cup, from cup to lip. Down from the roof hung gilded wheels each with a score of flaming candles in them, and in the walls torches burned, and not a fire was quenched, though the smokes wove endless patterns through the water.

In the body of the hall, not a place was vacant at the long tables. A full company of Knights and ladies dined together. And while they dined, proud dogs with collars of pearls lay by the tables or prowled about for scraps. The servers carved and the pages hastened on their errands, and the minstrels woke their harps. And on everything lay the irridescence of the lake. But under everything there lay a dimness and a shadow.

Perhaps several hours passed at the feasting. After this time a trumpet was sounded and a silence fell. Up the hall there walked a page clothed in black, pale as a plant of the deep woods, and carrying a dish of horn and onyx. On the dish lay a fruit from the aqueous orchards below the castle. Coming to Cedrevir, but no other, the boy kneeled: "Will you eat of this fruit, Knight?"

And Cedrevir hesitated. "Do you not come from Death?"

"If I do, it is not himself he sends you."

"What then?"

"The fruit, which is not forbidden, yet which is a fruit of knowledge. Perhaps a warning, perhaps a prophecy, perhaps a symbol or a test of heart or brain. Take the fruit, and see."

Then Cedrevir took the fruit, and at once the boy vanished. Cedrevir gazed long at the apple's satin skin, as he had outstared Death himself. And in the core of the fruit the Knight thought he saw a fire, but it was not impure or poisoned. So he put it before him and cut it open with his dagger.

Cedrevir started back in horror. For from the apple came a scaled worm, a serpent, which his knife had severed. Yet, it did not bleed, and both parts of it ended in a head, each having cold sad eyes that looked at him.

"You have wounded me," said the snake.

"Pardon me for that," the Knight answered. "I did not do it knowingly."

"You lie," said the snake.

"Not so."

"Do you not recognize me, then? I am the Serpent, that creature cursed of God and man. I am the Beguiler. I am Satan, your Enemy. Say now you do not wound me knowingly."

"If you are he," said Cedrevir, "then, knowingly, I would cut you from me, mind and body and soul, a hundred times over."

"It has been easy for you, this once," said the snake.

And then it shrank and shrivelled until it was no wider than a thread, and the thread went to ashes and crumbled, and was gone.

"What is the message of this, lady?" asked Cedrevir of Marismë.

"That you are already on your road. For no tempter would come to you if you had not entered the sphere of his sight."

Then she rose to her feet and the great hall grew vague and silent, as if a huge cloak had been thrown over it, and every light was smothered.

But at her side her brothers waited.

Marismë took Cedrevir by the hand, and led him out of the hall, and up a curving flight of marble stairs, into the well of a tower. At its summit was a chamber in which the windows were pillared by stone, but the casements were water where the fish swam in and out as they pleased. The two Knights took their stance, as at the pavilion, on either side the door, which then closed fast of itself.

"Now Cedrevir," said the Lady Marismë. "You are young and you are thralled in my spell. You are here with me, and blameless, and who is to see us?"

And she showed him a bed, scented with flowers and soft as snow, and hung with heavy curtains of silver stuff. Next, she threw off her gown, and stood in her shift, as translucent as the lake itself. But when she had done this, he saw through her, through shift and skin and flesh and hair, and she was made of bones, as the face of Death had been.

"Lady," he said, "I will lie beside you, but in no other way."

She nodded, as Death had done, and drawing back the covers of the bed, she revealed to him that a barrier of upturned blades ran down the middle of it, a palisade of steel. Marismë stretched herself to one side of this, and he on the other, the blades between them. And all at once Cedrevir slept, in that bed of swords, and in his sleep the fence grew higher and touched the roof of the chamber, which caught alight and fell down on him, and at that he woke.

He lay beside the lake, on the shore in the sunrise, and up the slope, where the ruin was, the patient horse cropped the grasses.

There was no sign of any other thing, for his hair and garments had no trace of wet. He was hungry and thirsty. The feast under the lake had not sustained him.

Yet, on opening his right hand, he found lying in the palm a little coal-black shell, and there fell from it one water drop, like a single tear.

The Knight of the Fellowship of the Circle rode northwards another month or more, and the summer waned from the land. He came among places of sterility where the trees were thin as famine, a burned country. In the valleys they had long since stripped the white corn, and the sun had withered off the grass and leaves. Only crows stood sentinel on the bald hill-tops. In the north, miles distant, were clouds that did not move, and these Cedrevir took for the mountains.

One noon, when the barren heat was very great, Cedrevir saw a church below him in the downlands, by a stream. The banks were shaded by walnut trees, and the water was fresh. The fruits on the walnuts were like stones, however, and when he smote on the church door it sagged wide. No one was there but lizards that rushed away like the scorched leaves over the floor. A window shaped as a wheel hung in the east wall; before it an antique banner dipped from a rafter, dark red, the fringes rusty. The altar was singular, a block of quartz, and in the depths of it might imperfectly be seen a war-axe though how it had come there there was no telling.

Cedrevir, going out again, tethered his horse, and stretched himself among the trees to rest through the heat of the day.

No sooner had he closed his eyes than he heard a weird wild pagan chanting, and shouts, and the tramp of feet coming towards him along the valley.

Cedrevir started up — and as he did so, the noises died on the air. Only the stream lilted in its narrow bed and the horse whispered to the plants under the wall's shade.

Cedrevir sat down again, and leaned his head on his hand and shut his eyes. Instantly he heard the chanting and the outcry, as before but louder still. Now he did not stir, but only waited, and presently shadows began to flicker and dance over his eyelids, as if a company of people passed.

Cedrevir opened his eyes a second time, and wide and grey they gazed on nothing but the arid afternoon.

A third time he withdrew his sight, and past him the people trampled, and bells rang and women shrilled. Now Marismë, the lady in the lake, had said to him: The name of your road is *I will*. So then Cedrevir said softly to himself, "It is to be seen if it is to be heard, and I will see this thing and what it is."

And as he had smitten on the church door, so he smote open his own eyes with the thought.

Then he saw this: Across the valley floor, following the course of the stream, came a band of men and women. They were summer-tanned, lean and ragged, but they had garlanded their heads with twisted briars. The women rang bells and the men brandished staves. In the midst was a cart which they pulled violently along, and in the cart was bound a young maiden, wan as if near death, though in her dark hair too was caught a crown, of vine-leaves and poppies. Plainly, she was to be a sacrifice.

Cedrevir got to his feet and loosened the sword in its sheath. It transpired that, as he had formerly not seen these people, they could not even now see him; he was invisible. Unhindered then, he trod behind them, and when they mounted a nearby hill, kept after.

There among the stubble was a ring of lifeless trees, from which the carrion birds rose at their arrival like flung, screeking stones. The ground under the trees, where they had been feeding, was littered by bones and bits of rotted meat. The spot smelled of death. As the men lifted the girl from their cart, she began to weep, but she did not beg for any mercy, judging it, seemingly, beyond them. They tied her fast to one of the trunks. She drooped there like a dying lily on a black branch. The maddened crowd ran about the tree, wailing and calling, and then an ancient man, cackling at the curtailment of youth, crept around the ring, sprinkling from a censer on the ground. It contained blood, which smoked and stank, and the crows, which had returned to the upper boughs, clapped their wings in greed.

When the ancient had completed his ritual, the people plunged together and swirled suddenly away. They went by Cedrevir, where he waited at the tree-ring's edge, without a look, and some even stumbled against him, but paid no heed to it. Their noise, which now had something more of fear than celebration, diminished and was gone. A vast silence settled on the hill. At this, the girl raised her drenched eyes and looked all about her. Her tears fell and she shook with terror, but nor did she make any sound.

Then there came a rumbling in the earth, under their very feet, and Cedrevir unslung from his shoulder the shield fronted with the *sarpafex*, and drew his sword.

In another second the ground bulged and split, and out of it there burst, flaming like a molten thing, a huge lizard, a dragon.

It was the colour of brass, and in size half the height again of a man. It bore up with it a fearfull smell of sulphur and decayed matter, and as it grubbed and pawed, discarding the soil, searching for the accustomed offering, from its jaws ran a venomous breath tinctured with fire.

Cedrevir stepped forward, and lifting his shield against the exhalation, called to it.

The dragon turned at once, and its orbs of eyes, that looked blind with unthinking malice, yet appeared to take him in.

"Before her, first you must be done with me, Devil-spawn," said the Knight.

"Now God be at my side, in Christ's Name." And he went forward straight at the dragon, but, as he did so, covered his head and breast with the shield. A wave of the filthiness and heat seared Cedrevir like a furnace blast. Yet he came on, and struck with his sword, upward, against the underside of the ribs. But the cage of ribs was a monumental thing. He bruised it, for the monster roared, and in the trees the waiting crows exclaimed and took flight. But no more than that he did.

Cedrevir fell back now, for the awful breath and fire of the dragon were greatly weakening.

It slunk after him, and raking at him with its forefeet continuously, inflicted instead horrid wounds in the earth, for he was too quick for it.

Then again, he struck at the breast, at its jaw that weaved above him, and one of the huge teeth in its mouth was broken at the blow.

Down the hill they passaged, the dragon sweeping with its claws and pouring out its bane-breath, Cedrevir avoiding its attack as he could — and here and there a tree stump or a boulder sprang alight in lieu of him, or cracked in pieces.

But it was in the thoughts of the Knight that he would lead it down, away from the damsel, to the stream below the church. The dragon's element was fire, but there lay water.

Among the walnut trees they passed, and Cedrevir stepped back into the stream and felt, through his mail, its blessed lesser warmth like coolness. The dragon baulked. It would not come on. It snarled, and the small stones of the walnuts might be heard popping and snapping.

"Is it water you spurn, or the holy church above?"

Then the dragon spoke to Cedrevir.

"You have wounded me. Is that not enough? Let me return to the maiden who is meant for me. I would not slay you. I honour your valour. You did not mean to wound me."

"Is it you?" said Cedrevir. "You were before a little snake."

"I? Who knows me, or what I have been, or may be?" said the dragon. The words came from its mouth, in a pure voice, shining like an organ-note in the flaxen air. The words came from it, yet no man could be sure it was the dragon which uttered them.

Cedrevir answered: "You are the creature of Satan, let him protect you. I call upon my Lord. You are the weapon of the Enemy. Oh God!" cried out Cedrevir, "send me a weapon here to meet this foe."

At that, the ground quaked, even as it had when the dragon erupted out of it. Above the stream, where the church stood, there came a sound of rending, and up into the air shot a beam of light. Cedrevir did not turn; he held his eyes on the dragon, and covered himself over with his shield. But also he let fall his sword, and raising his right arm high, opened his hand. And into it there came a heavy rounded haft, and at the haft's end a wedge of brightness like a jewel. It was the axe he had seen bedded in the altar.

"I will," repeated Cedrevir. He lifted up the axe and whirled it.

The dragon coughed out a spurt of livid fire, which enveloped Cedrevir, and seemed to touch his heart and shatter it. But yet still he let the revolving axe fling free and even as he sank down, he saw the axe-head meet the dragon's skull, and cleave it and become embedded in it. And he saw too that the skull seemed made of a substance like quartz.

The cool water laved the mail, the hair and flesh of Cedrevir. He lay under the stream, dreaming of the dragon's death. But he could not breathe the water of the stream as in the lake he had. He must rise up again and shake it from him.

He climbed the hill wearily, and the

crows berated him high above. (The dragon's corpse would be difficult eating.) Going to the dead tree, he cut the ropes which bound the maiden. She saw him clearly, as she had seen the battle for her life. She dropped at his feet. She clasped his ankles, and the garland of poppies slid from her shadowy hair.

"You are at liberty," he said.

"Yes, and I thank and bless you for it. But do not leave me here, for those savages of the region will themselves kill me. They have worshipped the dragon all the years of their lives." And she looked at him with the blackest eyes, and her mouth was red as the poppies. "I am called Melasind. A great lord is kin to me. Take me only to his kingdom. It lies northward. It is not far."

Cedrevir set the girl before him on the horse. She was slender and silent, no trouble for them, but for her beauty — which did trouble the Knight. For her beauty was of a subtle and uneasy sort, like smoke.

She gave no direction to the home of her kindred, the kingdom of the lord she had not named. Northward, she had said, northward they rode, and she was content. She did not question Cedrevir on any matter.

At night they slept upon the ground, and gentle Melasind made no complaint. She wrapped herself in her mantle and lay down, her cheek pillowed in her hand. Her slumber was discreet, but her hair strayed as she slept; it coiled and shimmered on the earth. She had been the dragon's bride, and her power over desire came from that, her virginity burned under the skin.

By day the sky was brazen. The landscape became a desert, flat-tabled plains where drifts of minerals sparkled. Not a tree grew. Water, where it was to be had, lay still in the cups of stones, and tasted of metal, granite, or cinders.

Then, as an evening came on after the sunset, the girl said to the Knight, "Do not pause now. For another hour's riding will bring us to the kingdom I told you of."

Cedrevir looked before them, to the north. He saw dim, folded plateaux and the vault of light. There was no sign of any road, any wall or tower.

"There, lady?"

"There," she said. "Where the stars are coming clear."

Then Cedrevir beheld a strangeness in the sky. On the height of it some stars were flashing out, a whole constellation, but it had a form which he had never seen before in any land, or place, nor ever heard spoken of.

It was like a spear or sword, but winged, the clustered stars thick like diamonds at its centre, raying away to glinting dust at the huge pinion-points, and the whole dazzling more fiercely than any other star of the sky, or the full moon even.

Cedrevir said nothing else to the maiden, and she nothing more to him. They rode on towards the winged sword of stars. And an hour passed, as she had said it must, but with no feature of the plain altering. Then, "Draw rein," said she. And when he had done so, she leaned forward and cried in a high voice thin as a wire:

"Ex orio per Nomine."

That done, she bowed her head meekly and clasped her hands.

But on the plain a mighty wind rose up. It seemed to lift the very corners of the world up after it; shards and dusts flew into the air, and in the welter of these things, soundless as an opening flower, Cedrevir saw a castle rising out of the earth. Its battlements and towers were pierced with lights, and banners curled about the tops of it. All was stillness as the wind died down. Then from the castle's walks the trumpets cla-

moured.

"Do not delay, we are expected," said Melasind.

So they rode forward, and as they went, the starburst of the winged sword was eclipsed behind the stoneworks, its point seeming to stab slowly to the castle's heart.

There was a gate, with torched turrets either side. The portals of this now began to open, and a Knight rode out. In the torches' light he was dressed in red, his mail red as new copper, and he was mounted on a red horse.

"You are welcome," he said courteously, and to the Lady Melasind he bowed.

With great surprise, Cedrevir heard her give a shrill merry laugh, and felt her shrink away between his arms. He looked, and saw that as the torches found her now, Melasind was a slender girl-child, some seven or eight years of age. She turned to him her laughing face and said, "In the world, I am wise. But here, in the house of my kin, I am as a child. Help me get down, Sir Knight."

So Cedrevir dismounted and lifted her down.

With misgiving, yet ever with the purpose of the Quest, he followed her under the great gate, into the castle which had risen from the Earth.

A night and a day, Cedrevir remained, the guest of an unknown host, in the Castle of Earth and Fire. And so it was. For by day, only the slightest sunlight entered through the embrasures, that were closed besides by panes of thick glass tinted with cinnabar. Constantly the lamps and torches and candles burned there. It was a place of great heat, and of leaping fire-cast shadows.

The servants of the Castle waited on

Cedrevir, as, in the mansions of his own land, he was wont to be waited on. There seemed nothing uncommon in it, though they did not speak to him of anything, nor did he interrogate them. At the ending of that first day, sunset filled the windows, and the Knight in red mail came to Cedrevir, greeted him with all proper forms, and asked him to descend the Castle to a hall of feasting.

Together they went down countless wide stairs of burnished basalt, by passages and chambers red with sunset and fire, and going always lower, until Cedrevir believed they had now passed under the ground. But he made no remark upon this fact, nor did the Red Knight speak of it.

At length the last stair ended at a door, which opened itself at their approach. Beyond lay a garden, most unusual and enigmatic in its looks. No daylight ever came there, it was far beneath the earth, but in the midst of it was a pool of ebony water from which proceeded a sourceless glowing light. On the water the whitest lilies rested, and sometimes, in the lighted dark, the gold fin of a fish would blink. The walks of the garden were laid with opals and other pallid fiery gems. Herbs and flowers stood in the beds, but they had no hue nor perfume. All across the garden, nevertheless, a tall rose tree had spread itself, and every rose on the tree was crimson. But when they came near to it, Cedrevir saw that these roses were made of rubies, garnets, and spinels.

Beyond the tree was another door, and through the door a hall.

They left the gardens and entered the hall, and stood on its threshold. A million candles were burning there, above tables covered with cloth-of-gold, and against hangings that ran with gold, on cups of sheerest crystal and platters trimmed with precious stones. But none sat down there, and presently Cedrevir perceived that the dust of years had gathered over everything. And, as the fish had winked in the pool, now and then a black rat would flicker under the draperies.

At the room's far end, the child Melasind sat on the flagstones. She wore now a gown of yellow scarlet, and her hair was crowned with the colourless flowers of the garden. In her lap she held an agate bowl and a knife of bone, and she wept.

Cedrevir went to her and kneeled down before her.

"Lady," said he, "why are you crying so bitterly?"

"The lord, my kindred, is sick," said Melasind. "Only this bowl, brimmed by the blood of a virgin, can revive him at such times. See, I have been nerving myself to it, but am afraid."

Cedrevir frowned. The Red Knight stood at his left shoulder, and said, "It is as she tells you. For long ago my lord, who is the lord of this kingdom, received a grievous wound. It does not heal. Only virgin blood can make him well, and that only for a little while."

"I do not ask the nature of the wound, nor how he came to it," Cedrevir replied. "The voice of fate, shouting or murmuring, is always to be heard on such a journey as mine. My vow is also of chastity. I have never joined with a woman, or committed any carnal act. I am as virgin as this child, and far stronger. Therefore I offer your lord instead my blood, without fear. For my soul is in profound safekeeping."

The lord's Knight, hearing this, bowed very low. "He will receive your gift with thanks," said he. And he withdrew from the hall. But the child-girl only stared at Cedrevir.

"You must attend me," he said. "When it is done, take your scarf and bind the cut tightly. Now give me the bowl, and if you wish, look away from what I do."

So Cedrevir opened a vein in his left arm with the bone knife, and filled the agate bowl with his blood. When the deed was finished, the child-girl ran to him and bound his arm tightly, not looking at the cut. But then, she dipped her finger in the blood.

"You shall take him this yourself," said Melasind. "I will guide you to my lord's chamber."

Cedrevir felt a little weakness from the loss of the blood, and he remembered how he had lain down in the stream after the dragon's death, and heard the water singing in his ears, but not as it had sung under the lake.

"Where does your lord lie?" asked Cedrevir. "In one of the great towers of the Castle?"

"No. He is below us, here."

Cedrevir followed her, as she bore the bowl of bright blood, and her steps were quick and light, his slower and less gladsome.

She took him through a narrow door, and beyond the passage sloped and widened, lit only by the raw torches in its wells. Till suddenly Cedrevir could see they were entering among huge hollow caves underground. Soon enough, the lighted corridor fell behind them, and on all sides unfurled the shining dark, like eternal night. Yet nevertheless he could tell their path, for a hot radiance beamed out from the agate bowl.

Shortly, Melasind led him over a bridge of flint, under which, miles down, an unseen river clashed its furious way. On the other side the bridge was a front of granite, in which a tall door of dull metal stood weirdly ajar. Through this slit went the maiden-child with her bloody lamp, and Cedrevir after her.

At once he seemed struck nearly blind. For though no light came out from the place beyond the door, yet light blazed there within. The means of the light Cedrevir could not discern, but the cause of its power he could barely miss. For the cavern that plunged away before him was piled with such treasures it would seem to beggar the richest kings of the world above.

"Come, follow still," said Melasind, and she led him on now up hills and along mountainsides of piled gold, made all of coins and chains and casks, crowns and swords and rings, and furnishings of every type. And through the gold ran streams of silver, and down its slopes rattled slips of jewels that their feet had disturbed. Until, coming over a ridge of this colossal wealth, Cedrevir looked upon a lake of sapphires, emeralds and rubies, so blue, so green, so bloodmost red, it seemed to boil and to flash lightnings. But in the centre of the lake, as the dragon lies upon its hoard, lay stretched a man on cushions of silk. And he was a giant, clad in black armour, his face turned away, so his locks of hair, that outshone the gold, flowed on the silk like fire.

Then Melasind gave a cry, and she ran down into the lake of jewels, and over it, and came to the giant and leaned above him. After a moment, she called to Cedrevir again: "Come, Sir Knight."

So Cedrevir walked out across all the jewels and when he reached the giant, gazed on his face. It was a countenance of such hideousness that none could look at it unmoved, nor without shrinking. For it was not the ugliness of any fleshly deformity, its horror stemmed from some inner twisting and torture. Then the eyes opened, and filled the face instead with an appalling beauty, but it was the endless beauty of agony that never ends.

"So you behold me, Knight," said the fallen one, and at his voice, no more than a sigh, stone and metal, skin and bone, heart and mind, were ravished and trembled and grew shamed and sick. "See what I possess," said the Lord of the Castle of Earth and Fire, "see what is mine. And see what I am brought to, that a child must fetch me gruel. I thank you for your charity, Sir Knight. Say now, may I drink?"

"Drink," said Cedrevir, "but I must

turn away," and leaning on a mace of silver that protruded from the lake of jewels, he hid his eyes with his hand.

After a moment, though, the wondrous horror of the voice whispered again.

"Your gift does me good. There is great vitality in you. Whom then, do you serve?"

"Only my Fellowship," answered Cedrevir. "And God."

The fallen giant drank again. The bowl was drained.

He said:

"I serve none. I will not serve, and so may never be free. Do you think my punishment has lasted sufficiently long? No, I am not punished. I need cry out humbly only once *Ut Libet.* But will not do it. It is my pride, not your *God,* that binds me. *Ut libet. Nunquam. Ut qui libentum.*"

Cedrevir, unable to prevent himself, had gazed once more into that awful face of a fallen dragon, and in the deeps of the golden eyes he saw printed those words — *Ut qui libentum.* (Seeing that *I will.*)

"Go now," said the mouth that had drunk his blood. "Go take your reward with this damsel. For I would not see this special virtue of yours wasted on another after I have had benefit from it."

"Lord," Cedrevir replied, "you know I may not take any pleasure with her in that way."

"That is to be seen."

And then there came up in the golden eyes a redness, like two dead suns that rose underground, and over the mouth, and all the features, went a ghastly flaring, as if wax melted in flame, and the being roared, and all the cavern seemed to break apart and the jewels rushed up over their heads like a storm of water.

Melasind took to her heels, and catching at his hand, she pulled Cedrevir after her. And in his terror, which

was like no other fear in the world, he allowed her to do it. Together they escaped the cavern of riches, and up the slopes of stone into the passage, and so back into the banquet hall with all its places laid and not a single guest. And beyond that they ran, to the subterranean garden, and here both the doors slammed on them, and cold silence fell.

Cedrevir felt a longing for water, and leaning to the lily-pool, he raised some to his face and lips. As the rings settled in the pool, he saw reflected, between the white chalices of the flowers, Melasind, and she was no longer a child, but a damsel again, with sweet high breasts and a rosy mouth, and hair that poured to her hips.

Then Cedrevir drew his sword and smote that image in the pool, so it smashed in pieces.

The damsel laughed.

"But did he not give me to you," said she, "and here I am and we are prisoners of this garden. Who is to see?"

"I should see it," replied Cedrevir. "I am both warrior and priest. I will not break the vows I made. They have fashioned me, in water and fire, on the anvil, as this sword was fashioned. Though I desire you, lady, which you, and he, both know too well, I have another duty, and a better lust than for your love."

"Alas," said Melasind, and she hurried to him, swift and sinuous as a snake, and threw her arms about him and sought his lips with hers. But he remembered her, how she had been a child, sexless and innocent, that cried at the notion of a wound. And desire left him and he put her away, though the heat of her body burned him through. Lifting his voice, he cried out then, as she herself had done on the night plain: "Ex orio per Nomine!"

But the Name invoked was now Another's, and all the power and passion of Cedrevir, which that place had stirred, turned otherwise, tore wide the enchantment.

With a screeching and thunder, the Castle of Earth and Fire seemed to burst, and up from the garden rushed the whirlwind, and taking Cedrevir in its grasp, hurled him through disintegrate stone and iron, glass and fire, on to the surface of the tindered land.

And as he lay on the breast of the world, the ground shook, and on the horizon a fiery crack, the shape of a serpent and two or three miles in length, healed itself, and thereafter everything was darkest night, without a beacon or a star.

But transfixing his palm, even through the steel of the gauntlet, was a blood-red thorn. And plucking it out, it left no mark on him. (And the cut from which he had filled the agate bowl had also vanished, leaving only a scar, a broken circle like the sickle Moon.)

In a dream, then he heard the voices sing:

First the Sword of Paining
Second the Sorrow's crowning
Third the Blood-Grail shining.

As, in the Castle of Towers they had sung, dulcet as silver bells.

And after these he heard the seeress Lady Marismë, who said, "Water inconstant and eternal, Earth and Fire that mingle, and the many Kingdoms of the Air."

When he wakened, the land was changed, as if swept by a mighty broom that had tumbled boulders, and the sky of earliest day showed the strokes of the broom in long riven skeins of cloud.

But northward, now, he saw the mountains sharp and clear as swords. Partially transparent they seemed, and hard as forged steel. Yet before the mountains was a vast forest lying on the land like the smoke of an old burning.

Now, this might be that forest called the Wood of the Savage Heart, and since he looked on it and found it there, Cedrevir so named it. Mounting his horse, which wandered docile on the plain, he rode north again, and in a few hours entered under the tangled branches.

In the stories, the trees of that forest were all dead, but the towering trees of the forest Cedrevir had entered, though leafless and often leaning with half their clawed roots from the soil — which was itself only of dust and stones — yet seemed to pulse and throb with liveness, as if with the very beat of hearts. And even those trees which had fallen seemed quickened by a strange force, and here and there the roots had driven back into the unnourishing ground.

There were no birds, nor any truly living thing which Cedrevir might see, or hunt for food. But, as a Knight of a fellowship, he was accustomed to fasting. As the noiseless days and silent nights went by, his thoughts grew only flawless and crystalline, and as for the horse, it survived by sometimes chewing on a kind of mastic that exuded from the trees. Of water there was no scarcity, for the nights were chill and brought a frost which, in the sunrise, melted in quantities, dripping off the boughs and gathered in the stones until midday.

The only flowers of that forest were the sun and the moon. There was, too, an overcast which hid the stars, and also that constellation of the winged sword. But probably this had been, in any case, a sorcery.

One dawn he woke from a deep sleep in which the bell-voices chimed. Not the length of a spear away, a creature was drinking at one of the water-puddles in the stones. It was a hart, cold white, but between the forked horns of it a gold blossom seemed stamped upon its forehead.

It appeared to Cedrevir that this was a magical beast, the genius of the wood, and so he rose and began to go towards it, but at that the hart tossed its head and ran away. Yet it ran only to a clearing some score of trees distant, and there again it stood, flickering in its whiteness like a candle-flame, as if awaiting him.

Accordingly Cedrevir untethered and mounted his horse, and rode slowly after the hart which, seeing him come on, began to trot before him.

In this manner the morning and the noon passed, the knight following and the white hart dancing before him. If Cedrevir should spur his horse, then the hart would run, so fleet the man seemed likely to lose it. However, if Cedrevir should lag, or pause, the hart too stayed itself, browsing on the dark mastic of the trees as the horse did.

When the afternoon came down into the forest, still the hart went on and the Knight rode after. It was a cheerless day, the season was no longer summer, nor anything, cool and dry, and without kindness.

There seemed no changes in the woods but for the natural alteration of the light. Later a pale amber westering glow flowed through the trees. Later yet, the dusk began.

Where did the creature lead him? In the crystal thoughts of Cedrevir, from which the fast too had sloughed most of the need for sleep or rest, the motive of the pursuit of the hart shone indivisible and immaculate. On a Vowed Journey, such things had all a reason.

Night won the land.

They had reached another of the hollow clearings, and now the hart stopped of its own accord and turned to face its pursuer. It gleamed dimly, even in the utter dark, and between its horned brows the golden flower was like a lingering speck of day. Then, a fearful metamorphosis occurred. The hart leapt abruptly high into the air, so its feet no longer touched the Earth, and as it did this, it seemed to leap out of its own skin, which pleated away into nothing behind it. From the skin of the hart there emerged a huge white lion, with a grey hoary mane like the spun frost, and eyes of flame. And in mid-air it sprang at Cedrevir, for his throat, and for his soul too it seemed.

The horse neighed in terror and plunged aside. The lion-beast, meeting the horse's flank in its spring, ripped with huge talons, but only the cloth and leather of the caparison were breached. The lion hung then from this vantage, glaring in the face of the Knight. And in the black silence of the forest, the hatred and blood-craving of the lion were like a torch. But Cedrevir had by now freed his sword. He swung it over and thrust it down, into the lion's jaws, until the hilt, where was engraved the sigil of the *sarpafex,* grated on the fangs. And the eyes of the lion turned to blackened coals. It fell away, and lay on the earth, still faintly shining, so Cedrevir beheld it was now only a flaccid pelt, without sinews, flesh or bones.

Cedrevir did not marvel, for he had come into a state of the marvellous, where nothing surprised him. But he bowed his head and gave customary thanks to God. Lifting his eyes again, he saw glow-worms in the wood, and then that they were not glow-worms, but the lit tapers of a procession of men and women, which wandered through the trees into the glade. As they drew closer, he noted also that they were garbed, the men as priests, the women as nuns. Reaching the spot where the skin of the lion sprawled, two of the priests raised it and bore it off. They spared no glance to Cedrevir, but passed him, chanting softly some litany he could not recognize.

Cedrevir leaned from his horse. He caught at the mantle of one of the nuns.

"Where is it that your mysterious company goes?"

She answered, "The Earth is fading. The sky will fall. You may follow us if you wish."

"But where, holy lady?"

"It is true, all places are as one in the World's death."

And with no more reply than that (though that perhaps reply enough), she slipped from him. And all of them had left him, the lion's skin carried in their midst.

Cedrevir dismounted and, leading the horse, went after.

Soon the way ascended. They climbed, the religious procession, and behind it Cedrevir. The trees thinned. The Knight looked about him, and saw they had emerged on a range of cliffs, which might be at the foot of the northern mountains, although these he could not make out. Though the forest had been stricken and non-verdurous, these cliffs were bare of everything but the rock itself. Presently, however, he might see the destination of the travellers. It was a skeletal chapel, roofless and wrecked.

A curious light came down. At first, Cedrevir took it for the glow-worm sheen of the tapers. But then, thinking over the words the nun had spoken, he looked up to heaven. And there was a strange sight, and one which filled him with a deep and sorrowing fear.

The night above had become a canopy, opaque and impenetrable, empty of moon or stars. Yet it was a canopy wonderfully adorned. Across the whole length of it, which stretched to the twelve quarters, ran scrolls and frettings of gold and silver, not in motion but still, as if painted there. And as Cedrevir gazed at this, the whole of it seemed always sinking a little nearer, so that indeed the sky, or this entity of the sky, was falling, by slow inches on the earth below. And from it nothing alive could fly away, but must be crushed beneath. Yet so beautifully fashioned it was, the great black coffin-lid of heaven, that now he saw gems of exquisite lucidity set into the metal, lilies of pearl and asphodel of the clearest topaz, and hyacinths of such purple corundum he could hardly bear to look at them. In his heart, Cedrevir wept. God, dismayed by the unrelenting wickedness of Man, let down the sky to end His creation. Yet, too, He honoured it with beauty. Not cruel water nor ravening fire would be the quietus of mankind, but black air flowered with jewels. Yes, Cedrevir's heart wept, and overflowed with pity for the Creator, and love and an anguish of fear, and resignation, also.

And so he followed the company into the chapel, and here they doused their lights, and were illumined only by the falling slow lights of the sky.

But where they had laid the lion's skin, suddenly there was also a fire on the earth. The pelt blazed up, and the flames divided. Out of them came daintily stepping a little snowy fawn, with a golden cross between its brows. For a moment it was clearly visible, and then it vanished and the glittering ashes of the fire snuffed out to nothing.

A wind blew through the chapel, among the silent watchers there. It was fierce yet strengthless, all the winds of the world flattened under the lid of the sky. After the wind had passed, dew or rain fell, but it died to dust even as it touched the ground.

Looking up again, through roofless walls, Cedrevir saw the canopy had come so close that every flow and decoration might be measured by the eye, huge in dimension, with gems set within gems. Then again, he bowed his head. And Heaven fell.

There was neither heat nor cold, nor sound nor vision nor thought. There was no pain or smothering. A vast *unness* covered all, and all was absorbed in it.

After the darkness, there was light. After the death of sleep, a second awakening. The Knight Cedrevir was as you have yourself seen him, well-made, and fair to look on, and he stood as formerly clad in mail and full armed, but alone, upon a mountainside. The world lay far beneath, or it was gone entirely to a ring of palest most insubstantial brightness, like the sea. The sky was all around, roseate blue with dawn, and clouds passed below and on all sides, moving leisurely as swans on a morning lake. And the sky too was full of golden flowers and silver flowers, like those which had fretted the lid of the Annihilation. But these flowers hung, as if woven in a tapestry, and as he began again to climb, now and then they brushed his face or shoulders, and they had only the touch of flowers, but they did not break or fall.

Above there was a castle which grew up from the mountain, and as it grew it changed to gold, so it was a thing of fire like the sun, and he could not keep his eyes on it. There was a road also under his feet, and it was laid with lapis lazuli and sapphire. While, at the roadside, trees sprang out of the mountain, and their boughs were all blossom, yet fruit hung from them that shone like mirrors and gave off a perfume like no fruit or bloom of the Earth.

By accident or by design it is not possible to come there, but by faith and will, sometimes, it is.

For Cedrevir had entered a kingdom of the Kingdoms of the Air, and before him rose Carba Bonem, blinding him with its glory.

As he approached the gate a horn blew within the Castle, a long and liquid note, and the doors of the gate opened without a sound.

Within lay a court. It was paved with marble, and on every side the towers went up blazing, and one tower above the others like a shaft of flame, whose head was not to be distinguished. At the centre of the court stood a tawny willow, the curved trunk of which was braced with silver. From its boughs depended the helms and swords, spears and shields and colours, of many scores of Knights, marked with their various devices, so it was a gaudy object, this brown tree. Under it there waited a maiden dressed in sackcloth. Her hair was white as salt, and her eyes the pallid green-azure grey of glass, but she was thin and twisted, and her face beautiless.

"Stay, Knight," said she. "You must leave your weapons and your colours here."

"As others have," said Cedrevir, "and not reclaimed them."

"Not all reclaim them, it is true," said the maiden. "But you have entered the *Azori Mundi Regna*, the Kingdoms of the Air, and must obey their laws."

Cedrevir unsheathed his sword, and unslung the shield from his shoulder, these he gave her, with his war-helm. And she raised the items as if they were no weight at all, and hung them on the tree.

"Who guards you, lady?" he asked her then, "are you alone, and still make this harsh demand of any man that comes here?"

"There is protection, though invisible. I am Morgainor, and it is I myself who guard this place, and its treasures, which you seek."

"So I do," he answered very low.

"Enter the tower then, the tallest of all, and go up the stair."

At these words Cedrevir went pale, and his heart thundered. He said "Is there no other preparation?"

"What is to be can only be."

So he left the maiden who had called herself Morgainor, and crossed the court, and the door of that tallest of the towers opened for him. He saw beyond a stair ascending. It was of polished ebony, inlaid with ivory. And in the tower too, the flowers of gold and silver hung in the air, brushing his face and shoulders as again he climbed upward. And he was filled by feverish lightness, and tears stood in his eyes.

Now as he climbed the stairs of ebony and ivory, it did begin to suggest itself to the Knight that, aside from the flowers which he might see and feel, the air thickened with unseen presences, and sometimes they too brushed him, as if with draperies or wings. Where the stair curled about itself, as it did very often, it seemed to him he detected voices also, soft and melodious, but they spoke in a tongue he had never heard.

At last he saw the light of the sky again before him, but, as he stepped off from the stair, he found the way was closed with a palisade the height of three men, and made from the bones of men, and the day streamed through them and through the eyeless skulls, which were very white and pure, as if fashioned of alabaster, but they were not.

This door would not open for Cedrevir. He paced before it, and saw dimly through its eyelets radiant day beyond.

Then a shadow moved in an inner corner of the door, and there was a stooped, gross woman there, dressed in sackcloth, her pale hair matted and her face very ugly, though her eyes were the eyes of the maiden in the court.

"You must give me a gift," said she, "or I may not open the way for you."

"What would you have? For I have nothing."

"Give me," she said, "a coal-black shell and a blood-red thorn."

Then he considered how he had remained true to himself and to his vows at the castle in the lake and the Castle of Earth and Fire, and how, waking, he had on both occasions found tokens left him, the shell and the thorn. So he took them from his belt and placed them on the ugly woman's palm.

At that she smiled, and she shook her head, and closed her hand upon the things.

"I am Morgainor," she said. "Do you recollect? You have met me before."

"If you are Morgainor, then you are she. I have given you what you asked."

"Yours is a heart that has no stain, nor any occlusion," she said. "I see through it, therefore. Alas, did you never question what you have been given, to give it up so easily in turn?"

"A shell," he said, "a thorn."

"Knight, I will render you one thing in exchange, and then will open the door of bone." And she held out to him her other hand, the right, and on the palm lay a golden needle. Cedrevir took this, and as he did so the door broke at its centre and folded wide for him to pass.

Beyond, the day was itself standing open, like a flower; it dazzled him, that upper sunshine.

The atmosphere was rare, thin as silk, and fragrant, and cold. The place was by the turret of the tower, its topmost roof, and so high a place the Castle itself had now vanished in the cloud below. A pavement stretched on every side, a round space without a wall, and at the centre of the pavement was a ring of white stones, each about half the height of a man. That was all, and the sun's rays smote on the stones, the pavement, and the gold turret, so everything was caught in a brilliant haze.

Then, from the brilliancy, forms began to shape themselves. Cedrevir stood immobile, and next he kneeled, for these creatures, though never wholly seen, yet appeared like angels, gleaming, and clad in robes of samite, with great wings, and having every one a

125

nimbus about its head. And these strange ethereal beings went to and fro in the air itself, not treading the pavement. (But they did not go inside the ring of stones.)

Cedrevir knelt and prayed then, for the dazzle of the sun and of the angel-beings had brought him all at once to a leaden weariness. As he prayed, too, every slight transgression, every weakness of his life, came into his mind, and he was ashamed. He began to believe that, like those others whose weapons and colours remained on the willow tree, he too would shrivel in this bath of light, and die. Flawed as man and as priest-warrior, he partly longed to leave the height, he could not bear the peerlessness he sensed hovering over him.

Then he heard the chime of bells, and startled, looked up. In the sky to the east he saw a sight.

A glistening barge came floating down the air. It had a sail that shone like red bronze, and the prow was carved like an eagle. A band of Knights rowed the barge through the ether with gilded oars, and young girls stood in the stern and rang bells in their white hands, and chanted dolefully.

Down and down the barge descended; it slipped over the ring of stones and landed weightless on the tower beneath the turret. When that was done, the Knights put up their oars. One, who was clothed in white, came from the barge, and with him an old, crippled, hag-like woman, dressed in sackcloth, who hid her face behind a veil. These two approached, and while the White Knight stood aside, the hag addressed Cedrevir.

"I am Morgainor. We meet a third time. Will you give me back now the golden needle, for if you do, I will then instruct you in the mystery."

Cedrevir rose from his knees. He looked at the White Knight, whose face was as splendid as sunrise and as uncarthly. Cedrevir looked at the hag who peeped hideously from her veil with faded azure-green grey eyes.

"Lady, before, you seemed to warn me that I had given up to you too easily the shell and the thorn. Shall I relinquish as easily this needle?"

"You must. And since you must, you shall."

"I believe I have begun to guess the riddle," said Cedrevir. He lowered his eyes and said, "The shell was symbol of the Blood Cup, and the thorn symbol of the Sorrow Crown. The needle is the Lance of Pain. I am unworthy of the vision which was sent me and so, unwittingly but at the design of God, resigned the key to these sacred relics. Nevertheless this needle I still hold, and if I do not part with it, perhaps I shall be granted one further sight of the Lance. Or, I shall be granted clean death upon the lance of a Knight more worthy than I, maybe such a one as he that stands before me now."

Then the hag said this: "Cedrevir, you must not presume. If God has chosen you, how do you dare to judge yourself unworthy? What is your knowledge beside the knowledge of Him? You see into your heart, but He sees much more. It is your soul He sees. Whatever is said to you, whatever you gain or lose, what do such things matter? Did the Christ not promise Heaven to a wretched thief?"

Cedrevir sighed deeply. He said, "I am in God's hand." And he gave the hag Morgainor back her needle.

She took it. She said, "Go to the barge. That is the mystery and the last test. There is no more to say."

Cedrevir went towards the barge, and as he walked, the White Knight with the archangel's face fell into step with him. And the White Knight said, "In the barge lies one under a curse, and you may free her from it." But his voice was remote, like distant music.

"What curse is that?" inquired Cedrevir, expressionless, and his heart ached within him, at the words of the hag Morgainor, at doubt, and *because* of doubt. He was not uplifted or comforted. His eagerness lay spent.

"That you shall see, the nature of the cursing. But to break it is, of itself, most simple. One lies within the barge, Embrace her, and kiss her, on the lips. All shall be well."

"That I may not do," Cedrevir replied, dully. "All and every intimate connection with women is forbidden me."

But now they had reached the barge. The beaked prow craned above, and the sail had netted the sun. At the stern the young girls stood with folded hands, bowed heads. The Knights were motionless. A ladder led into the midships of the vessel, and Cedrevir mounted it and stepped down into the barge. There lay a canopied bier, the hangings of which were blue silk.

"It is not to be, I can do nothing," said Cedrevir to the White Knight.

But, "Look on her. Perhaps you will pity her enough to do it."

Then, impelled, Cedrevir crossed to the bier and lifted aside its hangings. At the view he recoiled, unable to repress a groan of darkest loathing.

Then again, disbelieving, he stared, and could not take his gaze away.

On the bier there spilled a faintly-stirring mass. If it was a female it was the more terrible for that, for it was also reptile. The ripplings of its curded flesh, shapeless under a swathe of silk, gave way at the upper limbs to the little clutching arms of lizards, sheathed in lustreless metallic scales. And from the waist its lower part was a serpent, oozing in a slime. And round the whole slithered hair that lived, fatted worms, the snake-hair of a gorgon. The face grew from the torso — that had no scales. It was in truth a woman's face, but old as mummy, all fissured and crinkled, lipless and having no teeth but the four long fangs of its serpent side, these broken and discoloured. An evil stink arose from it as it laboured there at life, half-torpid and half-awake. And finally Cedrevir, sick with horror, dragged away his stare from it, but just then it spoke.

"You are wounded by the sight," said the voice, "But I by the existence."

And it was the voice of a lost child, that tore his heart.

"That is undeniable, lady," he answered.

"But you, if you would, with one kiss, might set me free. How long does a brief kiss last? How long my life?"

Then Cedrevir looked again on the monster. His gorge rose, but now for the first he saw her eyes. They had no colour and seemed mostly blind, yet in the windows of them shone the well of the world's tears. A hundred centuries of direst misery. Perhaps a hundred more if he should stint compassion.

To kiss her was not lust or longing, to kiss her was a kind of fearful death, and never sin.

So Cedrevir, keeping wide his eyes on hers, leaned down into the stench and shimmering shadow. He put his hand under her head, among the hair of worms, and he put his face to her face, and his lips upon her serpent mouth, and kissed her the kiss of all the love-desire in him that never once had he bestowed.

It was as if he had grasped lightning or the rushing sea. He opened his eyes yet wider, and lifted his head, and saw there in his grasp a maiden so lovely and so fair that not even the wonders of the Castle would outshine her. Her hair, flowing over his hands, was like spring sunshine on wild flax, her eyes were like marine turquoise, her lips were red and her clear-water skin as white as may. And all of her was slim and sweet and human, but quite perfect, so her gentle fingers that touched his brow fell there like petals, and with her perfumed breath she said to him, "Kiss me again." And in that moment he could not stay himself, and he did kiss her, in her beauty and in his great irreconcilable lust.

"I too am Morgainor," he heard her murmur then, as the Earth and sky wheeled about him. "And now you have given up to me all."

There was no thunderclap or shaking of the stones, but the light entirely perished. Everything was gone. The tower, the sky, the angel forms, the Knights and maidens, and the barge. Morgainor too, melted like water from between his hands. And Cedrevir was left in anguish and the dark.

But not for long. For presently, a new lamp was kindled. It was like the intimation of sunrise under storm.

Cedrevir, in his despair, looked yearningly towards it, and held himself ready, nearly gladly, for chastisement.

Next, through the smokes of the cloud, he beheld a searing hint of gold, and then of silver, of crimson, and of a depthless ruby green. Up in the air, anchorless, they wafted. He saw them hang in space, as if a thousand miles away — the Spear, the Thorn Crown, and the Grail. And Cedrevir, in his agony, covered his face and wept aloud, for he knew very well that now the culmination of his Quest was denied him. Even as he thought it, and other things more bitter, a burning wind passed by and colours stained against his tight-closed lids. After which the dark returned, without, within.

From the dark a voice spoke at last, at his right shoulder, and it seemed to Cedrevir that he had already heard it once, at the coming of the vision on Midsummer Midnight. But nothing now was to be seen.

"Cedrevir, were you not warned, and did not heed? It is your presumption that has denied you the final prize."

"Lord," Cedrevir replied, "it is my sin which has kept it from me."

"Who are you, before God, to judge yourself or how you sin? Know this. In

the moment of the second embrace, you had not lost the Quest. You lost it in the moment that you deemed yourself one fallen, and damned yourself."

"Fallen and damned I was. My vows were broken."

"And who are you to say you will never sin? Are you not a human man? Or are you a god, who is above sin?"

"I am a man. A sinner, and cast from grace."

"Since you must be perfect in your own eyes, Knight, perfect as God, it is your own grace that you have fallen from. It is not for you to know how God has judged you, blameless or to blame. But be assured of this, even the King of All cannot grant you what you stubbornly refuse to take. Go then, Knight. Go down again to the world. Believe this, your fault is forgiven, for a man has only to say *Forgive me* for his sins to be stripped from him. But you are proud. You say in your heart to God, Oh God, forgive me. But to yourself you say, *I* cannot forgive myself. *I will not.*"

After that the voice was silent, and a wan twilight came, and in the twilight Cedrevir stumbled down from the high place, over the stair of ebony and ivory, perhaps for many hours, and came at length into the court, the darkness gone, and another lesser darkness come, for already night had shut its wings.

There the willow cascaded to the ground, and on its ghostly weft the trophies of the Knights eerily spangled and swung. No figure was near, but three times round the trunk of the tree was coiled a silvery snake, which hissed at him. When the snake did this, the shield and helm and sword of Cedrevir dropped to the marble. He went and took them up, and in heavy grief turned from the Castle and descended the mountains.

THE KINGDOMS OF THE AIR

A night and a day he travelled, scarcely knowing what he did, and eventually he lost his way and his wits, and wandered some while.

In a valley of the world, kindly people found him, restored him as best they might, and brought to him a horse that was his own, lean and sad, which they had come on similarly wandering the valley a month before.

Of the Forest of the Savage Hart there was no sign, and the valley was set in verdant hills, flowered with fields and orchardland, though now the winter came on them.

Cedrevir rode south before the snow, which pressed behind him and covered the Earth with its white cloak. So, turning his head, he could yet see the snowy northern mountain-tops for several days, shining up in the sky like shed pieces of the winter Moon.

He saw, however, no unusual sights, and no uncommon adventures befell him.

Cedrevir returned, as you yourself have noted. And as he seemed, so he is. The Quest is more often resolved in such failure than in death. For now he knows the colours and the weapons on the willow tree remained of those who journeyed on to some explicit bliss he is denied. Or that he has, as the angel told him, denied for ever to himself.

— But tell me, then, since you have told so much, how do you know it all? His journey and his grief and loss.

— How do I know? How could it be, but that I too, long, long ago, have gone Questing. I too have striven and failed and fallen. I too have heard those awful words and known — not in heart and mind, but in my soul — the truth of them. God it is not, who is cruel. But we ourselves. *Mea culpa. Mea maxima culpa.* I, too.

N.B.: The Latin used in this story is the Mediaeval 'cat' Latin of the *Imperii Quattuorviri*, etc. ■

Dear Reader:

        If you aren't already a subscriber, please consider
becoming one. Not only will you receive all future copies in a
sturdy protective envelope hot off the presses, but you'll be
getting them at our low subscription rate, too -- which is the
only sure-fire hedge against inflation. Paper prices are
rising quickly, and soon our cover price is going to have to be
raised . . . but we'll be holding the subscription rate at 6
issues for $18.00 as long as we can.

        So, how's the magazine doing? Very well, thank you, is
our standard reply -- but you, the readers, certainly deserve
the full truth. We really are doing very well, especially for a
small, independant magazine. Circulation of our first issue has
topped ten thousand (more than most people were predicting!),
and we are pushing toward the twenty thousand mark through
display ads and a by-mail subscription campaign as fast as is
prudent.

        However (why does there always seem to be a catch?),
there is one small problem. Don't get alarmed, it's nothing
serious. It's simply that most of our circulation at present
comes from sales through specialty science fiction and comic
book stores.

        To be perfectly honest, we don't make much money from
copies sold by others (though we're happy to have them carrying
our products, since they're a terrific source of new readers).
Most of our income comes from subscribers -- and for Weird
Tales™ to be firmly profitable, we need more.

        How can you help? Very simply: take out a subscription
to The Unique Magazine, or (if you already have one), consider
giving one as a gift to a friend or local library.

        Obviously you'd be helping to insure Weird Tales™ is
around for a long time to come, and saving money while doing
so. But beyond that you'll be helping the magazine to grow and
expand: we'll be permanently increasing the size of the
magazine by 16 pages beginning next issue because of the number
of subscriptions we have now warrants it. And, once Weird
Tales™ is firmly established, we have plans for a companion
magazine . . . no definite commitments yet, but it will be the
revival of another famous pulp magazine, in the same great
"pulp format" as Weird Tales™!

        So, how about making sure you're there when the time
comes? Subscribe today!

                                        John Betancourt
                                        Publisher

www.Ingramcontent.com/pod-product-compliance
Lightning Source LLC
Chambersburg PA
CBHW070601180626
46817CB00005B/1946